Wretched
By Kelli Marlow

Blair,

For all the times you've rooted for the bad guy.

You've always said villains are simply misunderstood.

Sometimes I think we all are...

7 Days, 9 Hours, 23 Min...

The clang of metal bars awoke me from my dream. A face still teetered on the edge of my mind, remnants of the escape of dreaming. Another clang resonated through the concrete walls. I knew the sound intimately. It had been the only accompaniment to the endless drone in my skull for quite some time now. Another set of familiar sound followed soon after, the buzz of an unlocked door and the jingle of keys as they bounced against the hip of their owner.

The footsteps grew louder as they approached, signaling the time like clockwork. I must have slept longer than I planned. I'd been doing a lot of that lately, forgoing the waking world to escape into a place that was far less harsh and far less tedious. I stood and stretched as I counted the footsteps that approached.

...15, 16, 17, 18, 19...

Twenty steps to my door. Another clang and another buzz and I turned to the familiar face of guard number 1354679. I'd never bothered to learn their names. Numbers were easier for me anyway and at the end of the day they all looked the same. The same dark grey uniform, the same hard set jaws, the same judgmental eyes. They were the guards and I was the prisoner. They didn't honestly care if I knew their name. They knew my name, though. Everyone knew *my* name.

I followed the guard down the same pathway he'd taken to reach my cell. Cell number 2162. I watched the numbers recede as I passed. 2160...2158...2156... I never understood the need for the four digit numbers. There certainly weren't two thousand cells in this place. It was a large prison, but it wasn't *that* big.

Maybe it was intentional, a way to make the inmates feel more insignificant, just a number among a thousand others just like them. I wasn't like them, though, I was different. I was hated. And their feeble attempt at psychological manipulation was lost on me.

Twenty six steps and I was within the chamber that separated my wing from the rest of the prison. I was frisked, a custom I was now used to, and a new guard took the place of 1354679. I didn't know the number of this one and I didn't get the chance to peek at his badge before he led me through the second door.

Thirty three steps, a turn to the left, fourteen steps, a turn to the right, and finally the last 27 steps that led to the door of the interrogation room. The door buzzed and the guard escorted me into the 8X8 foot room with the single metal table and two folding chairs. I knew the space intimately. I'd sat in one of those chairs every day for three weeks.

There weren't any mirrors in this room like all the television shows depict. There wasn't any glass at all, save for the single hanging bulb above the center of the table. No cameras dotted the corners of the grey cinderblock walls. No one was listening in on what I had to say. No one cared.

The guard didn't care as he pushed me down into the hard metal chair and unceremoniously wrenched my handcuffs from my wrists. He wasn't the smartest oaf I'd met, leaning over me as he removed the second cuff. Had I had the inclination to try I could have easily pulled his weapon free from his shiny black belt.

We both knew I wouldn't though. Where did I have to go? No one escaped from where they'd put me, not unless they're in a body bag. Once you enter death row you only leave if you're very lucky or very well connected. I was neither. I'd only been lucky once, it hadn't ended well, and I didn't have any connections left. No one would save me, and if they did I'd still wind up dead one way or another. People have a funny way about exacting their revenge when you destroy their world.

One hundred and forty three days ago I'd unleashed a virus. Within a week it had infected half of the United States, and in the months since nearly one third of the world has become infected. They can't stop it, not before my goal is reached. Not before my revenge is exacted and the world pays for the crimes it's committed.

I was certainly going to pay for mine. I'd be dead in a week, a needle destined for my arm already on reserve somewhere in the prison I inhabited. Three injections and I'd be gone from this world, but my virus would live on. They might find a cure one day, but not any day soon. No one is saving them and no one is saving me.

The guard left me at last, shutting the door behind him with a clang and a click, telling me it was locked. It didn't matter that it was locked. Even if it wasn't, I wouldn't escape. I probably could, I was smart enough, but I wouldn't. I was ready to die; to leave this cruel world behind me and embrace whatever fate awaited in the next life. I only had seven days left. Seven days to breathe and think and feel. I didn't like feeling much. Thinking I was good at. Thinking is what got me to the very seat I was placed in. Thinking was the best part of being alone in a cell twenty hours of each day.

Eight minutes after the guard left, the door opened again, and the reason for one of the two hours of non-solitude I experienced flounced in with her usual flare. She was clearly trying to look more professional this time, I could tell. No doubt it had to do with one of my comments about her appearance that she seemed to take offense to on her previous visit. They weren't meant in offense, merely observation, but it seemed I'd struck a nerve.

Her hair, one of the points I'd observed, was slicked back neatly into a low ponytail. It must have taken a fair amount of effort considering the usual ferocity of her curls. I'm sure the wind I could just detect wailing beyond the walls certainly didn't help. A whiff of hairspray as she plopped into her usual chair opposite me suggested what *did* help. I wondered a moment if her hair would crunch under my fingers if I touched it. I surmised it would.

"Good afternoon." She greeted me. She rarely strayed from her overly cheerful greeting. Miranda Stevens was a reporter. One of those bubbly, pretty faces you see on TV telling you about all the horrible things that go on in the world. I suppose it all seems less grim when you're looking into one of those beautiful faces. Not that you ever saw faces on TV that weren't beautiful. That would just be unacceptable.

Miranda was pretty, not exceptionally so, but a genuinely handsome woman. Her wild curls, which I almost preferred to the smooth ponytail, always framed her heart shaped face. She had kind hazel eyes and dimples in her cheeks. A barely perceptible smattering of freckles donned the apple of her cheeks and I'd noticed over time that her eyes crinkled when she smiled, which she always did.

"Good afternoon, Miranda." I responded, shifting in my chair to a more comfortable position. I doubted there was a position obtainable by human anatomy that would make a metal folding chair comfortable. I'd decided a while back that the man who invented such a contraption was far more evil than I, and hoped he'd met a cruel fate in his end.

When I'd settled and Miranda had finished arranging her usual supply of equipment (notepad, three pencils, recording device, candy) she flipped through the pages of her notebook until she found an empty one.

"Shall we begin?" She questioned, pencil number one poised and ready to scribble away like it always did. I'd initially been quite fascinated with the rate at which the woman could put pen to paper. Her chicken scratch flowed across the pages nearly as quickly as I spoke.

Miranda was doing a story on me. She'd come three weeks earlier, exactly one month before my execution date, and asked my permission to interview me. What was meant as a onetime interview for a ten second blurb had turned into a full-fledged story that would air the eve of my death. I suspected the bubbly woman would get a book deal in the end, and she'd have no shortage of information.

I answered nearly every question she asked me. I had nothing to hide. For three weeks she'd come for the one hour of visitation time I was allotted and probed my mind for answers. I was still reluctant to reply to the first one she'd asked me and I knew a part of me was holding back the best part for last. After all, if I'm going to go out, why not do so with a bang?

"I believe when we stopped yesterday you were about to tell me a story." She recalled, tapping her pencil against her bottom lip. They were full lips, not grotesquely so, but soft and supple. Perfect lips for kissing. I had no interest in kissing them. I'd had no interest in romantic encounters for many years.

"Yes," I agreed, "I believe I was."

"Alright, shall we pick up where we left off then?" She suggested. I nodded and the pencil poised again just over the paper, the recorder already clicked on. Its green light blinked at me as I began.

Once upon a time there was a boy named Calvin. He was a nice boy, a little strange, a little different, but a nice boy. When Calvin, or Cal as he preferred, was born, his mother was very young, too young to be having a child. Her delivery was hard and by the time Cal was retrieved he was nearly dead. His mother hadn't been able to push him out and so the doctors cut him free from her. The doctor, in a rush to save the boy's life, didn't take heed to double check all of his instruments. He should have checked them. If he had this story might have gone a little bit differently.

Cal was born. He was very small. Eventually he'd learn that he would never be big or strong like the other boys. He would always be the runt, the weakling, the shrimp. He didn't care. His mother didn't care. She loved him with all her heart. Being small was a challenge, but there are worse things to be, like ugly. It seemed Cal wasn't so fortunate in that category either. He wasn't supposed to be ugly. No one was supposed to be ugly, not anymore. Our society took care of that problem long ago. Beautiful is better, so we made everyone beautiful.

Cal wasn't beautiful. Cal was scarred. Had the doctor double checked his instruments the day Cal was born he would have seen that the forceps he used had not been properly maintained. He would have used different ones, but he didn't, and when Cal was only three days old he developed a condition. An infection raged through his tiny body and threatened his already weak life. The doctor couldn't figure out what was wrong, the nurses did all they could, and as for Cal's mother, she prayed. She prayed that her beautiful little boy would live. He did, but not before the bacteria took his beauty away.

His scars weren't small. They weren't something you could hide with makeup or went unnoticed if you didn't look too closely. Cal's most visible scar ran from his temple to his jaw, red and clear and unmistakable. Now, in our society if you have the mischance of being born less than beautiful, or you happen to have some sort of accident to mar the beauty you were graced, with you have surgery. A skilled man or woman comes in and cuts the ugly away, disposing of the heinous disease. But surgeries cost money and Cal's mother didn't have any. Cal didn't get to have a surgery.

Despite his scar, Cal lived a fairly normal life. He played like children do and he learned and listened and scraped his knees. He discovered his love for art and that he had a talent with a pencil and paper. Even as a young boy he drew beautifully. His mother always wondered if his gift was the world's way of making up for the beauty it stole from his face. He would never be beautiful, but he could draw beauty. And he did. He drew every beautiful face he could find. In our society it wasn't hard to find them.

Though beauty surrounded him, he never resented himself or the face that stared back from the mirror. He knew he was different, but he kind of liked that he was. He liked being special. But every child likes being special when they're a child. Then you grow up and suddenly being different isn't so great anymore. Suddenly being unique is a burden. Being special isn't such a good thing. Cal learned this lesson the hard way, like most of us do.

"Why didn't Cal's mother sue the doctor?" Miranda interrupted, scribbling away in her notebook. She'd already finished half the bag of gummy bears she'd brought. I'd learned that the more candy she ate, the more excited she was about what I had to say. Apparently my story was good fodder for her tell all.

"Lawyers cost money, too." I replied. "And doctors have a lot of power." She nodded in response to my answer, writing down something I couldn't read from the angle I sat. I never could read what she wrote. Even when I had a clear view her scrawled handwriting was indecipherable. Honestly, it reminded me a bit of my own.

"Poor Cal." She sighed, popping another gummy victim into her mouth. "So how did Cal learn his lesson?" She asked, edging me back into my story. I smiled, allowing her to play her game. What did it matter if I told her a story? It was only a story.

"Cal went to school." I answered.

"Wait, he didn't before?" She asked, her eyebrows scrunching in the middle as her pen paused for the briefest of moments.

"No, his mother didn't want the other children to tease him so she taught him at home. He was a smart boy, exceptionally so, actually. He didn't need much help to learn." I told her, picking at the peeling grey paint of the metal table. I wondered why they thought they needed to paint everything grey. White was much more sterile. Of course, white also represented purity, cleanliness, holiness. White didn't belong in a prison. Bad things, dirty things, things as dingy as the grey color of the place belonged in prisons. Grey was an appropriate choice.

"Hello, earth to Doc." Miranda waved her hand in front of my face, breaking me free from the caravan of thoughts in my mind. It seemed I was getting sucked into it more and more these days.

Only Miranda called me Doc. My PhD's stopped mattering when I entered the concrete walls of the Holden Correctional Facility. I was no more a doctor than she was now, but I had been one once. I'd once been Dr. Andrews, head of the Allen Thomas Facility for Research and Development of Genetic Coding. I'd had a title once, respect, wealth. I'd had everything and I'd thrown it all away. The reason why was what Miranda sought, but I wasn't sure she'd earned her answer yet. I wasn't sure I was ready to tell it.

"Sorry." I apologized when Miranda called at me again, this time tapping a pencil against my knuckle. "I'm afraid my brain is a bit preoccupied today." She nodded and chewed on a few more defenseless fruit flavored candies. I couldn't remember the last time I had candy. I didn't like gummy bears, but just the thought of something different was enticing. Prison food, as you can assume, left much to be desired.

"May I have one of those?" I asked, pointing toward the bag. My inquiry seemed to catch her off guard for a moment, I never asked anything from her, but she quickly collected herself and offered me the bag. I tossed a small handful of the squishy things into my mouth and chewed. I didn't really like gummy bears.

"I'll bring extra next time." She smiled, taking the bag back. I swallowed the overly sweet lump and offered a soft smile. It was a nice gesture I suppose, but I didn't really want any more. "So, back to your story, how exactly did Cal end up going to school?" She shifted in her seat and awaited my response.

"Well..." I began, but the click of a lock pulled my attention away a moment later.The guard, leaned around the door and informed Miranda that her time was up.

"Yes, thank you." She replied, trying very little to hide the disappointment in her voice. With my impending execution she'd been trying to persuade the warden to allow her more time with me each day. She hadn't been having much luck. My utter lack of care seemed to not be to her advantage either.

She packed up her things, stuffing them into the black and silver messenger bag she always carried, and finished the pile off with the empty bag of gummies. The bags she brought always left empty. Before she slung the bag over her shoulder to leave she fished something out of the large pocket and slid it across the table to me.

"Here." She said. "I brought this for you. The guards said you can't have a pen, but I managed to convince them that you can't puncture your jugular with a crayon, so hopefully that will suffice." She beamed, a proud smile over discovering something without my telling it.

I looked down to the folded scrap of paper, the words New York Times printed across the top of the page that was torn along one edge. The Sunday Crossword stared up at me, its blank squares begging me to fill them in. Taped next to it was a new black crayon, sharpened to a flat tipped point.

"Someone's been doing her homework." I smiled, accepting her gift. I could already see the answers to at least three clues. There was a time when I'd considered this to be one of my favorite parts of the week. I'd always taken the paper out on the balcony of my high rise apartment with a cup of strong black coffee and whiled away my morning.

I hadn't seen a puzzle, or anything that might occupy my unusually busy brain, since I'd been brought to HCF. They didn't allow me such luxuries. Mostly my brain had to use itself for entertainment, useless knowledge plodding away constantly. Some of that knowledge spilled from my lips as I peeked at the questions itching to be answered.

“Theoretically someone could probably sever a jugular with a crayon if they applied the right amount of pressure, though the carotid would be more efficient.” I noticed the sudden tense of her shoulders as I spoke, and stopped before I spoke any further. She may be bubbly and far more interested in my story than most, but I was still a killer and she was still afraid of me.

“Thank you.” I concluded flatly and she nodded quickly before leaving. I had a problem with thinking before I spoke. A common affliction of genius.

I'd finished half the puzzle by the time the guard returned to bring me back to my cell. He allowed me to keep the gift Miranda had brought and I gazed over it as we walked, letting him to lead the way without a second glance. We reached my cell in the usual 120 steps and he quickly removed the cuffs and slid the bars closed behind him, locking the gate with a signal to his partner in the control room. I turned to him before he left, puzzle still in hand.

“What's an eight letter word for an unfortunate condition or circumstance?” I asked, peering at him through the steel-grey bars. I noticed his eyes were equally steely in color and his jaw was just as hard as the bars that separated us. He pondered my question a moment, tapping a finger thoughtfully against one temple.

"I don't know." He shrugged, turning to leave me alone again. I turned from the bars with the crossword in my hand and a smirk on my face.

"I do." I whispered.

7 Days, 6 Hours, 4 Min...

The crossword took mere minutes, the answers flowing onto the page almost faster than I could write. It wasn't a deck and there wasn't any coffee, but for the first time since I'd been inside the concrete walls I felt just a little bit normal, a little bit like my old self. Ninety-six days I'd spent within the walls, ninety-six days of feeling less than who I was, less than human, and a single black crayon changes it all. It's amazing how such a small catalyst can create such a drastic change...

..."Dr. Andrews, Dr. Andrews!"

The voice broke my concentration, the specimen below my microscope moving out of range the moment I took my eyes off of it. I heaved a heavy sigh at the encroaching man. Nigel never was very good with timing. Or finesse for that matter. In fact, as assistants went, Nigel wasn't much good for anything. He made a good cup of coffee, which was something, the voice reminded me again. I pinched the bridge of my nose, forcing the annoying voice back into submission. I didn't need another lecture from my own conscience.

"What is it now, Nigel?" I barked at him, annoyed by the loss of another specimen. Technically I could simply retrieve another from the cooler behind me, but it was the principal of the thing. I didn't like to be interrupted when I was working and Nigel had a habit of interrupting, and at the most inopportune times. My tone managed to relay my annoyance and the boy seemed to second guess his need to speak with me.

"I haven't got all day Nigel." I reminded him, setting my glasses down with a heavy sigh and rubbing at the bridge of my nose again. The migraines were becoming more common and I'd grown tired of them quickly.

"I didn't mean to…" He stammered, knowing full well he had messed up.

"Just tell me what you were blathering on about so I can get back to work." I was snippy, I knew it, he knew it. I chose to blame the pounding in my temples. I had no idea what he chose to blame, though my general antisocial temperament would have been at the top of my list of guesses.

"A letter came in the mail." He replied, sounding sheepish and looking at the ground as he handed over the piece of paper in his shaky hand. Another thing I didn't like about him. He was unsteady, completely useless in a lab, and clumsy to boot. I scanned the letter and ascertained the cause of his excitement.

"You've been accepted to the program you applied for at Johns Hopkins." I read aloud. "Congratulations." I told him, shoving the paper back into his hand and picking up my glasses. Grateful his recent outburst required little more than acknowledgement, I returned to the task at hand.

"Thank you." He continued to stammer. I ignored him, like I usually did, and went about procuring another sample from the large industrial refrigerator. I selected one at random as he prattled on still.

"I couldn't have done it without you; I mean you've taught me so much and that letter you wrote for me was so nice." I could tell he was getting sentimental, something I didn't do well with, and I sighed loudly. "I just don't know what I can do to thank you." He sighed as well, mistaking my sigh for nostalgia rather than irritation.

"Get lost so I can get back to work?" I suggested. He looked stunned for a moment, but as always his face crinkled into a smile and he folded the paper back up and stuffed it into his coat pocket.

"Can do, boss!" He exclaimed as he turned on his heel toward the door. I went back to my sample and microscope, but a moment later cried out in surprise when I found Nigel's arms wrapped around me, pinning my arms to my side. "I'm going to miss you." He sniveled.

Sentimentality was not my strong suit, and physical contact in any form other than a formal hand shake was beyond my realm of comfort. Unsure of what to do, which was also outside my normal realm, I awkwardly patted what little of him I could reach. I managed a couple of soft swats on his elbow and that seemed to suffice. He released me to my chagrin a moment later and smiled up at me with his big green eyes. His ginger hair was wild about his face, and for a moment I felt the urge to smile with him. It passed as quickly as it had come and I cleared my throat as I turned back to my specimen.

"Don't forget to send out those lab results like I asked you." I reminded him as he bounded out the door, knocking a coat rack over on his way.

"Sorry." He stammered as he put it back. It was at least the hundredth time he'd knocked it over and I cursed the bumbling oaf as he left. I did, however, manage that smile I'd thought about as I heard something else crash in the other room and a muffled "I'm alright!" following it.

I abandoned the memory with a shake of my head. More often, of late, I'd caught myself reminiscing of times passed, thinking back on people or places I'd long forgotten. Nigel was one of at least two dozen interns I'd had over my career, but for some unexplainable reason I'd always liked the oaf. The evidence of that fondness was clear in the smile that remained when the memory had gone.

Footsteps made me abandon the thoughts of the odd boy and I counted the thuds as they approached. Eighteen pounds later, I'd missed the first two being lost in thought, and the guard appeared in front of my door. The tray in his hand was familiar, the pale yellow color almost more off-putting than what I knew would lurk beneath the cover of dish it held. Prison food left a lot to be desired.

"Soups on." Guard number 9398114 told me, sliding the tray through its designated slot. With a wink and a smile he left, wafting the scent of the meal toward me in his wake. It smelled like spaghetti. I'd never really liked spaghetti.

Regardless of distaste I ate it, hunger being a driving force when it wanted to be. What did I care if it tasted as vile as it smelled, it was nourishment and nothing more. I was no longer able to indulge in the finer cuisines of life, forced only to choke down whatever slop they'd decided to toss at me that day. Nourishment was nourishment and in the case of prison cuisine, the cheaper the better. I momentarily wondered if the meatballs I consumed were even, in fact, meat. I doubted it, but decided it was something best left unanswered, for my stomach's sake.

When I'd finished what I could swallow of the meal and slid the tray back in place for pickup in 9 minutes, I turned my attention to a card pinned below the book that sat on the table under the window. I knew I needed to fill it out, to decide what I wanted for my last meal, but I couldn't bring myself to choose. There were things I craved, but nothing seemed right. If it was going to be the last thing I ate on this earth it should be something meaningful.

The problem was, nothing seemed meaningful any longer. Nothing mattered. I'd succeeded in what I'd intended to do. I'd been caught, though I'd never expected anything else, and I'd been sentenced to death for my crimes against humanity. I had nothing left in this world. No family, no friends, not even a pet to miss me when I was gone. *I* wasn't meaningful, just another face for evil that had plagued the world since its birth. Evil wasn't meaningful. It didn't care or love or feel, it only hated and destroyed.

I'd done my destroying. I'd left the world in turmoil. I'd completed my life's work. In all the books and all the stories that have ever been told, they forget to cover one thing. What happens when the subject reaches the end of what they've been fighting for? What exists in the aftermath of genius? There's nothing so great about genius when the genius has already completed their last task and has merely to count the minutes, the hours, the days until it's all over. In a week and a few hours it would be over. I would be free of this mortal coil. My final challenge lay in the days between. I didn't know what to do until I perished. What does one do when they have nothing left to live for and yet have no choice but to live?

6 Days, 15 Hours, 30 Min...

I didn't awake until the guard was rapping on the bars of my cell. I nearly fell off the bunk from the startle, and I heard the guard chuckle. I couldn't remember his number at the moment, being half terrified and still partially asleep, but I remembered the laugh. He liked to laugh, especially at the suffering of others. He wasn't my favorite guard. Not that I liked any of them particularly.

I was still groggy as I stuffed my arms through the slot in the bars and felt the slap of cold metal cuffs on my wrist. The buzz of the lock and the clank of the door helped to break the hold sleep tried to maintain, and soon I was following Chuckles down the hallway, counting our steps as we went.

...18...19...20...stop.

The door buzzed and I followed Chuckles again, down the same path I took every time I left the cell. There was only one time we'd left my cell that I didn't take this exact path. That time I'd been taken to the infirmary for an accident I'd had. They tried to call it a suicide attempt, but truthfully I'd merely been careless and had a bit of bad luck attached to it. I suppose though, if I were a medical doctor and a death row inmate walked in with blood spilling from their wrist I'd be suspicious too. I'd always been glad I wasn't a medical doctor, not a practitioner anyway. Blood made me very uncomfortable.

I was a different kind of doctor. My focus was genetics, and when all the other pre-med students went off to their internships and surgical schools I went to a lab. While my colleagues were perfectly happy to figure out what went wrong and how to fix it, I'd always been more interested in why it went wrong. I'd made figuring out why the body, or more specifically the brain, did the things it did my entire life's work. Some may call it pointless, others sacrilegious, but nothing made me happier than connecting another dot in the puzzle that is the human brain.

We are fascinating creatures. Constantly evolving and changing, creating new neural pathways. The brain can adapt better than any other organism on the entire planet. It holds more connections than anyone could fathom, and yet all the marvelous things our species is capable of only negates a small portion of our brain at any given time.

My brain was about to be dug through. At least that's what Dr. Gunderson always attempted when she came to visit. I knew it was her job, being a psychologist and all, but that didn't mean I had to like it. It also didn't mean I had to make things easy for her, and I didn't plan to. I suspected she knew as much by the look of dread on her face when they brought me into the interrogation room and unlatched the cuffs from my wrists. I rubbed at the places they'd chaffed. Chuckles certainly did like to slap them on hard.

"How are you feeling today?" The shrink asked. As always everything about her was perfect. Perfect blonde hair, perfect white teeth, perfectly toned yoga body under her pressed grey suit and blue silk blouse. Even her cherry red lipstick was perfectly applied, vibrant against the contrast of her teeth. She was beautiful right down to the shimmering blue of her eyes. Those weren't quite so perfect anymore. They hid the fear well, but it was there, just under the surface. She was afraid of being infected, and she should be, I designed the virus for people just like her. I'd put that fear in her eyes. She should be afraid.

"I'm the same I am every day." I replied honestly, dropping the corners of her mouth. I counted it as a personal victory. "Monotonous routine is the staple of prison life, but of course you know that already." It was my turn to smile. I hated seeing the shrink. It was mandated to ensure they weren't about to fry someone who is mentally unstable, but I still hated it.

My only joy came in wiping the smug smile off her face every time she realized I was smarter than she was. I suspected there were few she'd met that were, but I also knew where I was concerned, being smarter than most wasn't hard.

"You look tired today. Are you sleeping alright?" She inquired, the smug smile returning to its ever vexatious perch. She was on a mission today and I wasn't up for the competitive banter. I wasn't up for much of anything.

"I sleep as well as can be expected." I answered, folding my fingers together in front of me and resting my elbows on the edge of the cold metal table. Gunderson eyes me suspiciously, carefully choosing her next question. After a longer pause than usual, which only made my prideful smile deepen, she continued.

"What do you dream about?" She asked, poising her pen over the notepad in her hand. "Do you dream at all?" She smiled.

"I dream." I replied. "Everyone dreams, some people may not remember their dreams when they wake and some dream less often than others, but everyone dreams." I was less than thrilled with where her line of questioning was going. Most of our sessions revolved around my guilt, or lack thereof, and the occasional delve into my psychosis to determine whether I'm insane or not. So far she'd determined I wasn't, though I knew she had her doubts. No one could do what I did without remorse and not be at least unstable. I wasn't insane. I just had my reasons.

"You didn't answer my question." She pointed out. I'd hoped she'd let it be, but it seemed she wanted to dig a little deeper than usual. I wasn't so inclined.

"Actually, I did." I reminded her, coming off even smugger than I'd imagined. When had I become so arrogant? It hadn't been an intentional personality shift. Arrogance wasn't a trait I'd always possessed.

"Not all of them. As usual you picked around the more informative question and replied with a matter-of-fact scientific answer. You're avoiding the discussion of anything personal or intimate." She observed, more frankly than she usually was. I wasn't the only one who liked to dance around the issues.

"You want to be intimate with me?" I questioned snidely. I knew it was a cheap tactic, but an effective one based on the look of utter astonishment that struck her features.

"Hardly." She stammered while she regained her professional composure. I doubted I was the only patient to ever suggest something so inappropriate. "I want to understand you, to reach inside that brilliant mind of yours and figure out why someone with so much to gain, so much potential, would throw their life away for something so…"

"Evil." I finished her sentence for her. Perhaps it wasn't the word she would have used, but it was what she wanted to know. It was what they all wanted to know. How could someone so extraordinary do something so heinous? "I'm not evil, you know." I concluded, crossing my arms over my chest.

"There are evil people in this world, truly dark souls without care or concern for their actions, but I'm not one of them. You want to know how I threw it all away, you want to know why I did what I did, well here it is. I looked at my options, weighed my life and my own worth against the value of what the virus could do and I decided my life was worth less. It was simple math." I released my defensive stance and leaned back in my chair once again, composing the temper I'd not felt in a long time. It was actually quite nice to feel something so passionately again.

"How can people's lives boil down to simple math?" She asked, barely above a whisper. I'd shocked her. She was hoping for some all explaining tragedy in my past to explain my crimes. She could hope all she wanted, but I wasn't going to give her that. She didn't deserve it. None of them did.

"All people are is math. Chemical bonds forming perfect molecular equations. Laws and sciences that calculate likely trajectories. Life is calculated moves, statistics, and risk assessment. Of course people's lives boil down to simple math, life *is* math. When we determine a person's worth by the figure in their bank account or the symmetry of their face how can it be anything less?" I asked.

For once she didn't have an answer. She didn't even seem to have another pointless question, which I was grateful for. I'd finally managed to shut her up and I knew the smile I felt crease the corners of my mouth only added to the horrific image she was painting of me in her mind: a heartless killer who smiles at the brilliance of their own work. My work *was* brilliant.

With a great amount of satisfaction on my part, the guard came to tell her our time was up and she began to pack her things. When she'd gathered everything she rapped twice on the door and it opened for her. She started to step through and I reveled in watching her go. With any luck it was the last time I'd have to endure her, but mid stride she paused and turned over her shoulder to ask one final question.

"How can you be so cold?" She wondered, and then left before I could answer. I thought about it as the guard cuffed me again and lead me back to my 6X8 foot home, sliding the door shut behind me with a clang and a buzz of the automatic lock. I'd never considered myself cold. Antisocial perhaps, standoffish, but cold? I suppose from her perspective I was cold. A heartless monster. My virus hadn't been designed specifically to kill, but as intelligent as I am I knew people would die. I knew a lot of people would die, and I did it anyway.

How does one commit such acts and not be cold? I suppose I was cold. I could be cold. There were amazing things out there that were cold. Ice was cold and beautiful and strong. Winter was cold. I guess I could be like winter, harsh and unyielding, and what I left behind was a blanket of purity to hide the ugliness of the world.

I laughed at little of the irony of it. Ugliness wasn't what I had a problem with. I'd been ugly once. Surgery changed that, but I still knew the truth of my face, the scars that should have been there. They were gone, but I was still scarred. Surgery is a marvelous thing. A blade and a skilled hand can erase the evidence of trauma or poor genetics. They could smooth the surface and give you a new face. Not all scars stay on the surface, however, and those scars aren't so easily removed.

6 Days, 11 Hours, 7 Min...

Again I was startled as the guard approached, or rather stopped outside the door of my cell. It was unlike me to become so distracted, and yet I couldn't quite shake the fog that seemed to hover about me since I'd woken up that morning. I was glad to see the guard wasn't Chuckles, but the younger one with dark eyes and an almost pleasant smile. I liked him. His face wasn't symmetrical or perfect. He was short for his size and a little over what was usually considered the acceptable weight. I liked the way his uniform curved out a little in his midsection. He wasn't perfect, he wasn't beautiful, and therefore I liked him instinctively. Beauty, in all reality, was uglier than ugliness.

I thought about the short man in front of me as we trudged down the hallway toward the interrogation room, where no doubt a bubbly brunette awaited me, recorder at the ready. He was certainly below average height, shorter than me even, and I'm not exceptionally tall. I noticed as we rounded the second corner in our path that he walked with a slight limp, and a quick peek at the movement of his pelvis told my why.

"A chiropractor could fix that right up." I told him as he released the cuffs at my wrists. They weren't as tight as usual. They never were with him. Another reason I liked him.

"I'm fine." He grumbled, his deep voice mismatched with his small body.

"I could recommend a good one if you like." I smiled, rubbing my wrists methodically. It seemed the fog was accompanied with a lack of circulation. I hadn't been able to get my hands warm all day.

"Don't think I'd trust any recommendation from you." He replied honestly. I liked honesty. I nodded in acceptance of his remark and he left, holding the door open for the reporter who nearly knocked him over with her entrance.

"Sorry!" She muttered out of breath to the guard. "Sorry I'm late." She apologized, this time to me.

"Perhaps you should have left sooner." I recommended, knowing my simple logic would presume rude in her eyes. If she was shocked or offended she didn't let on as she spilled the usual contents of her bag across the table and made an attempt at organizing them. I'd never seen anything that accompanied her truly organized.

She shuffled the papers that spilled from her notebook into a haphazard pile and slapped them at an odd angle from her scribbled-in book. My fingers itched to reach over and straighten them, but I decided against it.

"Alright, shall we begin?" She asked, a question she repeated every day we met. I considered recommending a thesaurus, but doubted she'd listen. She plopped a handful of colorful candy into her mouth, jujubes this time, and flicked on the recorder. "I was hoping to discuss something today that we've yet to touch on." She sounded more professional than usual and I worried momentarily about where she might be leading to.

"And what, pray tell, do you wish to discuss?" I wondered. There was plenty we'd not touched on that she would want to know about and most all of it I didn't want to discuss. I suspected her line of questioning was leading to one of those topics I'd prefer to leave in the dark.

"I've been doing some research on you." She admitted, tapping her pencil against the notepad in front of her. "You're career is well documented and I've read everything you published that I could get my hands on."

"And you understood it?" I questioned haughtily.

"Well, no, not most of it," she stammered, "but regardless, I've read it. I've talked to colleagues and interns you've had. I even had a wonderful conversation with an old college professor of yours. He seemed quite surprised that one of his star pupils turned out to be a terrorist." She told me. Only one man came to mind, bringing with it visions of tweed and the faintest scent memory of pipe tobacco. I missed the old chap.

"How is Dr. Jacobsen?" I asked, genuinely interested.

"I even talked to a few classmates from your undergraduate career. One named Jason Evans seemed particularly unsurprised by how you turned out." She continued, ignoring my question completely. She seemed to be on a particular mission today and was relentless in her pursuit. I had a suspicion about where she was headed and it did not leave me particularly amused.

"Evans is a competitive, egotistic Neanderthal." I told her, picturing the dunce a moment before shaking all thoughts of him away. He wasn't worthy of my thoughts. None of them were.

"He seemed to have a few unflattering words to say about you as well." She smirked, blushing at the remembered words that no doubt would have made a nun faint. Evans wasn't exactly my biggest fan. I figured since I loathed him it was only fair that he harbor some animosity towards me.

"I'm not surprised." I told her. She nodded. "Did he tell you about the time I almost got him expelled for cheating and how he's hated me ever since?" I asked. She nodded and I knew what the story he'd told her would have sounded like. I'd heard it before.

"Did you?" She asked, tapping her pencil against her notebook and looking at me like a puzzle she was close to solving. She was nowhere near close. You can't solve a puzzle when you don't have all the pieces.

"If I had wanted Evans expelled he would have been." I replied, taking a peek at the dirt that was collecting under my chipped fingernails. There was a time when I'd have fired an intern for having such filthy fingers. My how the mighty do fall.

"He never did quite seem to comprehend that." I smiled over my fingers, recalling the idiot again. "Of course he always thought he was smarter than me, so..." I rested the hand back on the table and returned my attention to my interviewer.

"And he wasn't?" She asked, though I was quite certain she already knew the answer.

“Few are.” I answered. I knew I sounded arrogant. I *was* arrogant. Rightfully so. I’d fought my way to the top and humility was not the road that gotten me there. Of course, once I’d reached the top I’d done everything in my power to secure my inevitable descent into the very depths of hell, but of course that’s all semantics. I’d never had much time for semantics. If my pretentious response ruffled Miranda in any way she hid it well. Only a single eyebrow rose against my implication. “You didn’t come here to talk about Jason Evans.” I stated, letting her know that, as usual, I was a few steps ahead of her.

“No, I did not.” She replied. “I came here to talk about you. That’s what I always come here for, to learn more about you, about what makes someone like you do something so heinous.” Her honesty was what I always found refreshing about Miranda. She didn’t beat around the bush. Even the first time I’d met her she’d told me she straight out she was going to uncover all my secrets. I’d wished her luck, but I knew I’d never reveal them. They were secrets for a reason. Regardless, she tried time and time again, digging deeper and harder than anyone ever had. In another world, another life, I might have been truly fond of Miranda Stevens.

"You want to know about my life before college. You want to know who I was before I was a genius." I clarified for her. "You want to know what went wrong and where." She nodded.

"You are brilliant, clearly, and charming and attractive. You could have done literally *anything* with your life. People don't just throw that away without a reason. There *has* to be a reason." I could see the desperation in her eyes. I'd not noticed before but I saw it now. I saw that her repetitive visits weren't because she wanted to make a name for herself, but because she actually *needed* to know the answer.

"Who did you lose?" I asked. An educated guess for the reasoning behind her incessant drive to unravel my mystery. A glint in the corner of her eye told me I'd hit on something, but she brushed away the tear and the answer I was curious about with the back of her hand.

"Is there a reason?" She asked, though the spark had left her some. "Or are you just as insane as they all want to believe you to be?" I suppose being called insane wasn't surprising, but admittedly it stung a little more than expected. Of course they'd call me insane. That's what you do when something is beyond your grasp, but that didn't mean it is truly insane.

"I'm not crazy." I replied. "There is a reason. The theory of causality requires as much. I don't know that it justifies what I did to anyone but me, or that it will make anyone understand or provide any sort of closure, but there is a reason I did what I did." I watched the hope blossom in her eyes. "I just won't ever tell it." I smirked as I leaned back and watched the hope fall, and her smile with it. This time she sighed and set down her pencil. For a moment I honestly thought I'd broken her, finally rid myself of her prying, but then she pulled her bag closer to her and instead of stuffing her scattered piles into it, she pulled something out.

Three things to be exact, laying one on top of the other. First was a half inch thick paper bound booklet with the word 'Crossword' printed across the top in bright, bold lettering. On top of that she laid a box of fine-tip, washable markers. The final item she retrieved, to my surprise, was a fairly large bag of my favorite candy. The red and yellow figures on the front of the bright one pound bag smiled at me and waved with their gloved four-fingered hands.

"Someone's been doing their homework." I observed, forcing myself not to reach for the items she'd clearly brought for me. Seeing the smile on my face she reached forward and pushed them slightly closer.

"You want them?" She asked, inching the tempting items closer to me. I suspected an ulterior motive, but I played along. It only half surprised me when she quickly yanked them back to her when they'd entered my reach. "I want something as well." She stated, folding her hands neatly atop the pile in front of her.

"I've spoken with the warden and he's agreed to give me more time with you each day. In fact, he agreed that I could have as much time as you'd agree too, so..." She smiled, ripping the top off the giant bag of peanut M&M'S and plopping a small handful into her mouth, "This is yours, and more if you want it, as long as you agree to give me more time. And not like another fifteen minutes, a real allotment of extra time with you." She smiled, satisfied with herself, and crossed her arms victoriously.

I truly didn't need the items she offered. Wanted, yes, but not needed. There was something, however, that I did want and she might be the key to getting it. In a gesture that caused Miranda and the guard, based on the jingle of keys I heard, to jump, I reached toward her. With a smile I stuffed my hand in the yellow bag and pulled out a handful of colorful ovals, plopping a couple into my mouth before I responded. A wave of Miranda's hand had stopped the guard from coming in, though I could still see the fear pulsating in her carotid.

"I'll give you more time, but there's something else I want first." I told her, plopping another candy coated blob into my mouth and crunching away in satisfaction. She stayed silent, waiting for my request. I could hear the guard shuffling outside the door. Our time was nearly up. "What I'd really like is a little space. Some fresh air can do a lot of good."

"You want to go outside?" She questioned, clearly not expecting what I'd requested.

"Yes." I replied, finishing off the last of the candy in my hand. "I've spent most of my adult life in a lab. Here I spend time in one of two miniscule rooms. I'm tired of small, cramped areas. I think I'd like to spend a little time outside before I die. So that's my deal. I will give you whatever time the warden will allow me to be outside. However much time you can get him to agree to for me is yours to accompany." I smirked as the guard opened the door. "Times up." I smiled, sliding the pile of items to me and reveling in the look of disappointment on Miranda's face. We both knew death row inmates weren't allowed outside of the death row ward.

She gathered her things slowly as the guard fastened my cuffs and piled the items she'd brought into my arms. He then unceremoniously pushed me toward the open door, past where Miranda still sat. With a little effort and a hard pound of the guards hand against my shoulder, I paused directly next to her, leaning ever slightly toward her. She stood quickly, instinctively placing her bag between herself and danger. I was danger.

"Good luck." I whispered and then, with another encouraging shove from the guard, stepped forward again. I didn't need to look behind me to see the look of terror on her face. I knew people were afraid of me. I was a murderer, a terrorist. I was evil. I was also fairly certain I was finally free of Miss Stevens. I smiled all the way back to my cell.

6 Days, 7 Hours, 43 Min...

By midafternoon I'd already polished my way through half of the book of crosswords, starting from the back and working forward. I'd also eaten roughly a third of the M&M's. My stomach complained from the sudden assault of sugar, but it was worth it. What did I care if I had to suffer through a little indigestion? If you only have days to live, why not indulge in the good things in life? In my case, any luxury was an indulgence, and I intended to enjoy the few I managed to obtain.

I was midway through a medium ranked puzzle, contemplating a six letter word for the language of the Dead Sea Scrolls when a guard rapped on the bars of my cells. I scribbled the answer in the boxes before I laid the booklet down and peered through the metal bars. My contented expression fell slightly when I found Chuckles on the other side of the door.

"It's not dinner time." I told him, wondering what he could possibly want. I didn't have a clock in my cell, but the bright light that streamed through the 2X2 foot window told me it was five o'clock at best. Considering dinner was never served before six, I couldn't quite figure out what it was he wanted. Not knowing the answer to something was not my favorite thing, and by the time I strode over to where Chuckles waited, I was feeling a bit nervous.

"Hands, please." He commanded, shifting the cuffs around his chubby fingers. I squinted once more at the window on the far side of the cell, wondering where it was I was being taken. I knew the process of this week. I'd memorized the routine. This was not routine. "Hands." Chuckles grumbled again, tapping the metal cuffs against the bars and making my teeth hurt from the noise.

"Where are you taking me?" I asked, still hesitant. I'd not heard of, nor experienced, any brutality in this prison, but it still made me apprehensive, especially of this particular guard. If there was a grey uniformed man in the place that would take a prisoner to some remote corner and thrash them around, or worse, it would be chuckles. From the day I met him I didn't trust him. Something about the twitchy look in his eye didn't sit right with me.

"Warden wants to see ya." He grumbled, laughing his eerie laugh as he motioned once again for my hands. With a sigh I agreed. The warden was the one aspect of the system that I couldn't predict. He also was the only person who had the authority to move me about as he saw fit. As Chuckles slapped the cuffs on, a little too tightly as always, I pondered what it could be the warden wanted.

He'd already questioned me at length as to a cure for my virus. He'd offered me everything under the sun for it in fact. What he didn't seem to comprehend was that I already had everything I wanted. My life's goal was complete, my virus worked better than I could have expected, and soon I'd be rid of this miserable place once and for all.

Six days, I reminded myself as Chuckles led me down the corridor that split into a Y. The warden's and the security office lay to the right, the doorway to the yard on the left. Surprise struck me when we reached the split and veered left instead of right. I paused, but Chuckles pushed the heel of his hand into the blade of my shoulder and I moved onward down the hallway I'd never entered. Hope rose for a moment before logic squashed it back to its rightful place. People like me didn't have the luxury of hope. Although, in this instance, it seemed hope hadn't been that far off.

I rounded a corner twenty three paces from the fork in the hall and found Warden Green and Miranda waiting for me. The latter had what could only be described as a victorious grin plastered across her face. She clutched her leopard print messenger bag with eager fingers and nearly bobbled as I approached. The warden indicated for Chuckles to remove the cuffs and he did as he was told with a huff through his raggedly groomed mustache.

"I guess I'm luckier than you thought." Miranda quipped, sashaying in her spot next to the warden. I couldn't help but feel the corners of my mouth rise slightly at her. She was certainly more tenacious than I'd given her credit for.

"I'm going outside?" I asked, looking between her and the warden.

"I will allow four hours of yard time a day from now until the date of execution. I'll leave it to you two to determine how that time is allocated." The warden replied. I'd always found him a bit out of sorts with his job. Warden's generally emitted an heir of authority, but Green was much too soft spoken, and his kindly features didn't seem to help in any way. Regardless, I nodded in agreement to his proposal.

"Miranda will be accompanying me I assume." I observed.

"Yes, as per your terms, Miss Stevens will be allowed the entirety of any yard time to continue her questioning, as well as the previously allotted hour she currently receives." Green explained. "Of course a guard will be present for Miss Stevens' protection." He added, giving me a sly glance. His glance told me that the guard was required, but that he didn't believe I was dangerous. I suppose in this instance he wouldn't be wrong.

I was grateful to find that it wouldn't be Chuckles who accompanied us outdoors. Another guard, one I hadn't met before, led us both through the gate, passed the metal detectors, and through the door marked **EXIT**. Once outside the cuffs were removed and I closed my eyes against the sun that shone down from above. The air was crisp, it was only mid-April, but it was refreshing. I inhaled deeply, letting the corners of my mouth wind skyward.

"Happy?" A voice called from beside me. I peeked an eye over to where Miranda stood. She was closer than she'd ever been. Closer than anyone had been since my arrest, save for the doctor in the infirmary.

"One hundred and thirty seven." I sighed at the petite woman. Standing next to her, something I had never done for more than the brief moment when I wished her luck earlier in the day, I realized she was shorter than I'd thought. The top of her curl covered head only reached my shoulder. I was tall, but not ridiculously so. She couldn't have been over 5'3" at most.

"137 what?" She asked, digging in her bag. I assumed I'd see the flash of her silver recorder soon.

"Days." I responded, ambling slowly across the small section of grass I'd been allowed. I surveyed the area as I walked, Miranda keeping pace beside me. The four sides were blocked by fence and building. Once corner held a wooden picnic table much in need of new paint. There was a basketball court along the wall of the prison. The hoop no longer possessed a net and the rusted metal hardly looked like it would withstand an assault from a ball.

I spotted a semi-intact basketball beneath the bench of the table and guided myself toward it. I picked up the object in my hands, weighing it between them, and then turned and heaved it toward the rickety hoop. To my surprise the thing stayed firmly on the wall as the ball bounced off it and through the metal ring.

"Nice shot." Miranda offered, retrieving the ball from where it bounced and handing it back to me. She was certainly being braver than she ever had before. I assumed the guard that hung roughly six feet away at all times had something to do with that. His shiny black assault rifle didn't hurt either.

"It's been one hundred and thirty seven days since I've been outside those walls." I finally replied, nodding toward the cracking brick. “I don’t remember how long since I held one of these.” I smiled down at the ball in my hands. “Years at least. Maybe decades. Time doesn’t really hold much meaning anymore.” I sighed, sending another shot through the rusted circle before letting it bounce away across the pavement fractured with grass and weeds.

“You used to play?” Miranda asked, though I had a feeling she already knew the answer. She knew a lot more than I expected her to.

“A long time ago. Never on a team though. I just liked the physics of it all.” I smiled, making my way back to the table and sitting atop it, my feet planted on the bench and my elbows rested on my knees. Miranda hesitated only moments before she mimicked my stance, crossing her legs. This is the closest she’d ever been to me. This was the closest I’d been to anyone in a long time. I felt the unexpected weight of loneliness set upon my shoulders.

“So...” Miranda interrupted by thoughts, “shall we begin?” She sounded as hesitant to ask as I was to respond, but a steadying sigh brought a shake of my head in consent and I allowed her questioning to begin.

"I mentioned earlier that I knew a lot about you. I've talked to professors, colleagues, old college roommates." I nodded in acceptance of her statement. "What I haven't had much luck uncovering, however, is anything before that. From what I can dig up, and let me tell you I've done a lot of digging, I can't find a single thing about you prior to your freshman year at Yale. In fact, from what I can see, it's as if you didn't even exist before that."

The weight on my shoulders shifted at her clear direction of questioning. She wanted to know about my childhood. It wasn't surprising. Most people thought I was a sociopath at best. People always seek justification for the things they don't understand. There has to be a reason, some sort of abuse in early childhood, a traumatic event, something. Miranda was looking for the answers to why I became what I am.

She'd done an impressive job researching me so far. The fact that she'd made it all the way back to Yale was a feat. I'd moved around so much since then I'd hardly shed a second thought on my original alma mater in over a decade. She'd found it and much more, and now she wanted to go back further. Unfortunately for her, there wasn't any further to go. There was a reason she wasn't able to locate any information on me prior to

2034. I'd made sure all shreds of my life before that time had been long forgotten. There was nothing *to* find.

"You want to know who I was before I went to college?" I asked, leaning on my elbows and tipping my head to peer deeply into her inquisitive eyes. She nodded once, seemingly uncertain of her decision to sit so near. "The answer is simple." I shrugged, sitting up straight again. "I was a child." With my answer, one that no doubt irritated the woman behind me, I stepped off the picnic bench and began a slow trail along the edge of the perimeter. Once again the counting started. I reached 22 before Miranda caught up.

"That's not an answer." She grumbled, sliding her messenger bag up her arm as it slapped along beside her. "You said if I got you outside, you'd answer my questions, but you're avoiding them like usual." She was pouting. It wasn't becoming of her, especially considering she was well into her twenties. I stopped mid stride and turned very quickly toward her. Quickly enough that I noticed the guard's finger flick to his trigger in my periphery.

"I promised the time was yours to interrogate me. I promised nothing in the way of answering each of your inane questions. You're old enough and smart enough to know if the past is buried it's meant to be.." I hissed, digging into her wavering confidence with the steely blue of my eyes. "I intend for my past to stay buried and I will not answer any more questions about it." I concluded, turning again to continue my stroll. The counting increased in volume within my skull. 36, 37, 38, 39...

"You haven't actually answered any questions." She complained, catching up again. "At least not about your past. But if you say to leave it be, I will. It seems to be a moot point anyway, and I'd rather not waste what time I have left with you. So let's discuss something else." Her voice had taken on a soothing quality, something akin to a mother comforting her child. Was she attempting to calm me? Did she see the pain through the terror I was attempting to inflict? Did she care?

"What did you have in mind?" I asked, sitting again on the same picnic bench I'd left only a few minutes earlier. It had taken 83 steps to circle the yard and return to my seat again.

"Why don't we talk about the present instead?" She offered, poising her pen again.

"My present consists of a 6X8 foot cell and three barely edible meals a day. What about that could possibly be of interest to you?" I questioned. I'm sure it appeared as if I was being flippant, but in some honesty I was curious about her sudden increase in interest.

"Alright, fair enough, but what about the present you. The person sitting next to me. I am actually interested in learning more about you as a whole." She remarked, tapping her pen against the spiraling metal of her notepad.

"What would you like to know?" I asked, resting on my elbows again, though this time I didn't look her in the eyes.

"The little things. The details I can't find in scholarly journals or newspaper articles. The private stuff." She smiled. "Although not *too* private, I promise." She smiled wider, gesturing some sort of motion that I assumed was supposed to represent honor or something akin to it.

"Very well, ask and I will answer." I accepted.

"Alright." She said, the glee in her voice only mildly grating.

"You've never married." She stated. "At least not so far as I can find record of."

"I've never married." I answered.

"Why?" She inquired. "Have you ever been in love?"

"Yes, I loved someone once. I loved them more than life itself." My shoulders hung heavier with the thoughts I didn't want to think. I never wanted to think those thoughts, yet they were what had consumed me for many years now. The driving force behind my every decision.

"Loved?" She asked. "As in past tense?" I only nodded. "Will you tell me about them?" She prodded.

"No." I replied curtly. There were places I didn't want to delve. Some things should always remain private. Some things I would take to my grave.

6 Days, 5 Hours, 51 Min...

Miranda managed to secure us dinner out in the yard. I wasn't sure if it was the fresh air or something else, but the food also managed to taste a little better. It was still pathetic slop that barely passed for food, but a little better than usual. This particular evening's meal was pizza, or the rectangular slab of chewy dough covered in greasy slime they passed off as pizza. I was glad for the respite of silence as we ate. Miranda's questions were interminable and exhausting. I'd answered each of them, though, at least as much as I was willing to.

"Did you have any pets?"..."A goldfish once. It died."

"What about friends?... No."

"Why not?"..."I prefer solitude."

"What did you do outside of work then? Did you have any hobbies?"..."I liked to read. I ran a lot. Occasionally I'd watch movies I suppose."

"What's your favorite movie?"..."Breakfast at Tiffany's"

"Music?"..."Classical and Opera mostly."

"Who's your favorite author?"..."Shakespeare."

"Do you ever read or listen to anything from this century?"..."If it has merit, yes. I'm a bit of an old soul, though."

"Do you have any family still alive?"..."No. I don't have anyone."

Dinner had come and the questions had stopped with its arrival. I was thankful. These questions were easy, but I could tell neither of us cared much for them. It wasn't the information Miranda really wanted. To me it was a waste of time. A look around my apartment would have told her the same things. I wondered what happened to my home while I ate. Was it still there? Had they destroyed it? Did someone else reside within its walls?

"I have a question for you." I told the brunette who was scowling at the still untouched rectangle in her hand. So far she'd only managed to eat the corn they'd served her. I supposed the corn was the best part. The vegetables always were. It's hard to mess up something that comes in a can. It could have used a little butter and salt if you asked my opinion, but of course they wouldn't add those things. Who cares if prison food tastes good? Butter is expensive, and fattening. *And fat is ugly*. I smiled at the forkful of corn before stuffing it into my mouth.

"You had a question for me?" Miranda asked. I'd gotten lost in thought again. She'd abandoned her pizza during my mental journey and had taken to munching on her candy again. Today's victims were gummy worms. She decapitated one as she awaited my question.

"I had a home when I came here, an apartment in Essex. Do you know what happened to it?" I asked, reaching for a red and orange lump of chewy sugar for myself. For once Miranda didn't flinch at my reach, though the bag sat directly next to the elbow she'd propped on the table. She swallowed the last of her worm before she answered.

"As far as I know the apartment itself is still there. They confiscated a lot of the stuff in it for evidence, but as for the rest I'm not really sure." She shrugged. "Was there something you wanted done with it? I could arrange for a lawyer to visit you to discuss those things." She smiled softly. Again she seemed to be soothing me and it baffled me just as much as before.

"I have no more need for the place, or the things in it." I replied. "I was merely curious." I added, pulling at the rubbery candy in my fingers as I pondered another curiosity. "May I ask you another question?" I requested.

"You can ask me anything you want." She replied, tugging another victim between her teeth, stretching its body until it broke.

"How did you convince the warden to give you this time with me?" I inquired, sliding the trays to the side so that I could lean closer. I wanted to know if she lied to me. I suspected she wouldn't.

"He owed me a favor." She replied, smiling slightly, though only one corner of her mouth tugged upward, and only marginally.

"How does a prison warden become indebted to a common reporter?" I expanded. She'd spent too much time around me it seemed. She'd picked up my tendency for vagueness.

"If you must know, Jim is a family friend." She sighed, fishing the last worm from her bag. She scrunched her nose at the color combination and sighed as she laid it back onto the plastic wrapper. I yanked it away, chewing as I considered how she might know the warden.

"A family friend?" I raised an eyebrow, catching a slight hint of something in the tone of her voice when she said his name. The fact that she was on a first name basis with the warden also suggested something.

"He and my mom are, well I don't really know what they are, but I don't think I want to either." This time her tone made it clear she didn't want to discuss the matter further. I decided, for now, to let it be. Her family situation wasn't my business after all. "So," she redirected, "what shall we discuss next?"

"You're the one with a thousand and one questions." I told her. We both smiled.

"You're the one who likes to dodge those questions." She retorted, smiling wider. She had a nice smile, warm and pleasant. It suited her.

"Very well, ask me something you've been leery of asking and I'll tell you the truth." It was risky, but for some reason I found Miranda enticing. I was curious what she might ask if given the freedom. At first she seemed apprehensive, clearly not sure if she should trust my offer. She was smart to be cautious.

She and I both knew I was calculating whatever question she asked, judging how much she would learn from me. She was aware that there was a good chance that this question may determine how much information she gets in the future. Eventually she decided to accept my unspoken offer and she smiled, taking her time to think over the perfect question to ask. Finally she spoke.

"Alright." She leaned forward, crossing her arms to rest her elbows on the table. "One question, one honest, *straightforward* answer." I nodded in acceptance. She pondered just a moment more. "How did you do it?" She asked at last.

"How did I do what?" I inquired, not completely sure what she was asking. There were several things I'd done in my life that most would find confusing and complicated.

"How did you create the virus?" She clarified. A prideful smile spread across my lips. Though I was slightly surprised by her choice, as well as the fact that she'd not asked it sooner, it was one question I didn't mind answering. An artist is always happy to explain their work.

I'd been working in genetics since halfway through my undergraduate career. I loved everything about what I did. Genetics is complicated, but once you understand it its very predictable. I started out my career in Los Angeles, working in a lab that did gene mapping. I worked specifically with a gene called PSEN2, which triggered early onset Alzheimer's. I spent day in and day out pouring over the gene maps of infants and detecting which ones were candidates for the procedure my company was working on.

It took us five years but finally we, myself and the two colleagues who hired me, found a way to incorporate gene splicing theories and a new technique we developed to cut out the PSEN2 gene and create a procedure to basically eliminate the chances of early onset Alzheimer's in our patients. To my knowledge the lab is still doing the work, although I believe they've branched into cancer splicing now as well.

Regardless, when the challenge had been met and there was no more research to be done I quickly grew bored, and only months after our patent was accepted by the FDA I left the lab. I worked in New York for a time, but again the position wasn't challenging enough and I only stayed a few weeks. Then I got a call from a colleague in London. He told me he was working on something new, a project that could change the face of the world…literally.

I joined my friend, Dr. Allen Thomas, in his small private lab in Essex and he began introducing me to his work. Now I mean this with absolute respect for the late Dr. Thomas, but he was a disorganized, bumbling drunk. His research was brilliant, but he lacked the structure and follow-through to see it to fruition.

As it turns out, he never did see the results of his pet project. He died only six months after I joined him. Fortunately he left me his lab and all of his research, along with a small fortune in grants and backers.

I spent the next five years completing his work, and more than doubling my sponsors along the way. People are far more likely to back something run by a young, stable genius than an old, drunken one. I hired a small staff to see to the business side of things while I devoted myself to the science. Just three years after his death I broke through the initial roadblock of Allen's research.

You see, every gene in the human body has an internal map, a predetermined purpose if you will. The struggle science has had in the past is discovering what each individual gene is predestined to do. Allen had narrowed out a small section of genomes that he believed determined something he called the 'beauty factor'. He believed one of the genes in this set held the key to whether someone was beautiful or not. He also believed we could find a way to splice that gene and imprint it any way we liked, essentially making beauty as simple as an in-vitro injection.

Imagine the possibilities. Imagine that everyone in the world could be born beautiful, and with further development, beauty could even be given to those already born, for a price of course. That was Allen's dream, a cosmetic goldmine. He wasn't far off either. He was right; the gene that determined someone's outward beauty was within the sequence he'd isolated. It took many trials and a lot of error, but after three years of research and testing and hope, I finally found the right gene. Gene number AG99, the 'beauty' gene.

It took another two years for me to discover how to manipulate the gene from its sequence. Every approach I tried failed, leaving the gene sequence useless and ironically leaving the host with the opposite of the desired effect. I grew frustrated and more introverted by the day. I went through interns like takeout, which is what I mostly lived on, and then one day it just worked. One day the gene didn't die and I spent a month of nearly sleepless nights figuring out what I'd done right this time.

I can still remember the intern I had at the time dragging me, delirious, from the lab table after four straight days without sleep and forcing me to lie down on the couch I kept in the corner of my office. I slept better that night than I ever had. I'd reached the end stages of Allen's work. When I awoke, however, I had a certain sense of dread. My project had consumed my life for many years and I realized with a heavy heart that soon my work would be complete.

No amount of award or success ever made me happy. I didn't do what I did for recognition or riches. I'd surely win something very prestigious for my work, a Harper Avery perhaps, but I didn't care. It was just another piece of glass on another shelf. I had plenty of those already. The thrill for me was always in the discovery, in the potential of what I might create, what I might be capable of. I'd always pushed myself to do more, and so yet again I pushed.

I turned my sights to the genes, determined to find something new, something more I could do with them. I finished the research quickly for Allen's project and sent my team off to deal with the publishing of the work and what use it would be deemed for. I won an award, I gave a speech, but my mind was in my lab. My mind was on the next project, one that would no doubt earn me more fame that I didn't care about.

I decided simply correcting an underproductive gene wasn't enough; I wanted to change the gene all together. If I could improve the trajectory of the gene, why couldn't I alter it in some way? I wasn't satisfied to simply make the map clearer for the gene; I wanted to be the cartographer. I wanted to be able to determine what that gene did specifically. It took several more years of research and tests, but I did it. I found a way to cut open the AG99 gene and change its coding. I could use gene therapy to change someone's appearance.

It worked, too. I never published the work, never finished it really, but it worked. My intern, Nigel, can attest to that, assuming he's still alive that is. You see I grew impatient. I didn't want to wait for approval for human testing, and the FDA wasn't being very cooperative in it either. I suppose they didn't like the 2.3% fatality rate, but every procedure has flaws. Every scientific advancement has had casualties. They just couldn't see that, so I took matters into my own hands.

Nigel had worked with me for over a year at this point. I never did figure out why I kept him around. He was a nuisance and a terrible assistant, but one day, as he was beginning preparations to leave my service for a scholarship opportunity, I discovered his worth. You see, Nigel wasn't beautiful. In a world where beauty is so worshiped, such a necessity of everyday life, it was a wonder Nigel made it as far as he did. He was a fighter, though, and a perfect candidate for a human test. I offered, he accepted, and three months later when he left for Johns Hopkins he was a different man. He was a beautiful man.

After Nigel left I decided to create the virus. I saw what my work could do and I realized the mistake I'd made. I'd created something that would not only perpetuate the world's inane obsession with beauty, but I'd given them a way to solidify it, a way to truly divide the classes. I couldn't live with that. I destroyed the research. The only copy left was locked away in my brain and I used that knowledge to change my research.

I turned AG99 into the marker for the virus. The target my bullet was aimed at. It took time and a lot of different trials, but I knew it would work. The groundwork was there, I just needed the right materials. I needed the right virus. Soon I found that, too, and using the same technique I'd used to reroute AG99's mapping, I remapped the genetic information of the virus.

I made a genetic weapon and I made my biggest mistake it's perfectly hidden carrier. That's how I did it. That's why I'm sitting where I am. It's the reason I will be dead in less than a week. My virus, however, my genetic time bomb, well, that won't be quite so dead. A scientist lives for their work to outlive them. I guess you could say my life is complete.

6 Days, 3 Hours, 9 Min...

The clock read 9:51 when I passed back through the guard station that separated death row from the rest of the inmate population. I'd never seen the rest of the population. The only people I saw were the guards, the warden on occasion, the annoying Dr. Gunderson, and of course Miranda. Of the group, the latter was the only one I didn't mind seeing, although that had been a more recent development. Not long ago I would have counted her among the nuisances of my incarceration. It's funny how quickly things change when perspectives are altered.

The twenty step trek down the hallway lined with empty cells was silent as usual. Only the rhythmic patter of tennis shoes on concrete echoed off the surrounding walls. Before my foot fell a twenty first time the guard jingled the keys at his belt and motioned for the door to be unlocked.

Buzz...Whir...Click

The door opened and just under a minute later the guard's footsteps echoed away from me. Three minutes and thirty seconds later the bustle of shift change reached my ears and then a few moments later, at what would be precisely 10:00, the voices and jangling keys stopped and only silence reached me.

The nights were always quiet. Only one prisoner meant the guard didn't need to do rounds. I wasn't going anywhere. I lay in my bunk like I often did, feet resting on the cold metal of the frame, eyes peering at the small portion of sky visible through the miniscule window. It was a cold night; I could see the puffs of vapor rising from the boiler room across the yard. The sky was clear, the reason for the cooler temperature, and the blackness was alit with millions of twinkling stars.

It was nights like these I almost wished there was someone else who inhabited this ward. I didn't often yearn for conversation, I didn't often yearn for anything, but when the night dragged on and the silence hung about I sometimes wished there was someone or something to interrupt it. Of course, anyone in this ward wouldn't likely provide much in the way of decent conversation, but perhaps that didn't matter.

As the moon started to inch from my field of vision I felt my eyelids start to droop, countering the rise of the opaque orb. I yawned twice before I finally gave into my body's request and drifted into unconsciousness. Dreams of companionship consumed me.

I dreamed of romance, of a boy and a girl, both young, both naive, and both smitten. It was a warm fall afternoon, a Saturday, and they were in the park. A blanket lay across the grass beneath an ancient willow, the long branches dipping around them, blowing in the breeze and obscuring them from the rest of the world. This was their place, their safe haven. This was where the rest of the world didn't exist to mock and judge, where they could simply be themselves. This was their place.

The boy had a basket and the girl had a book. They both rested their backs against the trunk of the old tree, breathing in the crispness of fall air. They ate sandwiches and chips, sharing an apple between them, and sipped on Sunkist. It was a perfect day. They didn't get many perfect days. Not together at least. Not like this.

The girl read aloud as the boy yawned on his back, her knee the perfect pillow for his weary head. Her voice was sweet and he smiled often both at her story and the melodious tinkle of her laughter. They were happy. Young and blissful. They were in love.

Her fingers ran through his hair, scratching his scalp lightly with her nails. He was in need of a haircut. The girl couldn't remember him ever wearing it this long. She finished her story and laid the book down beside her, bending to place a kiss on the boy's forehead. He'd fallen asleep, but the brush of her lips across his skin awakens him and he smiles wide, crinkling the corner of his eyes. She smiles pleasantly back at him.

"I've missed you." The girl says to the boy, kissing him softly once more.

"I've missed you more." The boy replies. Has it really been so long since they'd seen one another? The distractions of life make the time blur by and neither remember how long it has been since they'd last sat under the willow.

This time it's the boys turn to brush the hair back from the girls face, gazing up into her bright eyes. He can see himself reflected there; see the love evident on his face. It's mirrored in hers and he pulls himself up by his elbow to kiss the smile that tells him she loves him.

"Is this heaven?" The girl asks when the boy relinquishes her lips. The boy doesn't answer.

He sits up against the tree once more. He pulls the girl into his lap, wrapping her legs over his, and tucking her head under his chin. He holds her tightly, running his fingers through her long locks. He breaths in the scent of her, the scent that always meant happiness.

"I've missed you." He whispers again. They sit like that for hours, talking, breathing, enjoying their time together. They both know it is brief, at least for now. When the sun dips towards its nightly home they reluctantly stand and gather their things. They pause for one last embrace.

"I've missed this most." The girl smiles softly, a single tear staining her cheek with mascara.

"I love you." The boy tells the girl.

"I love you more." The girl smiles back, genuine this time.

"I love you most." The boy whispers as he wishes her goodbye with a lightly brushed kiss.

I opened my eyes, finding only the ceiling before them. The moonlight drifted brightly through the small window, lighting my cell. I tried to sleep again, to no avail. The moonlight slid down the wall at a painfully slow pace. Finally the sun poked its head above the horizon, yawning sleepily with the dawn. I didn't yawn.

I arose, eyes heavy from a sleepless night. I drug a hand across them and found them damp. The drying tears still itched on my cheeks. I hadn't even realized I was crying. I couldn't remember the last time I cried. It had been a very, very long time.

The lack of light told me it was still early and therefore I would not have any visitors for quite some time. I wasn't sure if I felt relieved or discouraged by this realization. I plodded the circumference of my cell five times, tapping my fingers along the wall at equal increments. It had been a long time since I did that, too. OCD they called it. I didn't have it when I was born, it manifested later, but that's what it was. Obsessive-Compulsive Disorder, the constant need to count and straighten and organize. The parts of it that made my work immaculate were handy, the others not so much.

I stopped after my fifth round. Five circles, twenty taps. An even hundred. Even numbers were always best. I could still remember the first time I accepted I might have a problem. Freshman year at Yale. I was in an English Lit class; we were studying Kafka's Metamorphosis. It was one of my favorites, still is. I was just packing up my things after dismissal, ready to head back to my dorm room and work on assignments from my other, more tedious, courses. I was just about to walk out the door, my exit interrupted momentarily by an obnoxious gesture of public affection, when my professor called out to me.

"Andrews, may I have a moment?" Dr. Schmidt called to me. His eyes were still on the paper on his desk but his hand was outstretched, beckoning me toward him. I acquiesced.

"Is there something wrong with my paper?" I questioned. We'd just finished a unit on Proust the week before and I'd been left a little confused and unsure if my paper drew adequate conclusions. I peered quickly at the paper in his hand. It wasn't mine. "Did someone copy me?" Was my second thought and my second question of the professor in the grey tweed jacket.

"No, no." He huffed, dropping the paper onto the stack. "No one has plagiarized you and as for your paper, well, I was quite impressed. I could surmise that Proust was a stretch for you, but you did quite well, as usual." He smiled at me, finally meeting my gaze.

"I found him a bit obtuse." I frowned. "I don't always understand such abstract ideas. I like things to be concrete and obtainable. I suppose I never had much of an imagination." I admitted with a shrug.

"That is actually what I wanted to speak with you about." He sighed, heavier than when he'd dropped the less than

adequate paper marked profusely with red. "You're an extremely bright student." He said once he'd shuffled some of the papers in front of him nervously.

"Thank you?" I replied, not entirely sure how to respond. Afternoon specials on Lifetime kept popping up in my mind and I tried very hard to not feel uncomfortable. I liked this professor. I had no reason to be suspicious. Regardless, I caught myself nervously reaching over and straightening the three pens he had thrown haphazardly onto his desk.

Professor Schmidt didn't speak the whole while I did it. He sighed again when I'd finished, the instruments aligned perfectly, descending in height order. I placed my hand back where they'd begun and he pinched the bridge of his nose.

"Have you ever been to see a psychologist?" He asked me point blank. I gaped at him, shocked by his question. I was a sound, rational individual. I was intelligent, he'd said so himself. Why was he asking about my mental history?

"No." I lied. "Why do you ask?"

"I think you might benefit from a visit." He replied, placing his glasses back onto the place he'd been rubbing. "Honestly, I've been noticing certain habits you have, and I think you might have OCD." He was nothing if not frank. A part of me found it

slightly ironic that his name was, in fact, Frank. Frankfurt L. Schmidt, Ph.D,. that's what his letterhead read.

"You think I'm Obsessive-Compulsive?" I asked him, still shocked, maybe more so.

"Yes. I've had some suspicions since you started my class, but what you just did solidified them for me." He gestured toward the pens.

"I'm not a head case." I muttered, hugging my books slightly tighter to my body. "I like things to be organized." I added a little more sternly. "There's nothing wrong with that."

"I've seen you counting." He sighed again. "I think you should talk to someone. I think it could only help. Someone as brilliant as you shouldn't be hindered by a disease that's so easily treated." His eyes were kind. He really was trying to help me, I could see that. The rational part of me could see that, at least. My pride, however, was blind. Infuriated, insulted, and blind.

"I'm not a head case." I snipped at him, reiterating my previous statement before I stomped from the room.

I'd spent the entirety of that evening mulling over his suggestion in my dorm room. I'd gone from irate to hurt to insulted and back many times. After several hours I'd planted myself firmly in the middle of my bed and stared at the wall in front of me. I stared at it for over an hour, calculating whether it was overly organized or not. Sure each poster, calendar, picture, or schedule had a place. They were all straight. They were balanced, not one side of the wall more or less covered than the other. But that was normal wasn't it?

I peered at my bookshelf, scanning the spines in hope of an answer. Each one was carefully placed on the shelf, categorized by genre, subgenre, and finally author last name. It was as I stared at that shelf that Dr. Schmidt's words started to sink in. Was that normal? Was *I* normal? I looked back to the wall covered in my sparse decorations and it clicked. The logical part of my brain caught up to and restrained the irrational part and I suddenly realized he was right.

All the signs were right in front of my nose. Each item that adorned my wall was equidistant apart. My drawers, my books, any series of objects I possessed were perfectly organized and categorized. And I counted. He wasn't wrong. I didn't realize I did it most of the time, but I still did it. Steps, pages, pencils, the list went on and on. I even counted what I ate. An uneven amount of morsels hadn't passed my lips in many months.

As a final test I pulled open my sock drawer, dumped the contents on my bed, and shoved them back into the drawer with a sweep on my hand. I put it back in its place and waited. It took only twenty minutes for me to drop what I was doing, literally, and yank the drawer free. Then minutes later the drawer was as it should be and I breathed a heavy sigh.

I went to see Dr. Schmidt the following morning to offer an apology and ask for a recommendation. I'd seen a shrink twice a month from that day until the day I completed my virus.

5 Days, 15 Hours, 8 Min...

Just before nine a.m. the guard arrived at my cell, stopping me mid stride on yet another round about the cell. I was restless, anxious even, but I couldn't figure out why. Since I awoke I'd paced the cell a total of eleven times. I paused only to sit a few moments in between each round of 100 steps. I was on lap number four of round number twelve when the guard approached.

"Let's go." He instructed. It was my favorite guard, the one with the bad hips. For some reason he seemed to ease my anxiety some. Something about a friendly face I suppose. Though I hated to interrupt my pattern midway I obeyed his command and slid my arms through the narrow rectangle in the gate.

Snap-click, snap-click.

The handcuffs locked around my wrists and the guard pocketed the key. With a wave of his hand the gate opened and he led me down the hallway, out the wing entrance, and down the other hallway I wasn't yet familiar with. Like the night before, we veered left at the split in the warden's wing and stopped at the gate by the outside door. A quick pat down and another procession of snaps and clicks as the handcuffs were removed, and the friendly guard left me in the care of the surly one with the automatic rifle.

Miranda was already seated at the lopsided picnic table. Her pen was rested on her notebook and her recorder was set and ready to go. Before her sat two trays. A bowl with steam lifting off its surface was centered on each tray, accompanied by a small plate of grapes and a glass of orange juice. I sat down across from the pretty brunette and noticed the steam was coming off the oatmeal that filled the bowls. Caramel colored goo swirled about the mushy white lump. How did she know I liked brown sugar with my oatmeal?

"Good morning!" She greeted heartily as I took my first bite, careful not to burn my tongue. When I'd swallowed I returned her greeting.

"How do you know how I like my oatmeal?" I asked her, shoveling another gooey heap onto the spoon. It wasn't even plastic silverware for once. Inmates weren't generally allowed metal utensils. This had to be Miranda's doing. She certainly did have a lot of pull.

"I've done my homework." She smiled, scooping a thick gob of her own into her mouth. Even the consistency was just right, thick and stiff. Just this side of overcooked. I was impressed.

"So, what do you have in store for me today?" I asked, picking at a few grapes. Green, my favorite. "Another battering of mindless questions?" I smirked as I sunk my teeth into the crisp skin of the grape. They were perfectly tart. It was a nice contrast from the oatmeal. I was very impressed.

"You answered most of my questions, at least the simple ones, last night." She responded, sipping on a steaming paper cup. I didn't know she liked coffee. I didn't really know much about her at all. "I was actually hoping you would tell me some more of that story you started a few days ago." She concluded.

I sipped on my orange juice, savoring the spread I was actually enjoying. I couldn't remember the last time I'd enjoyed a meal. I couldn't quite remember what story I'd been telling Miranda either and I looked at her for further clarification.

"The one about Cal. You said he learned his lesson when he went to school, but I never got to hear how or why." She told me. Oh yes. Cal. I'd forgotten about telling her that. It wasn't a story I liked to remember.

The anxiety I'd felt all morning seemed to pick up again and I caught myself organizing the things on my tray twice. I also realized as I bit through the second to last grape that I'd been counting my food again. Unfortunately I was left with an odd number of grapes and I glowered at the small green orb left alone on the plate.

"Is something wrong?" Miranda asked. The smile dropped from her face for the first time since I walked out into the yard. "You don't look well." She observed. I ignored her, occupied instead with the stare down I was having with a grape. The uncertainty of what to do with it itched under my skin. I could eat it but that would mean eating an uneven number. I hadn't had a problem with it for a while, but I could tell this day that my compulsion wouldn't stand for that.

Leaving it was also troublesome because it meant a solitary object. I liked pairs. Plus it left an uneven number of objects on the tray. Spoon, bowl, cup, plate....grape. I touched each in turn, trying to decide what to do. Spoon, bowl, cup, plate.... Twice my fingers reached for the grape and ended up back in my lap.

What I really wanted to do was fling it across the yard, but I was afriad this would be seen as some sort of act of aggression and I'd lose my yard time. I counted again. 1, 2, 3, 4...spoon, bowl, cup, plate...hand?

I found fingers instead of a grape along my path and I followed their movement as Miranda slowly plucked the green nuisance from its place and plopped it into her mouth. She chewed slowly and with each bite my anxiety lessened. When she swallowed I swallowed with her, releasing the breath I hadn't realized I was holding. I closed my eyes, squeezing them tightly. How had I slipped so far?

"My brother has OCD, too." Miranda told me. I opened my eyes again and she was smiling kindly at me. "Have you had it your whole life?" She asked. I shook my head no.

"I was diagnosed in college." I admitted. "I haven't had an episode in a very long time." I was surprised to feel heat across my cheeks. I was ashamed, mortified. I felt vulnerable in front of her. It had been a very long time since I had experienced that as well.

"Is it just even numbers or do you have other compulsions?" She asked. I was mildly surprised that I hadn't noticed her jotting anything down into her notepad. The recorder remained where it sat as well, still switched off.

"I count." I admitted. When was the last time I told anyone this. "Steps, objects, food…" I trailed off. Miranda only nodded.

"Did you take medication for it?" She continued. "My brother did well with the pills."

"No. Therapy kept it in check." I replied. I couldn't remember the last time I'd been to see Dr. Nazari. Too long, I guessed. "I didn't know you had a brother?" I added, hoping to send her onto another path of discussion.

"That is probably because you are the one being interviewed, not me." She smirked, downing the last of her coffee with a sigh. "He's a couple years older than me. His name is Stephan. He's a lawyer." She shrugged. A lawyer and a successful reporter. Her mother must be very proud.

"You said your OCD didn't kick in until later in life?" She wondered aloud. So much for throwing her off track. I nodded in agreement. "Doesn't late onset typically stem from trauma? Is that what happened?" I didn't respond, but she clearly took my silence as admonition. "Is that the reason you did all of this?" She questioned, realization spreading across her face.

"Enough." I snapped. I saw her flinch and the guard stepped towards us. Miranda waved him away and he hesitantly wandered back to his post. I sighed heavily. "You wanted to hear more about Cal?" I reminded her. I prayed she'd sensed that delving further into my 'traumatic past' wasn't in her best interest.

"Yes." She nodded. She even managed a small smile. "Yes, I'd like to hear more about him." I nodded and launched back into my story.

When Cal was fourteen years old his mother became ill. Cancer, the doctors explained. Tiny little tumors that would slowly eat away at her body until it gave out. She was terminal. She sent Cal to live with his aunt, the only family she had left. Technically the woman, well into her sixties, was his mother's aunt. She was an absent minded old woman who cared more about her bridge parties than Cal. He hated it there.

Time and time again he begged his mother to let him come home. He visited her every day that summer, holding her hand in the hospital while the doctors pumped chemicals into her bloodstream. She grew weaker each time he saw her.

Three weeks before school started, before Cal faced public education for the first time, he went to sit with his mother like always. He walked to the nurse's station, checking in, though he didn't really need to anymore, they knew him by first name. The nurses were nice. On this particular day his favorite nurse was behind the counter. She was a pretty, petite woman with auburn hair and twinkling eyes. Cal had a crush on her.

He greeted the young woman shyly. She smiled before she even looked up from her paperwork. When she found Cal's face her smile wavered. Her eyes gleamed in the corner and Cal knew something was wrong. He asked if he'd done something wrong. He'd lived with the aunt for less than two months, but already he'd grown accustomed to being blamed for anything amiss.

She promised him he didn't. She called him her 'sweet boy'. He blushed then headed toward the elevators as directed. His mother had been moved. Level five, the pretty nurse had told him. When the door pinged open he stepped inside and pushed the button marked with a five. The label next to it read ICU.

He found his mother quickly, but she wasn't really his mother any more. Her eyes were closed and her face was contorted in pain. Tubes and lines and needles sprouted from all around her. The machines next to her bed beeped and hummed and ticked. Cal was scared. He begged for her to open her eyes, to tell him what he should do. She never opened her eyes again.

"She died!" Miranda shrieked. "Oh my god, poor Cal!" Her eyes were glistening and her mouth was slack. I nodded in agreement of her assumption.

"The doctors told him later that the cancer had taken a sudden, aggressive turn. She slipped into a coma overnight and died two days later." I filled in the missing pieces. The simplified pieces technically. Adenocarcinoma wasn't something I wanted to take the time to explain to Miranda.

"That poor boy. He really didn't stand a chance did he?" She wondered aloud.

"No, he really didn't." I huffed bitterly. I suddenly didn't want to talk about him anymore. "When is our time up?" I asked, hoping she'd take the hint that I'd had enough for one day.

"Oh..." She glanced at her watch. "We have about ten minutes left. Do you want to tell me more about Cal?" She asked apprehensively. She may be pushy, but she's also intuitive. The makings of a great reporter I surmised.

"No, not right now." I sighed. "I'd like to be done for now." I stood, stepping away from the table and starting toward the door. The guard looked more than a little surprised.

"Wait, Doc, I still have ten minutes!" She called, running to catch up to me. I didn't stop. I kept walking, intent on reaching the door before her. I didn't want to talk anymore.

Suddenly a hand closed over my elbow and pulled. I spun, nearly toppling from the sudden redirection, and found Miranda staring between her hand and my face. She clearly reached for me out of reflex. She hadn't been thinking about just who it was she was reaching for.

With a shout from the guard she dropped my arm, covering her mouth with the hand that had just been clamped around my elbow. She had a surprisingly strong grip for such a small creature. She looked as if she might cry and I prayed she wouldn't. I didn't do well with tears.

"You're tired." She stammered, stepping back from me. She didn't have much of a choice since I wasn't moving and her anxiety, and the guard, wouldn't allow her to remain in close proximity with me. She may be oddly fascinated with me, but she was still afraid. I was still a monster in her eyes. If only she knew.

"You should go rest. We'll pick this up later. Lunch?" She suggested, though she didn't give me the option of either accepting or denying her suggestion. She stomped determinedly past me and to the door. I did notice that she moved a little more quickly than usual. Had I really startled her that badly?

I waited until she'd shut the door behind her to advance again. I stopped just before the wall and held out my hands for the guard to cuff. He opened the door and passed me off to the other guard, the one I liked, who I followed back to my cell.

"What did you do to that poor girl?" He asked as he released the cuffs through the locked gate. "She looked like she saw a ghost or something." He shook his head. He suspected the worse. I didn't know why. What's the worst I could do to her with the guard standing right there, rifle trained and ready?

"I didn't do anything wrong." I sighed, more to myself than the guard. He grunted but didn't reply. When he'd walked back to the guard station I sat on the edge of my bunk. I thought over the conversation I'd had with Miranda, of the meal she'd brought special to me. What did she want?

I knew what she wanted. I knew what they all wanted. Answers. Explanations. A cure. Logic. I had it all. Everything they sought was tucked away in my brain. I wasn't going to give it to them, though. Not even her. What makes her worthy of that? None of them are worthy.

With a long heavy sigh I stood, peering out the window into pale blue sky. I shook my head and started to pace. Twenty steps, five trips, five rounds. 100 is a good number.

5 Days, 11 Hours, 44 Min...

I paced all morning. Back and forth, around and around. I couldn't remember the last time I was so anxious. I tapped my fingers along the bars as I went, counting each one. One...two...three...tap, tap, tap...four five six...tap, tap, tap. Back and forth, around and around.

Twice the guard came to glower at me. He didn't say anything. This one never did. He just glowered, saw that I wasn't hurting myself, and then trudged away. He didn't need to worry. I wasn't going to hurt myself. What would be the point?

About 11 a.m. I grew tired of the monotonous pacing and very aware of how far my control was slipping. I resolved to sit on my bed and meditate. It was a coping mechanism my first therapist had used on me. I hadn't done it in a while and it took some focus to remember the steps, but within twenty minutes I was breathing rhythmically and my mind was stilling. Dr. Nazari always had me focus on one thought while I meditated.

"Hone in on one image, one thought." She'd say in her thick accent. "Just focus on one thing. Hold that thing in your mind and let everything else slip away."

I decided to focus on a memory from my early days. A bright summer day. A bat, a ball, and the laughter of childhood. Happiness was what I needed to calm me. Happy memories, better days, fonder times. I focused on that perfect snapshot of childhood and blocked everything else out. One stress at a time clicked off like switches on a board. Click, click, click….on and on…until nothing remained but a single memory of sunshine and playful bliss.

I was remembering a ball sail through the air, my eye carefully following it so I wouldn't miss, when strong hands gripped my shoulders and pulled me from my reverie. I flinched, startled by the sudden contact. I leapt back instinctively, my subconscious wanting to distance itself from the cause of fear. I hit the wall at the back of my bunk at the same time I opened my eyes. I found warm brown ones staring back at me.

"I thought you were dead." The eyes muttered, stepping backward until I saw the whole face of the guard I liked.

I must have been so focused I didn't hear him call out to me. His voice was soft. Softer now that he was standing mere inches from me. Was it concern I'd seen behind his big brown eyes? More likely fear that he'd lose his job if I offed myself on his watch. If it was concern I'd seen, it was for me. That much I knew.

"I was meditating." I told him, carful not to move. He looked like a scared puppy as he leaned back against the wall across from me. His chest rose and fell rapidly as he got over his own fright. I don't think he expected me to jump when he touched me. He probably shouldn't have touched me.

"Oh." Was the only response I got in regards to the moment of shared fright we'd experienced. "The reporter is here to see you. She brought you lunch." He told me, sliding the cuffs from his belt and backing slowly toward the door. When he was what I felt was a safe distance away I climbed from the mattress and slowly walked over, wrists extended.

He cuffed them and lead me to Miranda. I was a little surprised that when we reached the intersection of the halls that led outside one way and to the interrogation rooms the other that we turned right. Miranda was waiting in the now familiar 8X8 foot room with the grey walls and grey table. She had a paper sack sitting next to her on the table. The smells coming from it were divine.

"Good afternoon." Miranda smiled softly. Her voice lacked its usual tenacity and I wondered if she was still leery from our earlier encounter. I sat, let my guard uncuff me, and then finally greeted her.

"Good afternoon, Miranda." I replied. "I see you haven't given up on me yet." I observed, though I was only half disappointed. It seemed the bubbly brunette was growing on me. She was driven if nothing else. Determination had always been a quality I respected. "What's in the bag?" I asked.

"Lunch." She replied. She slid the sack closer to her and pulled out several white containers. The red and gold lettering on the side said Golden Inn Restaurant. The spices that smelled divine were Asian in origin. Chinese food for lunch, an inmate could get used to this.

She produced two foam plates and plastic forks from the bag as well and set them down in front of her. She tossed a fortune cookie at me as she opened the containers, spilling an even more potent aroma into the room. From the smell of it she'd gotten all my favorites. Determined indeed.

"I've got mushu pork, mongolian beef and broccoli, szechuan chicken, egg rolls, fried rice, and orange chicken." She listed, peeking into each container as she listed them. "What would you like?" She smiled, knowing full well she had, in fact, gotten all my favorites. Well, all but one. I assumed the orange chicken was for her.

"I'll try a little of each I think." I replied, giving her a knowing look. She nodded, understanding the look, and plopped a helping of each on the place designated for me. I noticed she was sparing with the orange chicken, which I was grateful for. I didn't mind the dish, but only if prepared authentically.

Miranda slid my plate to me, along with a can of Dr. Pepper, and I stuffed a forkful of mushu pork into my mouth. I closed my eyes as I savored the deliciousness, sighing slightly. When I opened my eyes again, Miranda was watching me. I swallowed two more bites before I spoke.

"Thank you, this is delicious." I told her. She smiled and took a bite of egg roll.

"I'm glad you like it." She replied.

"I assume this cuisine has strings attached." I teased. I didn't care if it did. It was the best food I'd had in months.

"More like questions." She admitted shyly. "I've been doing some more research and I was hoping you'd clarify a few things for me." Out came the pad and pen, the recording device already poised and running.

"I suppose I could lend an expert ear to your knowledge, especially considering I happen to be the leading expert on the subject matter." I smirked, shoveling another heaping forkful. It really did taste fantastic.

"You're in a better mood than earlier." She observed. "Did something happen while I was away?" Her eyes sparkled the way they did when she thought she was onto a lead. A true reporter, always digging for that golden nugget of information.

"I took some time to meditate." I shrugged. I went in for another forkful of the Mongolian, but realized my plate was already empty. Was I really that hungry? I hadn't been hungry in months. Maybe it was the food. Maybe it was the company. Most likely it was because I had a new toy, a living breathing one that I could toss around at will. Mentally of course. I'm sure the guards would frown on me physically tossing the petite Miss Stevens around.

"I didn't know you meditate." She observed, scribbling something into her notebook. I nodded slowly at her observation. There had been a time when it was common practice for me.

"It's not a regular habit of late." I shrugged. My plate was still empty and my stomach growled in protest to the fact. Miranda, hearing my vociferous stomach, grabbed my plate and piled it full again. If I wasn't mistaken it seemed she was using food to get her way with me. Considering the state of prison cuisine it was a fairly clever ploy.

"Well, that's good. I've never tried meditating before." She told me, plopping another spoonful of rice onto my plate before sliding it back to me. "Do you find it relaxing?" She inquired. I took a moment to swallow a mouthful of what she'd dolled out before I responded.

"It quiets the mind." I nodded, greedily stuffing my face. What did I care if I looked like a pig with no manners? Miranda didn't seem to care. She nodded in understanding. "You had some questions for me?" I decided it was time for a change of subject. If possible I always liked to steer the salivating reporter away from the weaker points in my emotional defensive line.

"Oh, yes." She smiled, shuffling back through the pages in front of her. "Right then, I've been piecing together your time after Oxford and I was hoping to have you check some facts and fill in some holes for me." I nodded in acceptance of her desire and she continued. I could supply some facts while I stuffed my face. The Mongolian really was delicious.

"Alright, question number one...over the course of your time at Thomas Labs, LLC you employed a total of seventeen interns, is that correct?" She was being very reporter like again. I tried not to smirk at her. She would always seem like a child playing dress up in her mommy's clothes, pretending to be an adult.

"That sounds about right." I guessed. Had it really been that many? I couldn't for the life of me pull up a mental image of more than five or six. I could only recall the names of four.

"Why so many?" There was the girl I knew. The one who had no problem digging into the personal lives of other people.

"Some were incompetent. Some left for other careers. Some left for other reasons." I remembered one in particular, name unknown, who called me an egotistical, raging maniac with split personalities on their way out. I never said I was easy to work with.

"One intern reported you for harassment." She read from a copy of some official report. Her eyebrow quirked in response to the note she'd apparently just discovered. The face of said employee flashed momentarily in my mind. Again I couldn't recall the name.

"The complaint was dropped." I shrugged. Miranda looked at me with her patented 'I know you're not giving me everything' look. "That particular intern was a special breed of imbecilic and I simply took the opportunity to inform them of their shortcomings."

"The report states that you called him a brainless Neanderthal on several occasions as well as hurling a handheld microscope at his head on one occasion while you berated him in a foreign language." Though she was trying to appear stern I could tell she was amused by this fact.

"Like I said, he was exceptionally incompetent. I do believe the day I threw the microscope was the day he'd spilled several batches of tests onto the floor. Each one set me back over a day in work and I believe it was on the third slip I threw the microscope and told him to leave." The exact words I used were a little more explicit or course.

"So you'd consider yourself to be a difficult person to work for?" She dug.

"Only if you don't do your job correctly the first time. I expected my interns to be focused, organized, and diligently attentive to detail. Anything less than that was unacceptable, as it should be. In a lab there is no room for error. A missed comma, an extra drop, and the entire experiment is worthless. My work was far too important for carelessness." The more I spoke the more pompous I sounded, even to my own ears, but it was the truth. What I did was important. Nobody saw it at the moment, but one day they would. One day people would consider what I did a gift. One day.

"You consider what you did important?" Miranda half asked as she scribbled away. I was pretty sure I saw the words egotistical and perfectionist amongst her scrawl.

"Yes." I stated matter-of-factly. "What I created, the work I did, was very important. I found a way to change the world as we see it. What my work accomplished made it so that no human being would ever exist with any sort of defect or abnormality again. Everyone would be flawless, perfect in every physical way." I snort at my own inside joke. "Do you not consider that to be important work?" I asked, turning the tides.

"I think it could be a very valuable practice." She replied, looking coolly into my eyes. "Of course no one will ever know will they?" Her lips didn't twinge upward like usual. They were hard and set. She was catching on.

"I suppose they won't." I smiled, crossing my arms victoriously.

"Unless someone can replicate your work. But seeing as how you've destroyed all of it I doubt that will happen anytime soon." She went back to her scribbles, seemingly displeased with me again.

"Oh, don't you fret Miss Stevens. One day some other genius will come about and discover what I did. They'll publish the work, patent the theory, and make an insurmountable profit off of perfection. After all, we reside in a world that is obsessed with external beauty. One day my work will be replicated, and when it is, perhaps people will finally understand why it was I did what I did. Perhaps then they won't think me so much a monster." I said the last part to myself. Only barely audible, but Miranda clearly heard it based on the look of reserved pity she gave me.

"Do *you* think you're a monster?" She asked. The question was sincere.

"I think one's perception of identity is often skewed by others." I sighed. It was a coward's answer, an easy way out, but I didn't know the honest answer. I didn't know if I really considered myself a monster.

"So you think that because others view you as a monstrosity that you should as well?" She was digging.

"I think from an outside perspective the events construed by my catalyst can be viewed as monstrous. People died after all. It may not have been my intention to kill, but I killed none-the-less. Murder is a heinous crime, mass murder unthinkable. By societies standards what I did makes me a monster. The acts I've committed are, in fact, monstrous, but whether I believe an unavoidable outcome of a strategically implemented plan makes me a monster remains to be determined."

She wanted an answer, she got one. I doubt it's what she was hoping for. She'd have been happier if I simply said yes. Admitting to it meant I was evil, that I'd purposefully killed all those thousands of people. Proving I was a monster, a soulless thing, made killing me easier. It's ok to destroy something that's evil. It's a little more complicated when the evil thing isn't as evil as you originally thought. Grey areas are always the hardest to see through.

I could see Miranda thinking. I could almost hear the cogs in her head whirring and buzzing, churning out questions. There were always more questions where she was concerned. Despite her annoying probing I was quickly finding Miss Steven's brain quite interesting. I could see that she struggled with whether to villainize or victimize me. After a long moment of pause she sighed heavily.

"Did you know in advance that people would die?" She asked. Her eyes gave away her anxiety over the question she asked. I paused a moment before answering. I had a feeling said answer would quickly sway her decision of me.

"Yes, I knew the potential outcome of what I intended to do." I replied, steepling my hands in front of me.

"And you chose to release the virus anyway, despite the fact that people would die." She continued. The frantic increase of the taps of her pencil told me she was uncomfortable. I'd not seen her uncomfortable for some time now. It was both unnerving and exhilarating. I had such an effect on her.

"Yes. Every execution of new work has a number of calculated risks. In this case the value of the outcome outweighed the calculation of loss." It was the truth.

"You knew people would die?" She stammered.

"Yes." I replied. Finally we were getting somewhere. I could see specks of tears on the corners of her eyes.

"Thousands of people?" She swallowed.

"Yes, thousands." I nodded slowly.

"Then I think that does, in fact, make you a monster." She muttered, barely above a whisper. Her voice weakened, but her gaze never wavered. Miss Stevens was stronger than I'd thought.

"Then I'm a monster." I smiled. A tear fell down her cheek, solidifying her decision of me. I was a villain.

5 Days, 11 Min...

I didn't see Miranda for dinner. Technically she was still allowed two hours of yard time with me that day, but she didn't show. Instead I ate my dinner, or what they passed off as such, in solitude. I was gratefully still full from lunch and barely picked at the tatertot hotdish they'd slopped onto my 10X14 inch tan plastic tray.

It was mushy and barely warm. I managed to swallow one tatertot. The green beans that accompanied it were equally cold and soft, and seemed to be a grayish color. I wasn't aware green beans were meant to be gray. I'm pretty sure they're not. I did eat the two peach halves that completed the meal. At least they weren't hindered by cooking, or lack there of. I also swallowed the room temperature container of 2% milk they provided.

Ten minutes after consuming my 'meal' I happened to notice the date on the milk carton. It was at least a week past the printed numbers and I spent the next twenty minutes over the toilet with my finger down my throat. It wasn't shaping up to be a pleasant evening.

Once I'd retched up as much as I could I leaned back against the bedframe, wiping the spittle from my face with the back of my hand. My body was clammy from exertion and I felt hungry and nauseated at the same time. I began to wonder what I might have gotten to eat if Miranda had shown. I also wondered if I'd ever see her again. Both notions only added to my discomfort.

"You're getting spoiled." I told myself, pushing up with my forearms until I was seated on the bed rather than the floor. I lay back on the mattress, staring out the window at the starless sky. Clouds hung in their place. Dark gray ones that looked ominous and threatening. Soon enough their threats came to fruition and thunder rolled across the land while lightning scorched the sky. I could smell the electricity in the air. It seemed the weather was as anxious as I.

Time rolled on, ticking closer to another midnight. Another day closer to my execution. I found myself wondering about my last day a bit. I'd not given it much thought. It was an inevitability at this point so I'd figured it didn't warrant any further consideration.

As I lay there, however, I began to play the scenario over in my head. The medical aspects, the needles and chemical concoction they'd inject, those things I knew about. I knew it wouldn't hurt. I knew it would be humane. I also knew there were plenty of people who wished it wasn't.

What I didn't know was what would take place outside the small chamber that would house my body as it died. I knew the execution was not open to the public, but there were those that were allowed to attend. When the date had been set the warden had asked me if there was anyone I wanted there. I'd said no. I had no one left.

There would be reporters, Miss Stevens among them no doubt. There would also be representatives of the community. Under normal circumstances the victims or families would be allowed to view, but in situations like mine, where there were far too many of those to fit, a few select individuals were chosen as representation. I'd heard the guards whispering countless times about who might attend. Mine was a high profile execution.

I'd caught rumors that the governor was to attend. One guard had mentioned the President. I highly doubted it. The President of the United States had more important things to do than watch me take my last breath. I'm sure they'd merely send him a memo that the deed was done. A snapshot of my corpse perhaps.

That was the part I struggled to wrap my mind around. I'd be a corpse. I was leaving this world in only 5 short days and there was this group of people who were going to watch it happen. I'd been called monster, villain, terrorist, and yet these people were going to sit around and watch me die. They'd enjoy it, too, they'd find pleasure in my demise. They'd be happy to see me take my last breath.

I'd never watched anyone die. If there had been a way to avoid any casualties I'd have done it. There wasn't, though. The only way to spare the lives of those who'd died was to not release the virus at all. That wasn't an option. I'd always known, since the very first moment the possibility waltzed into my mind, that I'd release the virus, regardless of the consequences.

Maybe that did make me a monster. Maybe I was as evil as they all thought, maybe not. I didn't care. I'd done it. There was no going back. There was only an end left for me. Finality. I suppose in some way I found peace in this. Human beings spent so much of their existence wondering if, why, or when. I didn't have to anymore. I knew the why and the when, even the how. There was no more if for me.

The thoughts of my last day bouncing about my head made sleep unreachable yet again. I was grateful that I didn't resort to pacing again, but the weariness that set into my bones was nearly worse. At least pacing was mildly productive. Worrying was a waste.

The hours inched closer to midnight, only minutes away in fact, and yet I'd not been able to sleep. Thoughts of Hamlet flitted through my mind, mixing with the already present anxieties, and when I finally gave into sleep I dreamed of strange things.

I awoke, at first, surrounded on four sides by dark brown walls. The space was cramped. My fingers slid across the wall and it crumbled beneath my fingers. Dirt scattered about me. I was in a grave. My grave. Above me all I saw was stars. Bright, magnificent stars illuminating the sky. I marveled at their sight.

Quickly the stars gave way to darkness and something scattered across me. More dirt. I choked on it as more fell, shovelful after shovelful. I gagged and spit and tried to cry out, but every time I opened my mouth more dirt fell in. My limbs were soon covered. I could feel the weight of the earth upon my chest, mounded on top of me. I was being buried alive.

I cried out, but my scream was cut off midway by a blinding light. I shielded my eyes from it, peeking between fingers to glimpse its source. It seemed to be coming from all around me. I wandered, no longer trapped within the grave. I could make out others, figures amidst the light, but I couldn't see their faces. I tried to speak to them, to reach out and touch them, but they were always just out of reach.

I walked on, unsure what else to do. Soon the light began to dim. It faded in intensity until I was able to lower my arm and squint against it. The white had turned orange and all around me the colors of sunset blossomed. I turned my back to the sun, protecting my eyes from its rays. Night was drawing near.

As my eyes adjusted I noticed grass beneath my feet. Ahead of me lay large stones, aligned perfectly into rows. I stood between two of them. I began to walk, the sun still at my back. The stones seemed to go on and on forever, never turning, never changing. Giant round stones that bore no marks or significance. I felt frantic and as I continued onward, my pace increased until I was moving at a quick lope.

My feet skidded over the wet grass until suddenly I tripped on something and went sprawling onto the ground. My fingers clung to the damp earth; my lungs sucked the air back into my body. Finally, I made my way to my feet again. I looked to where I'd tripped and found a shovel. Beyond it was a rectangular hole in the ground, placed just in front of one of the boulders. A grave.

I didn't want to look. I didn't know what lay at the bottom of that grave, but I didn't want to either. I turned to walk away but a voice called out to me. A haunting name reached my ears, one I'd not heard in many, many years. As much as I didn't want to look, I couldn't stop myself.

I slowly crept to the side of the grave, careful to keep my feet and my wits about me. I peered over the edge and saw only dirt. The grave was empty. I sighed, but the voice called again. I peered closer, sure I'd missed something, and at the center of the bottom of the grave a small speck of light broke through. I squinted to see better in the thickening dark, but I couldn't make out what it was.

Again the voice called to me, louder this time, and I saw the light grow in diameter. Over and over the voice called and each time the light grew as the dirt crumbled away from it until the entire bottom of the grave was gone. What remained was an unfathomable pit, glowing with the fires of hell. Voices called my name, voices I no longer recognized. Voices that sent a chill to my core.

They called to me, fingers reaching beyond the broken earth. They beckoned me to them. I tried to pull back, but an invisible force pulled downward on me. I fought, digging my heels into the damp earth, but my feet slid across the soil. Finally I reached the edge of the grave, my toes teetering over. A final voice called to me and I fell.

4 Days, 20 Hours, 57 Min...

My body hit the ground hard. The cement was cold against my face and my nose stung from where it had struck. I rolled onto my back, lying flat on the ground, as I held my hand over my pounding heart. Though I knew it was scientifically impossible for a heart to beat its way out of a chest cavity I felt as if mine were trying its best to do just that. I felt the rapid pulse of it where my fingers rested on my sternum.

My breathing was equally as rapid. Quick, short breaths heaved my chest up and down. Fear had a strong grip on me. I couldn't remember the last time I'd been afraid. Actually, I could, but thoughts of that night only made everything worse, and so I ignored them.

Flashes of the nightmare played through my mind and my heart refused to abandon its erratic pace. I could feel the sweat sticking to my skin from the exertion of it. I felt like there was no escape, no way to run away from the terror that had suddenly attacked me. It had snuck up on me in a moment of weakness. In that moment that's exactly what I felt, weak. I started to cry. Another thing I'd not done in a very long while. Another terrible memory of another terrible night.

I lay on the floor, tears falling silently from my eyes and pooling on the cement below. I laid there until I fell asleep. I don't know when. I don't know how long I laid there or how long I slept. Not long I'd guess. I only remembered being woken up, and not gently.

Chuckles nudged my shoulder with his foot. I must have rolled onto my stomach while I slept. He kept nudging, more insistent and less gentle with each prod. I opened my eyes, wincing at the light and the dryness the tears had left behind. They'd also left a throbbing headache between my temples. Chuckles was lucky I didn't have a weapon.

I acknowledged his presence with a groan and rolled onto my back again, shielding my eyes with my forearm. My stomach growled and my eyes ached and I felt more defeated and pathetic than I ever had. Chuckles continued to prod at me, though verbally this time.

"Get up." He commanded. I sighed at him, ignoring the command. Had it been a request and a different guard I might have been more compliant. Maybe not. Not this day. This day I was irritable.

"Get up!" He commanded again, kicking out at me with his boot.

"Rogers!" Someone yelled from the hallway. The second voice prompted me to sit up and peer over my shoulder. I didn't recognize the voice. Curiosity was a powerful motivator.

I found a man of average build and height, with sand colored hair and warm brown eyes just beyond my cell door. He wore glasses, thick ones with dark rims, and was holding a clipboard in one hand. He wasn't dressed like the guards. He wasn't a guard. His clipped on tag read visitor. My curiosity piqued further and I got to my feet. Chuckles reached for his stick.

"Chill." I told the twitchy guard, crossing my arms and leaning against the bed frame to signify I wasn't making any sort of move toward him.

"Well, it's not dead." Chuckles grumbled. "Hands." He instructed. Again I ignored his request. Again he reached for his stick. I could see the fury my insolence flared in him, but I didn't care. Not this day. Not ever. Nothing would touch me today.

"Rogers." The man with the clipboard called again. He was dressed in well fit khaki pants, brown leather loafers, and a blue button down shirt that was tucked neatly into his belted pants. No tie. No name tag. Nothing to signify why he stood outside my door. He moved inside the cell with his second warning to the overzealous guard. Chuckles wasn't pleased.

He was even less pleased when the man reached a steady hand out and laid it gently on the bigger man's shoulder. Chuckles didn't like his authority undermined, and this gesture did just that. It also held a demeaning note, which only further increased my interest in this new man. I liked seeing Chuckles squirm.

"Perhaps if you asked nicely you might get a more compliant response." He told the red faced guard before turning his attention to me. "Might you please allow Mr. Rogers to cuff you so we may head to the infirmary now, please?" He requested. It might have been the most polite request I'd ever gotten. And all within the concrete walls of a prison. I acquiesced immediately, giving chuckles a sly smile. He replied by tightening the cuffs an extra notch.

By the time we reached the infirmary I could no longer feel my fingers. My hands were cold from the lack of blood supply and I rubbed them together best I could to stimulate them. I'd remembered halfway out the door the apparent reason for the new visitor. Prison regulations require a complete physical of an inmate prior to execution. I found it a bit redundant, but it got me out of the cell so I had little to complain about.

Chuckles was less than thrilled when the doctor asked him to step outside for privacy purposes. I wasn't what you'd call shy, I'm a scientist after all, but Chuckles was definitely the last person I wanted to flash my bits to. The added bonus of watching him squirm under the doctor's authority again was just the icing on the cake. I smirked at the irritable man as the door closed between us. I quickly heard the rhythmic clink of his keys against his thigh as he paced outside.

"Now that we're rid of him, let me introduce myself." The kindly man offered his hand. "I'm Dr. Neil Cichowski." His smile widened as I shook his hand quickly. His grip was soft, but he seemed nice enough.

"Hi." Was the only greeting I could muster. I was still reeling from the dream and the tears and sleeping on the floor.

"Well, before we begin, may I ask why it was you were asleep on the floor when we came to collect you?" He tilted his head to the side, reminding me of a puppy perplexed by a new toy. I wasn't sure how I felt about being his new toy.

"I fell out of bed and didn't feel like moving." I shrugged. This wasn't a psych consult, but that didn't mean I wanted to divulge any information that might stall the progress of my sentence. "It's not like the mattress is any more comfortable." I added for justification. He chuckled.

"I suppose you are right." He smiled, his brown eyes warming with his smile. "Well, shall we be on with it?" He asked with a sigh. I'd not noticed before but he seemed to have a slight posh accent. I couldn't place the exact origins, but he was certainly English, or at least had spent a fair amount of time on the island.

"Your accent, where is it from?" I asked frankly as I changed into the gown he'd given me. He had his back turned out of consideration, though I wasn't sure why he bothered. I could see his shoulders soften in the familiar memories of home.

"I grew up in Kensington." He replied as he turned back toward me. "I moved to the states when I was fifteen." I nodded in response. He pulled the stethoscope he'd acquired from around his neck and listened intently to my chest. "You spent some time in England if I'm not mistaken." He stated. I nodded again, not wanting to interrupt his examination with my words. When he'd apparently listened all he wanted to he stepped back and placed his hands on his hips. “So how long were you across the pond?”

“Six years total, though I split the last one between there and Venice.” I told him. He gestured for me to tilt my head back so he could probe my throat with his fingers and I did as I was told.

“Ah yes, Venice.” He sighed. Of course he knew the significance of it. It had only taken the government two weeks to track the virus back to its origination point. And just days more to track it back to me. It wasn’t hard. There weren’t many of us on the planet capable of it.

“May I ask, why Venice. Why not a more populous city such as New York or Beijing?” The doctor questioned. For once the questions seemed to be more out of curiosity than demand for answers.

“Its location provided the optimal breeding grounds. The virus was waterborne to begin with, genetically triggered to mutate into airborne upon incubation, and the entire city of Venice is built on water. It also is a highly popular tourist location and offered a more widespread outbreak pool.” I answered. He nodded, continuing to check my glands for swelling.

“You’re very intelligent.” He observed.

"I am." I agreed and he laughed.

"And modest as well, I see." He smiled as he pinched the skin of my forearm, checking for dehydration.

"Humility has always been wasted on me." I told him, watching the skin snap back into place. "I always figured if you have an accomplishment worthy of pride, you should be prideful."

"And you're proud of your accomplishment?" He asked. I didn't have to guess which accomplishment he was referring to. Though I'd made dozens of useful contributions to the scientific world in my career I would forever only be remembered for one. With a sigh I answered him.

"Yes." I retorted quickly. Perhaps not what he'd expected to hear, but he didn't argue against me. He simply nodded and continued on in his examination.

Twenty minutes later, almost to the T, he'd examined everything that could be examined. He'd drawn blood, listened to my heart and lungs, checked every orifice in my face, tested my blood pressure, and poked his bony fingers in my belly enough times I was sure I'd have internal bleeding before the day was out. To say he was a gentle touch would be a vast understatement. At least his hands weren't cold. I was grateful for that much as he pushed on and poked at my innards.

When he'd sufficiently examined, prodded, and tested the doctor began to pack up his kit into his little black bag. It reminded me of one you'd see on old television shows or movies. I couldn't help but smile at it. When he turned back to me, though, there was no smile on his face. I knew the question was coming before he even asked it.

"Would you like to tell me where you got those scars?" He asked, resting his elbows on his knees and steepling his fingers in front of his chin. I should have known we'd end up here eventually. The few times I'd succumbed to an examination they always asked. In a world where perfection and beauty is everything, seeing long, jagged scars crisscrossed over an otherwise unmarred chest is slightly shocking.

"They're from a long time ago. Long healed and no longer a concern." I replied, continuing to dress despite his attention. He was a doctor, he'd already examined 90% of my body, what did I care if he saw my underwear?

"And you never had them removed?" He seemed surprised. I found it comical that he found the fact that I'd chosen not to have scars removed from my body more shocking than my admonition that I was proud of the virus I'd released. He certainly was a strange little man.

"I didn't see the purpose." I told him, further confounding him. His head twisted back and forth, like a bird looking at a bug. I was starting to feel less comfortable around him by the minute.

"It's not as if you didn't have the money, or the contacts. You were acquainted with several physicians I'm sure that could have taken care of them for you." He continued as if he'd not heard me. It was starting to wear on my nerves. There weren't many of them this day to begin with. "If only I had the time." He sighed at last, tapping a long, boney finger on his chin.

"What's the point?" I said, raising my voice and ensuring he heard me this time. He looked at me as if I'd just asked him the most inane question on the face of the planet.

"Well, they're simply unsightly, and on such an attractive young person..." He felt sorry for me. He felt sorry for me for having ugly scars and diminishing my 'beauty'. It was the last straw.

"You know what's *unsightly* Dr. Cichowski?" I hissed, anger rising in my throat like bile. "What's truly unsightly is people like you who care more about a few scars than the fact that the person standing before you is directly responsible for the deaths of thousands of people. They may make me *unsightly* doctor, but my scars do nothing more than remind me of a past I've long left behind. They serve a purpose. They remind me each time I look at them why I did what I did. They remind me that I was right to release the virus, that I did it specifically because of people like you!"

The doctor staggered backward, grasping his chest as if I'd stabbed him there. I knew he could see the anger in my face, the hatred in my eyes. I did hate him. In that moment I hated the world again. I was glad I'd destroyed them; I hoped I'd destroy them all. I'd love nothing more than see the vain ingrates of this world writhing in agony.

I lunged for the doctor, compelled by rage and forgotten pain. I couldn't make *them* pay, but I could make him. I could squeeze his scrawny neck until the tissue folded under my skin and his eyes went cold. Maybe it would help. Maybe it wouldn't. I didn't care. In that moment I saw red, I wanted blood, but before my hands found purchase everything went black.

4 Days, 13 Hours, 37 Min...

I awoke in my cell, laid haphazardly on the mattress of my bunk. One arm was pinned under my body, numb. It also seemed an entire percussion section had taken up residence in my skull. At least that's what it felt like based on the consistent, rhythmic pounding that occurred there. It seemed they were keeping time with my heartbeat.

I groaned as I repositioned myself to free my pinned arm. I massaged the tingling fingers, encouraging blood flow into the starved appendage. My skull ached and every movement of my head or neck made it worse. I winced a total of three times before I finally managed to get into a sitting position, using the concrete wall to lean against. The sun was already higher than the window in my cell and I wondered where the time had gone.

More importantly I wondered where *I'd* gone. Last I remembered I was in the infirmary, but now I was back in my cell. I replayed the last few moments of memory and on the third rewind remembered feeling a blunt pain in the back of my head as the lights went out. My now reawakened fingers inched toward the back of my skull; reaching for the place I'd remembered the pain. I immediately withdrew them again upon contact.A sharp sting rang through the pounding. I wasn't sure what was worse.

My fingers came back into vision, sticky and darkened with drying blood. Someone had knocked me over the head hard enough to leave me unconscious for what I guessed was at least an hour. I wondered if I had a concussion, but the lack of dizziness and nausea told me I was probably fine.

I heard voices echoing down the hallway, reminding me of the cause of my waking. I'd heard raised voices. They seemed to continue still, and though I couldn't make out what they were saying, it seemed someone was rather unhappy. For a moment I thought it might be over what I'd done, that maybe someone was mad at Chuckles for conking me over the head, but that couldn't be. No one cared what happened to me.

The voices escalated and then I heard the patter of feet heading toward me. Their padding was much too soft for the guards and the pace much quicker than it should be. Whoever was headed for my cell was moving fast. I curled inward, preparing for whatever was coming. I assume it would be either someone come to get revenge for the pathetic doctor or someone who'd simply had enough of waiting for me to die and had decided to take matters into their own hands.

I closed my eyes and shielded my face as the pattering, now followed by the loud footfalls of the guards, drew near. I could hear the panting of labored breathing, the high jingle of keys slapping against the legs of the guards. Clothing rustled as the guards caught up to whoever was after me and grabbed hold of them. I wondered if they did it because they didn't want me to die or because they'd get in trouble for letting me die like this. I figured it was the latter.

"Let go of me!" A voice called out. It was feminine and familiar. I uncovered my eyes and found the determined Miss Stevens standing outside my cell, flanked on either side by very disgruntled looking guards.

"Unhand me you morons!" She yelled at them, jerking her elbows out of their grip. "I have rights, you know. What would the warden say if he knew you were manhandling me like this?" She spit and they each flinched, sighed, and then stepped backwards slightly.

Miranda straightened her clothing and brushed dust off her that probably didn't exist. She was being dramatic, but I found it amusing for some reason. I seemed to frequently find her amusing. When she'd straightened herself and given each of them a venomous look, she cleared her throat and turned her attention to me.

"Hi." She smiled. I smiled too, sliding forward to wander over. I only made it halfway vertical before the dizziness hit and I had to sit back down. Miranda gasped loudly. "My god, Doc, what did they do to you?" She asked. Each guard behind her got another evil look, though neither had been involved in my assault.

"I'm fine." I reassured her. "Just a bump on the head." Again I tried to stand and was more successful this time, though I still had to keep one hand on the bedframe for stability as I stumbled toward the door. Miranda's hands gripped the iron bars. Her eyes were full of a concern.

"Have you called a doctor?!" She questioned the guards behind her again. They both looked at the ground. Miranda groaned in complaint and whipped out her cell phone. I was pretty sure they weren't allowed in here, but I didn't see either guard move to take it away. It seemed Miss Stevens was feistier than I gave her credit for. Or perhaps the weight of her connection to their boss merely loomed largely over their heads.

"Miranda, I'm fine. I've not thrown up so I doubt I have a concussion. The cut will heal in a day or two." I reassured her. Her eyebrows reached skyward.

"Cut!" She exclaimed. I rolled my eyes and ran a hand across my brow. The pounding was still there but it seemed to be dissipating quickly, to my chagrin. "That's it, I'm calling you a doctor." She said, punching something into her phone. I sighed and closed the gap between us, grabbing hold of the hand that still wound around one bar.

"I don't think they'll let me see the doctor anymore." I told her as my fingers encircled hers. She jumped, startled by the contact and the guards were at her side in an instant.

"Good god, will you two go away! I'm fine!" She complained, elbowing the guards aside. I released my grip, raising both hands in the air as a show of complacency. When the guards returned to their previous spots against the wall she turned her attention back to me.

"Why won't they let you see the doctor?" She inquired, the cogs in her reporter mind churning. She could smell a story brewing.

"Because I tried to strangle the last one." I told her. No need for evasion. It's what I'd done. I didn't regret it. I regretted getting smacked over the head because of it, but I didn't regret the intention behind the grasp I aimed for the weasel's throat.

"And when did you do this?" She asked, catching on quickly.

"This morning." The guard answered for me. "Tried to kill poor Dr. Cinchowski and one of the other guards had to step in." The two looked smug. Apparently they were friends of Chuckles, or the doctor, or both perhaps.

"And by step in, you mean get violent?" Miranda shot over her shoulder.

"The doctor was turning purple!" The second guard told her. I smiled at the thought. It wasn't true. Chuckles had gotten to me before I'd inflicted any harm, but I still relished the idea of squeezing until the bastards face went blue.

"So that justifies bashing someone over the head hard enough to leave a laceration?" She scolded.

"And knock them unconscious." I added, enjoying the opportunity to toy with the guards who'd taunted me for weeks. Miranda gaped at me before turning on them again.

"Seriously!" She stammered. "Why didn't he just shoot?" I didn't need to see her face to know her eyes had rolled.

Apparently she didn't care for barbaric displays of authority any better than I.

"Maybe he should have." Guard number one mumbled.

"Would save the prison all the money they're forking over for those chemicals." Guard number two fist bumped guard number one. This time *I* rolled my eyes. Miranda remained less than amused.

"I think I'd like to finish the rest of my visit with Dr. Andrews in private." She hissed at them. They both opened their mouths, likely to protest, but she cut them off with a wave of her cell phone. "Should I call Warden Green? I'm sure he'd like to know I'm being harassed by some of his employees." They glared at her, but didn't budge. She sighed, a long whining expiration.

"It's not like Doc is going to get to me through the iron bars. I'm perfectly safe, now run along children." She waved them away like servants and I suddenly liked her even more. They grumbled, but obeyed.

"Maybe we should tell her daddy his little princess is breaking the rules." One of them mumbled on the way out. Miranda rolled her eyes again. I raised my eyebrows.

"Impressive, Miss Stevens." I smirked. "But why are we convening here rather than our usual local?" I asked.

"Well apparently because you have a terrible temper and go around attacking doctors." She quipped back. "I was informed by tweedly-dee and tweedly-dummer that you're on mandatory lockdown for twenty four hours. So no yard time for us today, but that's alright. We can chat just as easily here." She smiled, pulling her bag off her shoulder and plopping it on the ground in front of my cell door. A moment later she plopped herself next to it. I stared down at her.

"You intend for us to sit on the cement floor and chat like a couple of children?" I asked. I decided to leave out the fact that I'd slept on said floor the night before.

"Yes." She informed me. "And if you don't join me I wont give you the lunch I brought to share." She smirked. My stomach growled and I was on the floor with her a moment later, groaning as I eased my back against the wall. Her smiled softened and she dug a white paper sack from her bag. It smelled like heaven.

She pulled out two white Styrofoam containers and two paper wrapped burgers. She slid one of each to me through the bars. The burger was so big it barely fit through. Once I'd set them gently on my lap she slid a bottle of Coke through, and lastly, a handful of napkins. My fingers grazed hers as I grabbed them and she jumped again, though less this time.

"Sorry." I sighed, pulling the napkins away. She set up the rest of her stuff, recorder, pen and paper, soda of her own. I focused on the delicious meal in my hands, the still warm burger was more than enticing. Sauce dripped down the corners of my mouth as I bit in. I groaned in satisfaction. Apparently Miranda found this amusing and I rolled my eyes at her for laughing.

"Someone's hungry." She observed. I nodded, wiping my mouth.

"It seems I slept through breakfast this morning." I admitted. That or they'd simply forgotten to feed me. I wouldn't have been surprised either way. She only hummed at me, biting into her own burger.

Each bun contained two beef patties, four slices of bacon, two kinds of cheese, lettuce, tomato, pickle, and some sort of spicy sauce I didn't recognize, but which tasted delicious. The Styrofoam containers contained fries, also still warm, and seasoned with a variety of spices that complimented the heat of the burgers perfectly. I was glad Miranda had brought me a bottle of Coke this time, rather than a can.

"So," she began when she'd finished half her burger, "may I ask why exactly you decided to attempt to strangle a doctor this morning?" She pulled out her pad and paper and I knew the questions were just beginning. It also appeared that whatever mood had consumed her the day before had dissipated, which I was glad for.

"He was being a pompous moron." I informed her, stuffing the last bite of burger into my mouth. I reminded myself to ask Miranda where the burgers were from. I might've just determined my final meal, although I think I'd add an ice cream sundae as well, with sprinkles and a whole can of whipped cream. Miranda's tapping brought me back from my visions of food. Apparently I'd missed something.

"Doc, are you alright, you seem kinda out of it today?" She asked. I shrugged.

"Haven't been sleeping well." I admitted.

"Is that why you went after the doctor this morning, because you're not sleeping?" She gave me a look that told me she knew that excuse was full of it. I shook my head no. "It's not like you to be violent." She stated, the smile waning.

"I've killed thousands of people." I reminded her.

"Yes, but not yourself. Your virus did the dirty work. You, yourself, aren't violent. At least not physically." She pointed out. She wasn't wrong. "I mean, don't get me wrong, I wouldn't want to be up against you in a verbal sparring match, but I'm pretty sure if I was inside that cage with you I'd be just as safe as I am right here on the outside. Am I wrong?" She raised on eyebrow. She was testing me, I could see it in her eyes. She was trying to figure out just how volatile I was.

"No." I sighed. "You're not wrong. I wouldn't lay a finger on you." She smiled in response. "There are those I might though, people who have it coming." I told the fries before shoving them in my mouth. I imagined Chuckles grinning face on each one as I bit into them. *He* was lucky I was in this cage.

"Did the doctor have it coming?" She asked.

"Yes." I replied. At least by my standards he deserved whatever horrible fate befell him. I hoped it was bloody. I wished it would be my doing. I doubted it would be.

"What did he do?" Miranda probed further. Again I sighed. This was where it got challenging. I could tell her and hope that she'd see it my way. I doubted it. I could lie and make something up. She'd just learn the truth later. I decided to ignore the question all together. It was the safest route.

"You didn't come last night." I redirected. I could see that she saw straight through my ploy. I could also see that the thoughts it brought about were less than pleasant. Despite them, she answered.

"I had a funeral to attend." She told me. I weighed the possibilities. Surely this late in the game my virus couldn't be to blame. It only killed on initial implication and only because its effects were designed to onset quickly. The government had been warning people for months to stay home if symptoms appear. Yet as I looked at the sadness that I'd not noticed in her eyes before, I knew this death was connected to me in some way.

"Who was it?" I asked. She flinched, sighed, and then held my gaze again. A new fire burned slowly behind her eyes.

"My uncle." She replied. "He died when the outbreak first hit this area, killed by a driver whose symptoms hit suddenly. He was just out walking his dog and then he was gone. We hadn't been ready to give him a proper farewell until now. My mom was still coming to terms with everything. He was the only family she had left." I nodded.

"Was it a nice service?" I asked. This time she nodded.

"We scattered his ashes in his favorite place. I think he would have been happy with it." A tear crept down her cheek and without thinking I reached through the bars and wiped it away with my sleeve. She gasped and I froze, tear soaked hand still against her face. I could see the fear in her eyes then, raw and real. I scared her. I didn't blame her for her fear.

There was something else in those eyes as well and I started to understand the sprightly reporter in that moment. She was driven to me by her family's loss, but it wasn't what kept her coming back with more ferocity each time. She was intrigued by me. She needed to solve the puzzle before the timer ran out. For a moment, I almost wanted her to.

"I'm sorry for your loss, Miranda." I whispered. The first and only apology I'd given for my actions. Her eyes searched mine, trying to find any hidden motive or agenda. There was none. I was genuinely sorry for the pain I'd caused her.

"You've never called me Miranda before." She stated.

"I'll try to do that more often." I smiled. If ever there were a creature on this pathetic planet worthy of the truths I bore it was her. I could trust her, I knew that then. And, as her fingers reached up and wrapped around my outstretched hand, I knew she trusted me as well.

4 Days, 12 Hours...

Miranda left shortly after our moment of connection. She promised to return shortly and she did. The watch that wrapped around the warden's wrist read 12:00 on the dot. His face read defeat while Miranda nearly skipped in victory next to him. If I were to make an educated guess, I'd say she spent our time apart in his office fighting for her time with me. I stretched and joined them at my cell door.

"It seems you had quite the morning." The warden observed. His narrowed eyes told me he was less than impressed with my violent outburst.

"It would seem that way." I replied.

"You can say that again. Do you know which of your stupid guards it was who attacked..." Miranda started to chastise, but the warden ignored her.

"I won't stand for any more of that business, do you understand me?" He asked. Miranda glared in annoyance. I nodded in acceptance. "Very well." He sighed. "It seems Miss Stevens is unhappy with her agreement being violated and assures me that you're outburst was some sort of episode." It sounded more like a question than a statement.

"I told you Jim, OCD can cause sudden fits of..." Again she was cut off. Again she glared.

"I will allow the visits to continue, but know this, if you so much as think of touching a hair on her head I'll have you locked in solitary for the remainder of your stay." He fixed me with a stare that said he meant business. I suspected his allowance of Miranda's visits wasn't known by his bed partner. I also suspected he'd like to keep it that way.

"I won't touch her." I said. "I promise." Miranda opened her mouth to say something, but closed it again. She didn't want to be interrupted again.

"Alright, then you two can convene as usual this afternoon and again this evening." He stated, motioning for a guard. I could see Miranda's eyes light up in triumph.

"And you'll give us an extra hour outside this afternoon to compensate for the missed time?" She asked. I could tell she was testing her limits and pushing his. He grumbled, scratching at his close cropped beard, but eventually he heaved a sigh.

"Oh hell, what difference does it make?" He threw his hands up. "Take whatever time you want Miranda." He ruffled her hair but she ignored the childish innuendo and clapped her hands together in glee. The guard ordered me to turn and stick my hands through the slot. I obeyed.

Ten minutes later Miranda and I were seated at our picnic table. She was fishing around in a large tote bag for our lunch and I had my head back, eyes closed, enjoying the sun on my face. The smell of melted cheese and butter brought me back to reality.

Miranda had set out a plate and bowl for each of us. A perfectly browned grilled cheese sandwich sat on each plate and I watched as she poured tomato soup into each bowl. The steam rose from the creamy surface. The scent of basil reached my nose and I smiled. When the thermos was empty she opened a bag of oyster crackers and dumped a handful into her own bowl. I did the same, careful to reach long after her hands were safely returned to her side of the table. I didn't need to give the twitchy guard any reason to shoot.

I tore my sandwich in half and dipped the edge into the creamy soup. I took a big bite and felt warm liquid drip down my chin. Miranda offered me a napkin. I wiped my face and took another bite of the deliciously greasy sandwich, this time sans soup.

"If I didn't know any better I'd think you were trying to fatten me for slaughter." I joked. Miranda didn't laugh. She gasped and her spoon froze halfway to her mouth. I thought it was funny. "Sorry," I smiled, "too soon?"

"How can you be so glib about it?" She asked, filling two Styrofoam cups from another steaming thermos and handing me one. The scent of strong black coffee reached my nose instantly. She was definitely trying to get on my good side. I shrugged as I sipped.

"I suppose I figure that there's nothing I can do about it, so why worry?" I answered her, drinking the coffee slowly. I wasn't sure how well it went with tomato bisque and grilled cheese, but on a cool afternoon it tasted fantastic.

"I guess you're braver than I am." She sighed. "I'd be terrified." I nodded. There was no doubt in my mind that she'd be a mess if she were about to die. There was also no doubt in my mind that she'd never do anything to warrant an execution.

“So what do you plan to probe my mind for today?” I asked, ready to move on from the topic of my death. I knew it was coming, I’d accepted it, that didn’t mean I wanted to dwell on the fact.

“Oh, right.” She said around a mouthful of cheese and bread. “I was actually hoping you’d continue that story you’ve been telling me; the one about Cal.” I nodded, memories of distant voices pulling my smile downward. “You don’t have to if you don’t want.” She insisted, sensing my sudden shift in mood. I shook my head.

“It’s fine.” I lied. “Remind me where we left off?” I’d replayed the story so many times over in my mind I’d lost track of where I’d left off with Miranda and where I’d left off in my own memory.

“Cal’s mom died and he was living with his horrible aunt.” She reminded. I nodded.

“Yes, I remember. Adenocarcinoma is a nasty thing.” I sighed.

“Is that what she died of?” She asked, scribbling in her notebook. “Adeno-whatever you call it.” I laughed.

“Adenocarcinoma.” I corrected.

"How the hell do you spell that?" She inquired. I laughed again and gestured for the pen and paper. She obliged and I scribbled it down on the page. I took the opportunity to peek at her other scribbles as I did so, at least the ones I could make out. The woman had terrible penmanship.

I did manage to read a few instances where she'd written 'who is Cal?' over and over with a lot of question marks and exclamation points. She hadn't figured everything out just yet. I had a feeling her suspicious were on the right path, though. I slid the notebook and pen back to her and started my story.

Cal started public high school just over two weeks after his mom died. His aunt took him to the principal's office the first day and told him that Cal had been home schooled by her idiot sister and she was almost certain the boy would need to be in the most remedial classes available. The principal seemed less than enthused and even less interested when Cal argued that his mother was a good teacher. The tears that accompanied his exclamation were the only thing that caught the principal's attention.

Unsure of what else to do with the boy the principal, Mr. Smith, dragged Cal to the guidance counselor's office. The counselor, Miss Gonzales, was much nicer than Mr. Smith, and Cal liked her instantly. She also took a shining to Cal, seeing past the scars and tears, and they built a quick friendship.

Miss Gonzales had Cal spend his entire first day taking tests to determine where he should be placed. Age-wise he would be a Freshman, but she had no idea where he was intellectually. Cal did as she asked, grateful that for at least another day he didn't have to face the boys and girls that trod past Miss Gonzales's door all day.

He pretended to not see them leering at him every time they walked by, he pretended not to see them at all, but he did. He watched carefully, taking note of all the new faces he would see on a daily basis. They were all beautiful, as children should be. Something his aunt had reminded him that morning.

Children, young adults, they should be beautiful. Beautiful people were important. Cal wasn't beautiful. Cal wasn't important. He never would be. What he was, though, was smart. Miss Gonzales discovered just how smart he was as she corrected his tests after lunch.

Her face blanched in shock when she looked at the final scores and IQ results. Cal was more than smart. She smiled even wider at him than before. She knew she'd seen potential there. She spent the rest of the afternoon scheduling Cal into every advanced placement class she could manage and then they talked.

First they talked about his mother, about her death and her life and how much he missed her. Then they talked about school and all the new things he would be facing. They talked most about his fears of this new place and how he was worried no one would like him. Miss Gonzales assured him he was extremely likable and would make new friends in no time. Miss Gonzales was wrong.

Six months passed and Cal had no friends. He ate his lunch in the bathroom everyday because the cafeteria was too hard. If he was lucky he could sneak to the back corner of the library before anyone left the lunchroom for free period and hide there until class. In class he worked hard and tried his best to ignore the other students. His teachers liked him, which was something. He wished it was enough, that it didn't matter if the other students called him names and taunted and teased him. It did matter, though. It mattered a lot.

The time in between classes was the worst. This was when Cal couldn't slip away early or focus on the work. This was when he had to walk amongst the beautiful people knowing he'd never be like them. This was when he struggled the hardest to not hear the names they called him, but he always heard. Even if he didn't, they'd etched enough of them into his locker and amid the bathroom stalls that he knew his new name… Fugly.

The kids weren't imaginative with their demoralization. They didn't have to be. If words weren't enough to keep the unwanted in line a little shove here and there would help. If they were particularly stubborn or just particularly ugly a carton of milk over the head or spit in the face should do the trick. Needless to say, Cal was not particularly liked. There was a reason the cafeteria was avoided. They couldn't throw food at you if you weren't in the room with the food.

The worst time of all was gym class. Cal spent a total of one day in gym his second quarter. He didn't even make it onto the basketball court. He never made it out of the locker room. He wanted to. He wanted to show the perfectly sculpted jerks that they didn't bother him, that even though they'd held him down and pulled his clothes halfway off and peed on his face they wouldn't win. They did win, though. They always did and Cal didn't need a broken nose to prove that. Going onto that basketball court would have gotten him a broken nose. They promised as much.

Instead Cal slumped off to Miss Gonzales's office, wet and filthy, his clothes torn from where they'd pulled at him. He didn't want to go. He didn't want to tell her what they'd done. He hadn't told her about any of the other things. But he couldn't go to gym and she was the only one who wouldn't make him go to gym, so he went to her office and knocked on the door.

Miss Gonzales hugged him, pee and all, and told him she was sorry. She was a nice lady. She had a good heart and good intentions. Unfortunately good intentions don't always constitute good results. Her good intentions pulled the three boys that had peed on Cal into her office and scolded them, sending them each home on a suspension.

It worked, for the three days they were gone. When they came back, however, her intentions landed Cal in the dumpster behind the cafeteria. His nose apparently did need to be broken for them to win. And so did one of his ribs as well.

Miss Gonzales had good intentions, but her good intentions couldn't save Cal. She thought they did, but the boys just got smart. Instead of messing with Cal in the halls or the bathroom they kept their antics for afterhours, outside the eyes of Miss Gonzales. Her good intentions landed Cal in a dumpster every day for a year.

"Those boys were jerks." Miranda sniffed. I looked up from where I'd been staring at my empty plate. She had tears streaming down her cheeks. "How could anyone treat another human being like that? How could they be so cruel?" She wiped at the tears with her sweater. I knew she was worthy then.

"People are cruel." I told her. "People see difference as a handicap, an excuse to treat someone less. Our world revolves around perfection and anything less than that is lesser than those that are. People do worse things to the less fortunate than throw them in dumpsters." I looked down again. I didn't need to join Miranda in her teary state. People could do much worse.

"Doc?" She called, pulling my attention back to her. Clearly she wanted to ask something, but I could tell she was treading lightly. I appreciated that. My nod gave her the permission she sought. "How do you know this story? Did you know Cal?" She asked. I nodded again. "Were you two friends?"

"I guess you could say that." I smirked.

4 Days, 9 Hours, 31 Min...

For once I wasn't eager to walk away from Miss Stevens. The way the story of Cal moved her impressed me. Impressing me has never been an easy feat. It seems I'd perhaps been wrong about the over zealous reporter. She may just be worthwhile after all.

Once the guard left me in my cage I flopped down onto the stiff mattress. My body was tired from the lack of sleep the night before and my head still swam a little from the earlier blow. Miranda had promised to return with dinner later and I had a feeling she intended to take advantage of the warden's promise of all the time she wanted. I had a feeling there was going to be a lot of Miss Stevens in my near future.

The fact that said near future would only last four more days surprisingly saddened me. I swallowed twice to choke back tears yet again. I really didn't know what was happening to me lately. I'd never been an emotional person, not in my entire life.

There'd only ever been one being who'd been able to pull the softer side out of me, though I suspected I'd met a second that, if she had the time, could do the same.

I worried that suppressing my fear of the impending end was the cause. Every shrink I'd ever seen had told me not to suppress my feelings. I'd never listened to them. Pushing the painful thoughts and memories from my mind was how I survived the day.

I wasn't about to let those pains bubble up now, not this close to freedom. I forced them away again and closed my eyes against the sun's rays. A nap was all I needed to pull myself together. A little rest would let my body finish healing whatever rift was buried deep in my skull. A little nap would do me well, so long as the dreams stayed at bay.

The connection wasn't great. Driving through this part of town was always bad for cell service. You'd think after all these years they'd come up with something better. I wished they would as I strained to hear the voice on the other end. It was broken, though I couldn't tell if it was due to the reception or the tears I heard in the snippets of conversation I did catch.

"I can't...anymo...it's too hard...I can't...wanna live..." The broken voice said, words missing. Crucial words.

"What, baby, I can't hear you?" I pleaded. "Just hold on until I get to a better area."

"Can't wait...just wan...over." The voice sobbed. I started to feel panicked. This person wasn't someone who was ever irrational or dramatic. Rarely emotional. I was worried.

"Baby, listen to me I'm on my way, just hold on and I'll be right there." I promised, pushing the accelerator harder into the floorboard. Just twelve more blocks. I heard crackling silence on the other end. "Baby?" I yelled, "Baby are you still with me?" More silence.

"I'm sorry." I heard at last. "I lo...you." More silence. Worry changed to panic. My heart raced, my foot pushed harder. My whole body felt the wrongness in the voice. Something bad was going to happen, I could feel it. Only five more blocks.

"Baby, I'm coming, I'm almost there, please don..." A ringing sound echoed in my ear. The sound of a lost call. A peek at the screen confirmed my auditory assumption. I'd lost the call. "Damn it!" I yelled at the phone, at the car, at anything that was keeping me from where I wanted to be, from where I needed to be.

I hit the number I'd just been disconnected from. Silence pounded and then ringing. It rang six times and then I heard the familiar voice. "Hi, you've reached..."

"Damn it!" I yelled again, stabbing the end call button. I tried again. More ringing, another voicemail message from the familiar voice. Only two blocks now. A red light and I tried to call twice more while I waited. As the light turned green I dialed again. Ringing, voicemail.

"Come on, baby, pick up!" I yelled at the unanswered phone. "Please just pick up!" I cried. My cheeks were wet. My heart was heavy with dread. I rounded the last block and tossed the phone onto the seat next to me. I parked the car, not even killing the engine, and opened the door. A loud bang reverberated through the air, stopping me midway out of the driver seat.

My heart sunk with the sound of the gunshot and my body froze. I heard no other sound after that. Not the car alarms the shot had set off. Not the barking dogs whose ears were ringing. Not the sirens in the distance, responding to a neighbors call. I heard nothing. I felt nothing.

My body moved without command. Get out, shut the door, run up the pathway. My hand found the key that was always hidden under a ceramic turtle. The key found the lock and the door opened under my fingers.

I didn't hear my footsteps on the hardwood, but I felt the weight of every step. The floor felt as hard and cold as my heart did. I don't know what guided me, I only felt pulled along. The brain is a marvelous thing. Even when the parts that hold emotion and rationale quit functioning, the rest keeps going, pushing you onward. Mine pushed me to the bedroom at the top of the stairs.

Everything in the house should have been beyond familiar to me. I'd spent countless hours within its walls, but that day it felt alien. It felt like everything I saw, that I was so used to seeing, had been shifted just slightly. I nearly tripped over the last stair.

I smelled something strange as I reached the door I'd helped paint. The doorknob still had splatter on it from the brush strokes. I touched the speckles on the crystal knob before I turned it. I'm not sure whether an hour or an instant passed before I opened the door. Time didn't exist then. Everything seemed both instantaneous and everlasting at the same time. It made my insides turn.

My stomach betrayed me when I opened the door. The police came soon after. I saw their faces change when they saw the scene beside where I still kneeled on the ground. I don't remember when my legs gave out. I didn't care. I didn't care that I'd fallen or that my hand was covered in sick. I didn't see it.

All I saw was the red and the crumpled body on the bed, and more red. It was everywhere. It touched everything in the room. It tainted every memory held within those walls, turning them dark with its horror. I saw red for days after, years even. I never tolerated the color again.

I watched as the body was pulled from the red pool and hidden away in a black bag. The officer spoke, but still it all fell on deaf ears. Two sets in the whole place, but only mine were still alive.

A woman came and wept on an officer's shirt. A man in uniform pulled me from the ground and walked me outside. He sat me down in the back of the ambulance. Another man in another uniform wiped away the vomit that stained my jeans.

I stayed in the ambulance until the men in blue shirts with radios on their belts carried out the bag that held the body that was crumpled on the bed. The woman who wept was still sniffling as she followed them out. I didn't weep, I didn't follow. I only sat in the ambulance, waiting for the sound to return. It didn't matter how long it took. They didn't need the ambulance anyway.

4 Days, 6 Hours, 14 Min...

I was awoken by the sounds of footsteps. They were approaching from the other end of the hall, where the guard station was. I must have a visitor. Miranda must be back from her appointment. Dinner in tow, I hoped.

I sat straight up from the mattress. My eyes were sore and my face was wet with tears. My chest ached and my heart felt heavy. I rested a hand on it as I used the sleeve of the other to wipe the evidence of emotion from my face. I wouldn't be weak. Not now. Not this late in the game.

Miranda appeared outside the cell door a few moments later. Chuckles stood beside her. Neither looked too pleased with their company. I tried to smile at their discomfort, but the heaviness in my chest weighed down the corners of my mouth. I sighed and stood.

"You know the drill." Chuckles grumbled, giving me an irritated look. I wasn't sure if I disliked him more or less without the stupid humor. Maybe less. Miranda smiled as I approached the door and slid my wrists through the rectangular slot.

"Hey." She greeted me. "How was your afternoon?" Chuckles grumbled at her pleasantry, but remained silent for the time being.

"Oh, you know, the usual, rock climbing, swimming, got a massage." I smiled. One corner obeyed this time.

"No parasailing today?" She teased back. It helped edge the other corner higher.

"Nah," I replied, "thought I could use a change of scenery." I smirked, fully at last, and Miranda giggled.

"Oh, for the love of god." Chuckles complained as he rolled his eyes. Apparently he didn't approve of the camaraderie building between the reporter and I. I determined not to let him sour my new mood.

"Sounds like someone's jealous." Miranda half whispered, obviously shielding her mouth with the back of her hand. It earned another eye roll. She stifled a laugh all the way to the exit. When we walked out into the surprisingly warm yard she sighed. "I don't think that guard likes you very much." She offered as she sat down. I joined her.

"I don't think he likes anyone too much, except himself of course. I call him Chuckles." I told her. She laughed.

"Appropriate." She nodded. "So how was your afternoon really?" She inquired. Her eyes told me she was searching for something. I heaved a sigh. She was very perceptive.

"I don't really want to talk about it." I told her as I picked at the paint peeling off the picnic table. Would it kill them to sand the thing down? An inmate could get lead poisoning. They could probably even shank themselves with one of the splinters sloughing off the antique thing. I pulled one of the splinters loose and looked it over carefully before throwing it a few feet away.

"You really are struggling with something, aren't you?" Miranda pulled my attention back to her. I looked deep into her warm eyes, seeing the genuine concern that rested there. I wanted to tell her, but I didn't. It didn't matter. I sighed and rested my elbows on the disintegrating table, crossing my arms over my chest.

"I hope you brought dinner." I told her instead. "I'm starving." She sighed softly, but smiled.

"Of course, I wouldn't want you to starve." She teased, pulling a square box from a bag I didn't notice before. Even my powers of observation were off today. She flipped the lid of the box and slid a paper plate to me. I lifted three pieces of pizza onto my plate. The cheese pulled away in long strings and steam curled off the top. I was still perplexed how she managed to always bring me hot food.

"It's still warm." I observed, pulling a pepperoni loose and sliding it into my mouth. I licked the combination of grease and sauce from my fingers. "How do you manage to keep our meals warm?" I asked. Curiosity was a useless trait unless one was willing to search out the answers.

"I have one of those insulated cooler bags in my car. I pick up the food on the way over and keep it in there until I come see you." She replied. "I suppose it wouldn't matter. I'm sure even cold, what I bring you is better than the slop they serve in there," she nodded at the prison wall, "but I figure if I was about to die I'd want a few good, hot meals before I went." I smiled at her.

"Well, thank you." I smiled, biting into my first slice of cheesy goodness. It was still a little too hot, but I didn't want to wait. "My papillae are grateful to you." I added once I'd swallowed. Miranda stopped mid bite.

"What's a Papillion?" She asked. I laughed so hard I nearly spit out my food. She didn't find it so funny. I wiped my mouth and forced myself to breath before I responded.

"A Papillion is a breed of dog." I corrected. "What I said was papillae, which are taste buds."

"Oh." She said and then started to laugh as well. "Well no one ever said I was going to be a doctor." She shrugged, stuffing another significant bite into her mouth.

"I'm glad to see you don't starve yourself like most women." I told her. She looked surprised and then slowly sat the pizza down and wiped her mouth looking sheepish. I rolled my eyes with a sigh. "It was meant to be a compliment." I huffed.

"Why would being a pig be considered a compliment?" She asked, eyeing the pizza. She clearly wanted to continue eating it. Her hunger won out and she ate while I explained.

"It's a compliment because far too many women these days starve themselves or live on trash just so they can be perfectly beautiful. You care more about the internal beauty." I observed. "It's a rare quality." I sighed. If only the world's population were more like Miss Stevens. There might be more of them still around.

"You really hate the idea of physical beauty, don't you?" She asked. I nodded. She studied me for a moment and then sighed. "I guess I just don't understand why." She continued.

"You're a very attractive person yourself, why hate beauty? Why hate something so much that's a part of you?"

"I don't hate beauty as a concept." I told her. "I know I'm considered 'beautiful', but I think a person's true merit lies within them. An intelligent brain or a kind soul should be more valuable than flawless skin or the size of your clothes." Miranda nodded. I could see she understood. I could see she truly *was* good. I hoped the virus would spare her.

"That's a really beautiful notion." She smiled. "If only more people thought that way." She sighed. I joined her. "Of course if more people thought like you we might have a lot smaller population." She said. Her face was expressionless and I was taken aback for a moment. She shocked me with her bluntness and I almost retorted coolly, but a twinkle in her eye made me pause. A moment later she was laughing.

"Did you just tease me about being a terrorist?" I asked, stunned and laughing as well. She shrugged and stuffed half a slice of pizza into her mouth. She moaned as she chewed, enjoying the food, and then laughed again.

I noticed then that she had a particularly pleasant laugh. She laughed with her whole self, never holding back. It reminded me of another laugh, one that had haunted me for seventeen years. My smile dropped and I looked at my plate. A perfectly timed drip of sauce landed on the white paper, splattering red across the surface, and my heart sank to my feet.

I watched the pizza fall from my hand in slow motion. Catching the edge of the plate and sending it all crashing downward. The plate bounced on the seat next to me and a spray of red sauce splashed across my knee. The next thing I saw was the grass below me as I retched up the lunch I'd just consumed. I really hated the color red.

4 Days, 5 Hours, 49 Min...

I jumped when Miranda's hand landed on my shoulder. I didn't realize she'd run around the table and crouched by my side until she was helping me to my feet. The guard was yelling at her to back away from me. His finger was nervously twitching around the trigger of his gun. She ignored him and focused instead on me. Finally he walked over, but she shooed him away.

"Doc, are you alright?" She asked me when he accepted her dismissal. I looked at my hands, seeing red everywhere. It was on my arms, under my fingernails. It stained the front of my jeans. It was everywhere. I was covered in blood. I felt dampness on my face and I reached to wipe a blood streaked hand across it, but Miranda stopped me.

She raised her own hand and wiped at my cheek with her sleeve. I waited for it to come away red, stained like the rest of my world, but I was shocked to find it clean when she reached past my shoulder for the napkins. She handed me one, but I just stared at it. I couldn't wipe the red away no matter how hard I tried. I'd tried for 17 years, to no avail.

Miranda took the pile of napkins and set them between us on the picnic bench. Slowly and gently she lifted one after another to wipe at my face and hands, removing the wetness that resided there. When she'd run out of napkins she tossed the lot into a pile on the ground, right next to the vomit I'd left there.

I stared at the red that made me ache. Something wasn't right. There was something in the red, other colors, pieces of things, things that didn't belong in blood. I looked closer, leaning toward the pool of red and tan and yellow. Miranda's hand rested on my shoulder again, rubbing soft circles with her fingers. She was a good friend.

I looked at her finally, seeing her this time instead of seeing through her. She was smiling softly, her hand still rested on the curve of my shoulder. Again she raised her sleeve to my face to wipe away the wetness that wouldn't go away. Again her sleeve came away clean. I reached for it and ran a thumb over the fabric that had touched my face. It was damp. Wetted by the tears she's wiped away. I ran the back of my hand under my eyes and it came away wet as well. I hadn't even realized I was crying. Miranda's voice reached me finally.

"Doc, whatever it is, it's going to be alright." She promised. If only she knew. She wouldn't promise. She couldn't promise something that could never be true.

"Thank you." I told her, blinking through the tears that suddenly stung. She smiled.

"Are you alright?" She repeated. I nodded. "Did you feel sick earlier?" She asked. "Do you think you have a concussion?" She asked quieter. I shook my head at both.

"I'll be fine." I said, scooting away from her a little. It was more for the guard's sake, but her proximity was making me anxious. Everything was making me anxious. And nauseous. "I don't suppose you have any water I could rinse my mouth out with, do you?" I asked the ground.

"Coming right up." Miranda replied. A moment later she handed me a small, clear bottle and I cleaned the taste of throw up from my mouth. When I was satisfied that I didn't taste anything vile anymore I took two sips and regained my seat at the table. Miranda waited on the other side.

"I bet your papillae aren't quite so grateful right now." She joked. I smiled and then laughed. My stomach protested and I rubbed it as I sipped more water.

"So, Miss Stevens, what did you want to poke at today?" I asked with a sigh and some more water.

"Well, Dr. Andrews, I was hopping we could discuss so more of your work. Why did you choose genetics as your field of study? What drew you to it? What do you consider your greatest accomplishments?" Her voice dropped on the last question. She had a good idea what I considered my greatest accomplishment. That didn't mean I wasn't proud of others, however.

"Well, Miss Stevens, it seems you're in strict reporter mode today." I observed. She shrugged and I smiled at her aloofness. "Very well, you wish to know what sparked my passion for genetics?" I asked. She nodded. "Very well, you see it's very simple. It was the words of an old man that changed my future..."

I was a sophomore at Yale. I'd spent the entirety of the previous year working towards a political science degree, but I was satisfied. Sure, the work was challenging, but it struggled to keep my attention. Like any young ingénue, I wanted to change the world. And I thought I could. But the more I worked toward that degree the more I realized the world couldn't be changed through politics.

You can't change the world with words and empty promises. Discussion would never make a difference. Going into sophomore year I was feeling defeated and lost, and I was very close to dropping out all together. I had other talents, I could make a living. I toyed with those thoughts as I made my way to my first class of the new semester. It was one I actually looked forward to.

Science had always come easy to me. Something about the rigidity of it always felt comfortable, yet it had that ability to surprise you from time to time. I was glad that I'd selected it as my fall Gen. Ed. Class. I needed the familiarity. And so off I went to Biology 116 with Dr. Stuart Jacobsen. I would soon learn I wasn't headed to any old biology class. Dr. Jacobsen wasn't any old professor.

I knew it was going to be different when the professor insisted we call him Stu, not Dr. Jacobsen. He insisted he was far too young and handsome for such labels. Considering the man that stood before us was eat least in his late fifties the class seemed to find this quite funny. They laughed. I didn't. Something about him instantly demanded my respect. I wanted very badly to learn from him.

He noticed my lack of humorous expression and called my name. The entire class looked my way. I looked at the pen in my hand. He asked why it was I didn't laugh with the rest of the class. I replied that I didn't find it as funny as they. Again he asked why. I replied,

"You're only as old as you feel."

He smiled at me, thanked me, and set into his lecture on the wonders of the human brain. It may have been a biology class but according to the syllable Stu handed each of us, the only biology he was concerned with lay in a three pound package.

After class that day Stu stopped me. A momentary flash back to being stopped by another professor made me leery, but I liked this guy. I trusted him for some unknown reason. When I approached as he requested he motioned for me to sit with him. I did as he asked.

He proceeded to ask what I was majoring in. I told him. He laughed. I wasn't sure what he found so funny and I ducked my head in shame.

"What's a brilliant mind like yours doing wasting it's time in a pointless field like that?" He asked. I told him I didn't know. He then inquired why it was I'd chosen that particular.

"I want to change the world." I told him, blushing at the absurdity. "I guess that's kinda dumb, huh?" I shrugged.

"Those who are crazy enough to think they can change the world are the usually the ones that do." He smirked. I would eventually learn it was the closing line of a quote he cherished. I instantly loved it as well. I was instantly a crazy one.

Stu concluded our little meeting by asking if I'd be interested in taking another class with him, a more advanced one with a more specific focus. I asked if he thought I could handle it and all he did was tap a single stuffy finger against my forehead and say he recognized a good brain from a mile away. He then gave me the paperwork to get into his class and sent me on my way.

A week later I'd changed my major to genetics, dropped all my political classes for Chemistry, Anatomy, and Advanced Biology, and started my private tutoring with Stu. There was no turning back from the path of genetics. Though I only worked with Stu for a short while he sparked my passion and set me on the path that shaped the rest of my life.

"So one man changed your life?" Miranda asked. I nodded, a sad smile playing on my mouth. It's funny how a single being can change everything. "What about the rest. You touched some on your other accomplishments before, but I'm sure there were other projects that you worked on. Maybe some left unfinished. What of those?" She surely was in reporter mode today.

"All scientists have unfinished work. Theories can only be tested so far as we have the technology to test them. Sometimes ideas must be abandoned until the rest of the world catches up." I told her.

"I highly doubt you've ever waited for anyone to catch up to you." She smirked as she dug into her bag again. Little to my surprise she produced a small bag of red gummy candies in the shape of fish. I could smell their overpowering flavoring as soon as she pulled them open. She offered me some.

"No thanks." I rejected. She dug deeper into her seemingly bottomless bag and finally tossed a packet of peanut M&Ms at me.

"Maybe these will suit your fancy." She smiled. I nodded in thanks and tore the corner off. I dropped a half dozen of the candy coated droplets into my palm and shoved them into my mouth.

"You're right." I told her when I'd finished half the bag. "I've never waited for anyone to catch up. Few ever can. It's meant a fairly solitary existence, but I'd rather live alone than diminished."

"I get that." She nodded. "So, Dr. Andrews, what *is* your unfinished business?"

"How long do you plan to sit here?" I inquired with a smile and another handful of chocolate.

4 Days, 23 Min...

Miranda and I talked until the guard insisted we go inside. The sun had long set and the night air was chilly. We never did get around to discussing my unfinished business. Unfinished work, yes. Theories and trials I'd abandoned when my obsession over the virus had taken over, but none of that mattered now.

We left the topic quickly. Miranda didn't understand much of it anyway. Instead we discussed more of my story of Cal. It seemed Miss Stevens had taken a liking to my story and had as many questions about it as she did about me. I obliged as much as I saw fit and elaborated where I felt it was necessary. By the time we parted she seemed genuinely pleased with me and I said goodnight with a smile and a wave. She reciprocated.

The young guard that I favored led me back to my small domicile and wished me goodnight as well. I thanked him and eased my tired body down onto the mattress, making myself as comfortable as possible. It wasn't that comfortable.

I tried to focus on the walls around me, to keep my mind occupied with other tasks, but I couldn't stop my subconscious from reaching back to where I'd retched in the grass earlier. I saw red every time I closed my eyes, though I couldn't be sure of its source, and it made my stomach start to churn again.

I decided sleep was out of the question and stood from my cot, pacing around the room to keep myself awake. I was grateful that my pattern seemed completely nonsensical, no counting, no tapping, just meandering movement to keep my eyes open.

I kept up the game into the wee hours of the morning, walking, stretching, moving muscles for no other purpose than to keep moving. Fifteen minutes without movement and you fall asleep. I doubted, in my unrested state, it would take more than five. I had to keep moving. When my body slowed, my brain trying to quell the movement in search of rest, I resorted to talking to myself.

Over and over again I recited anything I could pull to mind. Shakespearean sonnets, whole articles I'd written, even a few scenes from movies I'd seen over the years. I talked and talked, kept the noise flowing, the movement of my jaw adding to the slogging of my tired feet.

I would win. I would beat the night and avoid sleep. I wouldn't close my eyes longer than to blink. I was determined to make it through the night. I would see the dawn rise into the sky. I would let the light burn away the red behind my eyelids, replacing it with the pink of a new day. I had a challenge, a goal laid out before me, one I was determined to reach. I would succeed!

I failed.

I don't know when I fell asleep. I don't know *how* I fell asleep. But I did. And when I did I dreamed...

My eyes opened to a face. The lines and planes of it were familiar to me. The feel of them as recognizable to my fingers as my own face. I smiled at the face. The eyes brightened, shining down on me as fingers pulled unruly hair from my eyes. Words were whispered..."I love you"..."I miss you"..."Hurry, baby"...

With the last words the face vanished. I stood, searching for its familiarity again. Round and round I spun, feeling like I was just missing it out of the corner of one eye. I stilled, listening, waiting. I closed my eyes again, hopeful that when I opened them the face would reappear, that I would see the shining eyes looking down on me, calling me to them.

I traced the curve of that face in my mind. The high cheekbones, the slender nose, the soft lips I'd kissed innumerably. The voice returned, whispering to me yet again. "Baby…baby…" I opened my eyes but the face wasn't there.

"Where are you?" I called out. "I can't see you, where have you gone?" The world was turning dark, fading from white to grey to black. Pin pricks of light dotted above me, shimmering in the night sky. The ground grew hard under my feet, cracked here and there. Walls rose around me, signs and windows I almost recognized in the dim light of the midnight moon.

"Where are you?" I asked again. "Where am I?"

The wind picked up, blowing things past me, crumpled pages of discarded newspaper, abandoned bags of white plastic. A foam cup rolled along beside me, my only companion in the darkening night. I pulled my arms around myself, holding in the heat my body produced. I walked, searching for something familiar, for some sign I might know.

I blinked my eyes. The world seemed to be blurred at the edges, everything made smooth and distant. Just unreachable by the fingers of my memory. I walked further. Still searching, kicking at the cup the wind had stopped blowing. My only companion. I didn't want to lose him.

I listened to the noises of the night. Distant tires on pavement. Wind making its way around the buildings. The scrape of garbage rolling across the ground, tin and plastic and paper, all blown from one place to another. The sounds of the animals that inhabit the dark reached my ears, screeches and hoots and scurries. And then a voice.

A well known voiced called to me yet again. "Baby…" I quickened my pace. My heart pounded in my chest, though I didn't know the cause. "Baby…" The voice came again, a ghost in the darkness leading me onward. "Baby!" It cried. This time not a ghost, not a beckoning, but a cry for help.

I ran. I slammed my feet into the pavement below, slapping hard and fast as I forced myself onward with more urgency. The voice cried out twice more, calling for me, needing me. I knew it was in danger, I just knew.

"I'm coming, baby, I'm coming!" I yelled back. The pounding of my feet matched the pounding of my heart as I raced down the ally that seemed to continue on forever. No twists, no turns, nothing but an endless line of walls and signs I almost recognized.

I ran, searching for the source of the voice that had called to me. I grew more frantic by the minute. I had to find it. I had to save it. I had to get there in time. I looked back over my shoulder, wondering if I'd missed something and then turned back in time to see the wall that seemed to appear out of thin air.

In the middle of the wall was a door. In the middle of the door was a handle. I grasped it and it turned in my hand. I hesitated before I pulled on it, something warning me. Something else I almost recognized. I pulled it anyway.

The door opened and darkness fell out of it. A darkness that was deeper than the night around me. The heat of it spilled over me like the exhale of a giant monster preparing to engulf me completely. The door was a precipice. I teetered on the edge, but a voice pulled me over and I fell headlong into the mouth of hell itself.

The air was heavy there, wet and damp, but it chilled me to the bone. I ambled blindly in the darkness, searching without sight, listening without ears. I was stuck inside a void, a great vacuum of sound and light and air. The silence was deafening. The air was being slowly sucked from my lungs. I was blind. And then there was the most infinitesimal shaft of light breaking through.

I followed its call, finding the source in a cracked door. I pulled on the handle of the door and I was sucked further into the hell that surrounded me. I was sucked back and spit out in the middle of a night I'd never wanted to relive.

A voice cried out. A face, the *face, turned to me, begging me to save it, to make it stop. I couldn't. I couldn't before, I couldn't now. Another voice drowned out the cries with an evil laugh, deep and bellowing, joined by a chorus of excitement, the song of the diabolical.*

I was frozen, held back by an unseen force. Unable to move, unable to flee, unable to look away. I watched the face, slick with tears and blood. I watched the scene unfold. Dishonorable acts committed, horrible things done, lives ruined, virtues destroyed, and blood spilled across the pavement.

One by one the droplets splattered against the cobblestone. Little by little the grey turned red, a stain that would never wash away. The worst kind of stain, left by only the vilest of acts. Invisible to the rest of the world, inescapable to those who yearned most to escape it.

Little by little the world turned red, the dream washed in the blood that ran from the acts even it wanted to escape. Little by little the world darkened, the light losing out. Little by little the beauty gave way to the truth of the ugliness within and true beauty was marked by its evil. As the world was engulfed by the redness of hate, I saw the face once more. Its planes still familiar, its lips still soft, its eyes dulled forever.

3 Days, 20 Hours, 24 Min...

I rolled from the cot I didn't remember lying down on. My knees and hands caught my weight as I landed on the cement below. The momentum urged the vomit the last few inches up my throat until it splattered against the floor between my thumbs. It didn't really need the added assistance. I would have vomited where I laid after that dream.

As I heaved onto the floor I could still see the images behind my eyelids. The contorted faces as they enjoyed the destruction they wrought. I could hear the cries of a woman destroyed, of a man broken. I couldn't make it stop. I couldn't make *them* stop.

When my stomach had emptied I sat back on my heels, pressing my hands into my eyes in an attempt to rub away the sights that couldn't be unseen. When rubbing didn't work I slammed them against the sockets, crying out, hoping to drown out the screams in my head with one of my own. My hands were wet with tears. They choked my throat and burned my lungs.

Nothing I did made them go away. The faces swirled in the blackness behind my closed eyes. I cried out over and over, banging my head against the metal frame of the bed behind me when my hands no longer aided me. I heard a distant sound, like the rhythmic beating of a drum, but I didn't listen. I couldn't hear it over the screams and sobs of agony that filled my ears.

I heard another sound, a scraping, grating sound like metal on rock. Another voice joined the cacophony in my head, but I didn't hear the words it bellowed. I couldn't hear anything. I didn't want to. The voice that had joined called out to another, one that responded a few moments later with crackles and beeps.

I felt hands on my arms, pulling me, hauling me upward. I was limp, unable and unwilling to move for fear of making the visions worse. The hands that pulled were strong, though, and soon I was on my back, rocking and crying and screaming as strong hands held me down.

I thrashed and cried for help and kicked out at the hands that held me. I was convinced they wanted to hurt me. "No!" I cried, over and over. I begged, I sobbed, and still the hands held strong. But I was strong, too. I kicked out again, striking my elbow against something that was both soft and hard at the same time. The hands let go.

I scurried away, tucking my body into the corner of the bed as tightly as I could. The hands came again and I rolled myself over, falling once more to the concrete floor. I crawled, pulling myself with bloody elbows, to the farthest corner I could reach. There I pulled my knees to my chest and yelled for help again. The hands yelled, too.

They didn't grasp again, not until another sound of drums echoed in my ears and another voice joined the owner of the hands. Someone called my name. Hands reached for me again, cautious this time. A third voice joined and cursed. My name was called again and the beckoner urged me to open my eyes. I hadn't realized they were shut.

I peeled the lids from the eyes that kept betraying me, controlled by the mind that meant to destroy me. That had. My vision was blurred by tears and the pounding in my skull. I saw faces, warped at the edges like a dream. I thought I might still be dreaming, but then I remembered the vomit and the pain. This was reality.

One of the voices called my name for a third time. The tone was soothing, gentle even, but I didn't trust it. I didn't trust anyone. I lashed out at the misguiding voice. Strong hands grasped me yet again. Four hands this time, and they held me down; pinned my cheek to the cold ground and held me there with a knee. I heard talking and the click of plastic. There was a bright sharpness in the side of my neck and I opened my mouth to cry out, but the sound was silenced before it escaped. The world fell into blackness.

3 Days, 14 Hours, 52 Min...

When I awoke everything was too bright. White light pierced my eyes like needles and my mouth felt like I'd swallowed a desert. I blinked and turned my head. A clock next to me read 9:08 in blinking green lights. I turned away from it and closed my eyes again. Even closed, the whiteness of the room hurt. I tried to pull my hands up, but they stopped short, something cold biting into the skin of my wrists.

I heard a voice nearby, muffled by something. It was an irritated voice, one I knew well by this point. It seemed Miranda was displeased about something and I pitied the poor sucker she was blasting. I couldn't make out everything she said, but what I could was not so nice.

"I don't give a damn what your policy states." She shouted, suddenly coming clearer. I thought I heard a door open, and her voice increased in volume, no longer muffled by the separation. She continued to berate the person as she drew nearer, her voice getting louder with each step. "I was given permission to see Dr. Andrews anytime I want, and I want to see Dr. Andrews right now!" She demanded.

I wasn't sure why she kept repeating my name like that, but it was amusing. Even though the decibel of her voice hurt my already sore head I couldn't help but smile at her. Her quick steps drew closer, followed by another set whose words I wasn't listening to.

"That sounds like an excellent idea!" She exclaimed, sarcasm dripping form her voice. "And while you go get the warden I'll sit right here." She said. I felt my body lilt slightly as she sat on the bed with me. "Psychotic episode my ass." She muttered.

I felt a pressure around the fingers of my left hand and realized she was holding it. I tried again to open my eyes. The room was still blindingly bright, but it seemed more tolerable this time. I blinked a couple times, forcing my pupils to adjust to the sudden assault. The light dimmed some when a head full of brown curls leaned over me.

"Welcome back, Doc!" Miranda greeted enthusiastically. I winced at the volume of her voice. "Are you in pain?" I nodded, my throat too dry for speech.

"The bastards probably won't let me give you any pills, but there's water here. Not that that helps any." She sighed. I squeezed her fingers and nodded, hoping she'd understand. "What?" She asked.

"Water." I managed to squeak out, my voice scratchy and hoarse.

"Oh, you want water." She realized. A moment later a cup was at my lips. I was half drowned by the time Miranda let up, water running down the sides of my face and onto my chest, but the coolness was refreshing and my throat no longer felt like the Sahara.

"Thank you." I squeaked when she set the glass down again.

"Sorry." She giggled, wiping the water from my face with the corner of my pillow case. It didn't take much to put together that I was lying in what looked like a hospital room. The infirmary I guessed.

"What happened?" I asked Miranda. She shrugged, finally relinquishing my fingers.

"You tell me." She insisted. "When I got here this morning they told me you had a psychotic episode last night.

They said they found you foaming at the mouth and banging your head against the bedframe. It took two of them to hold you down so the doctor could sedate you." She looked back at the hand she'd released and grabbed it once again. "They said it looked like you were trying to hurt yourself." She sighed.

"I wasn't." I told her. "Well, I guess technically I was, but not in the way they think." I sighed. "It's complicated."

"Isn't everything with you?" She teased and we both smiled. The door flew open with a bang a moment later and the warden came stomping in, followed closely by a man in pale blue scrubs and a white overcoat. Neither looked pleased.

"Miranda Annabeth Stevens." The warden yelled. "What the hell do you think you're doing?"

"I'm visiting with Dr. Andrews." She replied obviously. "You know," she added, "like you said I could." He huffed into his moustache.

"I said you could have visiting time, that didn't include terrorizing my staff, ignoring orders, and sitting within stabbing distance of a dangerous criminal." He yelled again. I half expected him to add a 'young lady' to the end. He certainly sounded like a father chastising his daughter. Miranda only rolled her eyes, unintentionally playing along with the scenario.

"The *dangerous criminal* is handcuffed to the bed." She reminded, standing and facing him. "And I wasn't terrorizing anyone. Your so called doctor was harassing me." She folded her arms across her chest and the doctor's mouth flew open.

"Sir, I was doing no such thing." He insisted.

"Whatever." Miranda quipped, surveying her fingernails. "Still," she sighed, looking back to the warden, "you specifically said, and I quote "take whatever time you want". End quote." She enunciated sarcastically. "This is me taking the time that I want." She smirked. The warden rolled his eyes.

"You are as infuriating as your mother, you know that right?" He asked her.

"It's a family trait." She shrugged. She sat again on the edge of my bed, her hip next to my elbow. "So when are you going to let Doc out of here? I have important questions to ask and your moron nurse here is cutting into my time." The doctor looked like he wanted to stab her with one of the syringes on the tray next to him. The warden looked like he might just let him. I wondered if somehow this was Miranda's way of protesting her mother's relationship.

"I'm a doctor, for one thing." The tall man snipped at Miranda, who stiffened next to me. "And furthermore, this inmate has had a severe mental break in the last twenty four hours. You can't honestly expect me to just release the cuffs and send you both on your way, can you?" He asked, though it wasn't clear who the question was aimed at. Miranda looked down at me.

"Dr. Andrews," she called and I looked at her, "this man claims that you suffered a mental break last night. Do you concur?" She asked. I tried to stifle the smile she was also attempting to hide. Neither of us had much success.

"You can't be serious. A patient isn't capable of diagnosing themselves." The angry doctor exclaimed. He sounded utterly exasperated.

"Uh, hello, did you not catch the Doctor part?" Miranda quipped. It seemed the warden had checked out of the conversation. Probably smart on his part. Miranda was a force to be reckoned with.

"A doctorate does not a physician make." He retorted. "I spent over a decade studying the human body, including an internship at a psychiatric hospital, I'm pretty sure I know a psychotic break when I see one. And another thing, missy..."

"For starters," I interrupted the arrogant prick, "I have a doctorate in both biology and genetics. I also specialized in the study of infectious and genetic diseases, which I'm pretty sure qualifies me to make a diagnosis just as much as you. Furthermore, I'm almost positive my IQ is superior to yours. If nothing else, your pathetic excuse of a diagnosis proves just that." I fixed the doctor with a withering stare and he reddened. Clearly I'd struck a nerve.

"Then what, pray tell, do *you* think is wrong with you, oh superior one." He mocked. Clearly he thought I was bluffing. It would only make wiping the smug look off his face that much more satisfactory.

"Night terrors." I stated. "Vivid dreams resulting in unexpected waking often accompanied by paranoia, hallucinations and crippling fear."

"Score one for Doc!" Miranda smirked, crossing her arms victoriously. I half expected her to stick out her tongue.

"I don't see the difference, or the point for that matter. It's still psychological and I still shouldn't release you." The doctor grumbled, playing on the only power he still maintained, my freedom, or as much freedom as a walk in a fenced in yard allowed.

"Where did you graduate from?" I asked him. He looked surprised by the question, but he answered.

"UCLA, not that I see how that's relevant here." He insisted. I laughed. He looked less pleased.

"Well, doctor, let me clear things up for you." I spit. UCLA could kiss my Yale/Oxford ass. "The most common cause of night terrors is sleep deprivation and extreme emotional stress. I'm pretty sure the fact that I've been attempting to sleep on a rock they pass of as a mattress around here and that I will knowingly be put to death in just over 72 hours probably plays more of a factor than my psychiatric health, especially since the shrink saw me already this week and gave me a clean bill of mental health."

The room fell silent when I finished. Miranda looked pleased. The doctor looked pissed. And the warden looked out the window, completely oblivious to the fact that I'd just mentally eviscerated his on call doctor. I was delighted. Finally the doctor opened his mouth to say something, but was cut off.

"Enough, John, let it go." The warden sighed. "There's no use arguing with a genius and there's no winning against Miranda. Trust me." He smirked. "Release the inmate and have the guards take them both to the meeting room." He instructed.

"Jim, I think we agreed to yard time." Miranda interrupted before he could exit.

"It's raining, Miranda." He gestured toward the window that was, in fact, covered in raindrops. "When it quits I will have the guards escort you outside, alright?" He asked. She nodded and he started toward the door.

"Jim" She called again before his hand reached the handle. He sighed and peered over his shoulder at her. "Thanks." She smiled sheepishly. He nodded and stepped out. The door clicked behind him and his footsteps echoed down the hall.

"Well, you heard the man." Miranda yelled at the defeated doctor. "The cuffs aren't going to unlock themselves." She exclaimed, resting her hands on her hips and tapping a foot impatiently. She was a force to be reckoned with indeed.

3 Days, 13 Hours, 57 Min...

Miranda's breakfast turned into a brunch by the time we got to the interrogation room. While I'd gotten dressed into a fresh uniform she's coerced the cooks in the kitchen into reheating the meal she'd brought. When I sat down at the table she'd already dished up a steaming plate of French toast, sausage, and bacon, all smothered in syrup. There was also fresh strawberries in a separate bowl and orange juice in a plastic glass.

"You're beginning to make me feel spoiled." I told her as I stuffed the first sticky bite into my mouth. It was buttery heaven dipped in cinnamon. "Where did you get these?" I asked. They were delicious.

"A little diner near my house. They have the best breakfast." She replied, biting off a chunk of bacon.

"I think they might." I agreed. I was insanely hungry and devoured the entirety of my toast in half a dozen bites. Miranda giggled.

"Well glad to see night terrors haven't messed with your appetite." She observed with a wink. "Did they mess with anything else?" She asked. Her curiosity was as insatiable as my appetite.

"I'm fine." I told her. "A bad dream isn't going to diminish my brain."

"Do you want to talk about it?" She asked, nonchalantly sipping at her juice. She was trying to make it seem like she wasn't dying to know what I'd dreamed about. Her eyes gave away the truth. A reporter always wants the scoop.

"Not really." I sighed. "Why don't we just talk about whatever it was you planned to discuss today." I suggested.

"And if I planned to discuss night terrors and bad dreams?" She teased.

"Be my guest." I smirked. "What exactly haunts *your* dreams?" I asked.

"Touché." She smiled. "Alright, how about you tell me more about Cal instead? Last I heard he was being bullied terribly. Did things ever get better for him?"

"Yes and no." I told her truthfully. "Things got better, for a while at least, but good things always come to an end." It was the truth. I'd experienced it myself many times. It seemed the better the thing the quicker the end.

"So what was Cal's good thing?" Miranda questioned. "What made his life better?"

"A girl." I told her. She smiled and I delved back into the story.

By the time Cal was a senior he'd gotten expertly good at avoiding the boys who'd bullied him for years. He still had no friends. His Aunt still ignored him, at best. And halfway through his junior year he lost Miss Gonzales to a child of her own. She had promised to return the following year, but when senior year started a new teacher resided in her office. This new teacher was no Miss Gonzales.

Cal avoided the new counselor. Cal avoided everyone. He'd made a routine, found a route through the treacherous halls that provided the least exposure to their torture. He'd been forced to suffer through Gym the previous year, but thankfully that meant it was over with. Cal could focus on his plan of avoidance.

He took all AP classes by this point, so avoiding the boys wasn't hard in class. It was between classes that got challenging. He'd learned to study them, to map out their patterns, and thus avoid them. It usually meant taking the longest way from class to class and often a strange short cut through the cafeteria or the back door of the library.

Lunch was the easiest part. Cal abandoned any thoughts of eating a hot lunch halfway through his first year there. Instead, each morning he'd get up before his aunt and pack a lunch that he would hide in his backpack. She still gave him money for lunch each day, but he stowed it away. Cal saved any money he got his hands on so that he could one day escape that horrible place.

When the rest of the students left for lunch Cal would take his time in the back of the classroom, carefully putting each item back into the backpack he carried with him everywhere. The teachers all saw, but no one said anything. Once he'd made sure the halls were clear he'd sneak into the library. No one noticed him there, tucked away in the back corner between the stacks that held the reference books. No one noticed you when you were invisible.

That is where Cal spent every lunch, and everyday after school he'd return to his hidden sanctuary among the dusty encyclopedias, eat a snack he'd brought or purchased, and read a book until all the rest of the student body had gone on their way. Then he'd sneak out through the back door and walk the long way home through the back alleys where no one else went. Cal didn't mind. He was invisible to the drug dealers and crack whores, too.

It was at the end of one of these days that his life changed. About a week into his senior year Cal was eating his apple and reading to himself behind the row of Encyclopedia Britannica, when a voice interrupted him mid bite. The librarian's voice was clear and well known to Cal, but the second, sweeter voice wasn't one he recognized.

Afraid of getting in trouble for both loitering and eating in the library he hid behind a desk tucked beside the shelves. The old librarian plotted into view in her orthopedic shoes and knee length tweed skirt. Beside her was a girl. She was Cal's age, with fair hair and eyes the color of the sky.

Cal thought she was the most beautiful creature he'd ever seen. Considering most of the world was beautiful, he considered that a feat. The librarian pointed out the book the girl sought. Cal assumed it was for an assignment. No one every came this far back in the stacks for leisure reading. The librarian left and Cal watched the girl as she carefully plucked the books from the shelf one by one.

He was mesmerized by her. The way she stood, just hunched enough to be humble. The way she gracefully took each book with care in her long, delicate fingers. She had what his mother would have called pianist's hands, slender and graceful, with long, curved fingers and short cropped nails. They were painted the same soft pink as the sweater she wore. It matched perfectly with her matchstick jeans, cream colored ballet flats, and the delicate silver charm bracelet around her wrist..

Cal was smitten. Before he could learn anything more about this girl he was certain he'd never seen before, she turned and left the stacks. He exhaled, realizing he'd been holding his breath, and stood from his hiding place. He pulled his bag over his shoulder and headed for the back door. It was a little early to leave, but Cal didn't want to risk the librarian coming back, or the girl for that matter.

He couldn't imagine what he'd do if he came face to face with her. Something stupid he supposed. He was nearly out the door when something caught his attention, a spark of light on the carpet where the girl had been standing. He walked to it and bent down to see. A single charm, a butterfly, was lying on the carpet. He knew it must have broken off the girl's bracelet before she left.

He picked it up, turning it over carefully in his palm as he stood. A voice startled him and he jumped. He looked toward the sound and found the sky looking back at him. The girl of his dreams was standing not two feet away, smiling sweetly at him. Not through him, AT him.

She spoke again. It took a moment for the words to register in his mind. He was distracted by the sky. Finally she pointed and his brain caught up with his ears. He attempted a smile and handed her back the charm he'd found. She thanked him and frowned at the bracelet.

Cal's mouth told the girl he could fix her charm. His brain froze in panic at the boldness of his mouth. She smiled again, further paralyzing his brain, and handed him the unclasped bracelet. He turned and sat at the desk he'd previously hidden under. The girl followed and sat on the corner nearby.

A few minutes later he handed her back her bracelet, the charm returned to its rightful place. The girl hooked it back where it had dangled before and thanked him enthusiastically. His mouth had been silenced by his brain for its treachery, and all he could manage in response was a nod and a crooked smile.

The girl gave him one more smile and turned to leave. Cal grabbed up his bag again and headed for the door. He stole one last glance at the departing girl before he did the same. When he did she turned back and smiled at him again.

"I'm Lily, by the way." She told him in her sweet voice before disappearing all together. Cal was late getting home that day. He got lost three times on his way home, distracted by the thoughts of the pretty girl named Lily who'd looked at him and actually seen him.

"Cal fell in love." Miranda interrupted. "That's so sweet!" I nodded in agreement. She was picking at the last of her strawberries, pulling the leaves off one by one. She looked thoughtfully at the berry a moment and then back at me. "Have you ever been in love, Doc?" She asked with a serious face.

"Once," I answered, "a long time ago." She nodded again, slower this time. "Have you?" I inquired. Again she shook her head, side to side this time.

"No, I've never been in love." She told me, relinquishing the strawberry at last. "I've dated," she expanded, "I've told people I love them, but I've never actually felt it, you know?" Her question was rhetorical, but I nodded in agreement regardless. She sighed, picking up the strawberry again and biting it in two. "So," she redirected as she chewed, "what about Lily and Cal? Did they have an epic love story?"

"I suppose you could call their story epic." I smiled softly.

"So, what happened?" She asked, finishing the strawberry and wiping her hands.

"All in due time, Miss Stevens," I smirked, handing her a napkin to wipe the juice from her chin, "all in due time."

3 Days, 8 Hours, 22 Min...

The sun came out about one o'clock. Miranda and I were escorted outdoors and after she insisted they retrieve towels for us to sit on, we sat at the picnic table enjoying the sun. By three the majority of the moisture had been burned away and we both had our sleeves rolled up to our elbows as we talked about miscellaneous things of little import.

As usual Miranda chomped away at a bag of gummy bears. I shook my head as she popped her third handful in the last ten minutes into her mouth. I snatched the bag away, scouring the back with my eyes.

"Do you even know what's in these things?" I asked her. I eyed the back side of the package, reading over the ingredients. "You're basically eating wax and artificial flavoring, with preservatives on top." I scrunched my nose.

"You like M&M's." She pointed out.

"Chocolate comes from a plant and they have peanuts inside, at least they provide a modicum of nutrition. These are just fruit flavored junk." I tossed the bag back to her. She picked it up and eyed up the same things I did. She them slapped the bag down on the table and jabbed a fingernail at the white box on the back.

"Look, they have protein in them, so there." She stuck her tongue out at me and I laughed.

"Wow, a whole 3%, you could practically live on these babies." I rolled my eyes. "You would, too, wouldn't you?" She smiled and shrugged. I shook my head at her and crossed my arms over my chest, resting my elbows on the table and stretching the tired muscles in my back. "I don't suppose you could twist your pet warden's arm and get me a massage, could you?" I stretched again.

"I'm pretty sure I'm temporarily out of favors from Jim at the moment. He wasn't so pleased about this morning, but he owed me one so he couldn't say much." She answered, popping more gummy death into her mouth.

"Why'd he owe you?" I asked, curiosity getting the better of me.

"Let's just say I became privy to some information he'd most likely not want my mother hearing about." She smirked.

"Blackmailing your mom's boyfriend." I whistled. "I'm impressed."

"I'm blackmailing the warden of the prison who happens to hold my current focus of interest, technically." She corrected. "The fact that he's also sleeping with my mother just makes things easier." I laughed at her and she laughed as well. "Hungry?" She asked and I nodded. She then whipped out a sleek black phone, swiped in a couple things, and put it to her ear.

"Yes, hello, I'd like to place an order for delivery. We'd like two orders of the Curry of the Day, an order of Gai Med Ma Moung, and a large side of Sweet Rice with Mango." She put a hand over the receiver long enough to ask if I wanted anything else. I shook my head no. "Yes," she continued with the person on the other end of the line, "that will be paid in cash. You can have it delivered to the warden's office at the Holden Correctional Facility. Yes, for Warden James Greene." She smirked and said thank you before hanging up.

"And they say *I'm* a criminal." I teased. She shrugged and went on discussing what we'd been talking about before the gummy bears.

Half an hour later the warden himself came striding out the door and across the yard. He was carrying a fairly large paper sack with red printing on the side. He didn't look very pleased with Miranda.

"I suppose this belongs to you?" He asked her. She looked up from the notebook she hadn't touched until he opened the door, a look of utter indifference on her face. I bit my lip to keep from laughing.

"Oh, yes, thank you. We're quite hungry." She smiled innocently, taking the bag from him. He held onto it a moment longer, staring her down. Her smile never wavered, though a glint of mischief shone in her eyes. He sighed at last and relinquished the bag.

"Very well, enjoy your dinner." He told her, ignoring me completely. "You could have at least ordered me spring rolls." He grumbled as he walked away. The moment the door shut behind him we both burst into laughter. It didn't quiet until Miranda had finished doling out the food. Then our mouths had other things to do.

"Good?" She asked, pointing a fork toward the heap of food I was about to shove in my mouth.

"Delicious." I replied around the chicken and cashews. "I love Thai."

"Me, too." She smiled. "So, do you think we can talk while we eat?" She asked. I nodded. "Good because I want to know more about Cal and Lily." She insisted, pouring me a glass of Coke.

"Alright." I agreed. "What do you want to know?" I took a long sip of the Coke. The bubbles tickled my nose and cooled the heat of the curry on my tongue. If nothing else Miranda sure knew how to order great takeout.

"I want to know everything." She smiled. Her eyes sparkled with anticipation and I decided to share a little more. I finished my Coke and started in as she poured me more.

Cal didn't see Lily up close for another two weeks after the meeting in the Library. He never stopped thinking about her, though. He did all he could to learn who she was, and thanks to his skills on a computer he came up with quite a bit.

Lily was a transfer student. Her parents had divorced the year before and she moved with her mother. She was a senior, like he thought, and according to her transcripts she was almost as smart as he was. She was an only child. She liked strawberries, orange soda, chocolate pudding, and her favorite color was mint, just like her favorite ice cream.

Cal watched her, feeling slightly creepy for it, but he had to know more about her. He wasn't brave enough to venture into the cafeteria, but he watched through the window. He noticed that she sat alone. The most popular kids frequently sat down with her or wandered over to talk to her, but she never initiated it.

The boys that had bullied Cal for years swarmed around her like bees. Cal couldn't blame them. She was just as beautiful as the flower she was named for, maybe even more so. She, however, seemed mostly content to ignore the peacocks and the preening doves. She talked to them, but not for more than a moment or two.

Cal quickly learned that Lily never went anywhere without a book tucked under her arm. It was usually Shakespeare, but one day he'd seen her with a copy of Tolstoy's Anna Karenina. Apparently she liked the classics.

Finally, after watching for weeks, Cal decided to be bold. He waited until after school had let out and the parking lot had emptied, and then he snuck from the library. Earlier that day he'd feigned a migraine so he could sneak into the office when they weren't looking and find Lily's locker number. He found locker number 262 and pulled his backpack from his shoulder.

Inside he found the piece of paper he'd carefully tucked away, the drawing he'd worked on since that morning, a perfect likeness of her face. He folded the paper carefully and slipped it into an envelope he'd stolen while looking for her locker number. On the outside he'd written a quote from the book he'd seen her carrying the day before. He sealed the envelope and carefully began sliding it through the grate of her locker.

Halfway done with his task a voice echoed down the hallway, calling him the name he hated most. In his fear he dropped the envelope and turn to run regardless. Big hands stopped him, hauling him roughly against the metal of the lockers. The steel locks dug into his spine and he bit his tongue to keep from crying out. He couldn't show weakness.

The largest of the three, a boy named Anthony, pressed his forearm into Cal's throat, holding him in place while he gestured to one of the other boy's to pick up what Cal had dropped. The one he indicated, Owen, did as he was told and elbowed the third, Will, as he read the front. They snickered together.

"What have we here?" Anthony taunted, yanking the paper from Owen's hand. "He could not be mistaken. There were no other eyes like those in the world. There was only one creature in the world who could concentrate for him all the brightness and meaning of life. It was she." *He read from the envelope.*

"What the hell is this?" He spat, waving the envelope in Cal's face. "Love poems?" He asked. Cal cringed, preparing for the blow. It didn't come, not yet anyway.

"What's inside, hmm?" The boy asked. Cal's eyes flew open. He begged, pleaded for the boys not to open it, but of course that only made them want to open it more. Anthony held Cal against the lockers by his shoulders while the other two ripped open the envelope and yanked the drawing free. The envelope fluttered to the floor as the two boys whooped and hollered over their discovery.

"You're gonna wanna see this." Will told Anthony, handing him Cal's drawing. The larger boy's eyes darkened and he turned to Cal with malice in his smile.

"Someone's got a little crush?" He asked. Cal swallowed and tried not to cry. His face was red with shame and the tears fell regardless of how hard he tried to swallow them. The other boys just laughed harder. Cal closed his eyes to them,

embarrassed and afraid. Anthony released his grip on Cal's shoulders long enough to sink a fist into his gut.

Cal doubled over, clutching his stomach, and Anthony brought his knee up into Cal's face. Cal fell to the ground, blood dripping from his nose onto the floor. Anthony kicked out, forcing Cal onto his side with a blow to his ribs. Cal looked up into the eyes of his tormentor. They were full of excitement and pleasure over his pain.

Anthony held the picture over Cal's head, one corner in each hand, and pulled slowly, ripping it in half. With a laugh he ripped it in half again and let the pieces flutter to the ground in front of Cal's face. Cal hated him then, hated him more than he'd ever hated anyone or anything before. He looked up at the boy with that hatred in his eyes and all Anthony did was laugh.

"She could never love you." He hissed at Cal, squatting down next to him and leaning closer. "Girls like her could never love an ugly freak like you." He spit into Cal's face, making him cringe in disgust. "No one could ever love you." He said, standing again and pulling his leg back for another kick.

"What are you doing?" A voice yelled, stopping the foot that was aimed for Cal's face. Cal curled into himself, covering

his face with his arms, and waited for the blow to land. A voice had never stop Anthony before. Nothing ever stopped him..

"Just teaching the freak a lesson." Anthony told the voice. "No need to worry your pretty head." The voice yelled at him again, angry and vengeful. It told him to get lost, that it was calling the cops and telling them what it saw if he and his friends didn't leave immediately. Anthony tried to reason, but Cal heard a loud crack and then the sounds of three sets of heavy boy feet walked away and a door shut hard behind them.

"Are you alright?" The voice asked. It took Cal a moment to realize the question was for him. Slowly he peered beneath his fingers and jumped when he saw Lily's face hovering over him. She smiled kindly and reached for him. He winced out of habit. She frowned. "I'm not going to hurt you." She promised.

She grabbed his elbow and helped him to his feet. When she released him she pulled a small package of Kleenex from her pocket and pressed the lot to his face. She grabbed his hand, making his heart leap, and pressed it to where she'd placed the tissue, telling him to hold it there. She was kind and gentle and didn't seem to care at all that tears still fell from his eyes, or that his body still shook from fear.

"I'm so sorry they did this to you." She told him. He looked at the floor. She couldn't have known it wasn't the first time, or the worst for that matter. She asked him why they did it and he blushed, looking down. He saw the paper still lying on the floor. One edge of it was tinted with blood that had fallen from his face.

He watched as Lily's graceful fingers bent and picked up the pieces of paper form the floor. He tried to stop her from seeing, tried to say no, but it was too late. She crossed to the bench on the other side of the hallway and laid the pieces out like a puzzle, fitting them back together. He watched in horror as she did.

When she finished she gasped and looked at him. He looked at the floor in shame. She knew. She knew what he'd been trying to leave in secret. She knew how he felt. He wished he could die. Slowly he watched her pink shoes cross the hallway, stopping just in front of him. He lowered both hands and waited for the slap, the let down.

Her hand rose and he cringed again. He could see the pieces of paper still clutched in her other hand. He felt her fingers against his chin and she tugged upward, pulling his eyes up to look at her. When he did he was surprised to find tears in her eyes and a sad smile on her face.

"This is the most beautiful thing anyone has ever given me." She told him, wiping the tears from her eyes. She thanked him for the picture, told him it was beautiful, that he was very talented. And then, without warning or reason, she kissed him.

3 Days, 3 Hours, 14 Min...

As I'd finished my story the rain started up again and Miranda and I were ushered inside. She insisted on accompanying me to my cell and asked a million questions along the way. Did Cal kiss Lily back? Was Cal hurt? Did he and Lily start dating? Did she tell him she loved him too? What happened to them? Did the boys who beat up Cal ever pay for their actions?

I smiled and told her the answers. Cal and Lily did start dating and quickly fell in love. They kept their relationship a secret because Cal didn't want Lily to get hurt because of him. Each day after school they would meet in a secret place, hidden from the rest of the world. Cal would draw and Lily would read. They'd have picnics and talk and do the things teenagers do when they're alone. They were happy. They were in love.

Miranda had tears in her eyes by the time we reached my cell. She told me she was glad Cal had found someone to love him, that Lily could see the real beauty hidden behind his scars. She said she wished she could have a love like Cal and Lily's one day. She asked if I would tell her the rest of their story and I promised to the next time we were together. I knew she'd cry then, too. I only wished it would still be out of joy.

She told me before she left that she wouldn't see me the next day. She said she had a work obligation she couldn't get out of. She promised to have no fun at all and made me promise the same. I asked a quick favor of her before she left and she agreed. She then handed me a present she'd bought me and, after the guard checked it over and approved, she left me and it in the cell as she waved goodbye.

So, there I sat some time after she left, peering down at the present in my hands, the wrapping discarded on the floor somewhere. I ran my fingers across the leather bound surface of the brand new sketchbook. The pack of charcoal pencils and shading tools sat next to me on the bed. My fingers itched to open them, but my mind was otherwise preoccupied.

I spent the better part of an hour trying to decipher the motives behind the gift. What exactly gave Miranda the idea for such a gift? There wasn't a soul still alive that knew I sketched. I destroyed every pencil mark I'd made some time ago. I thought and thought, but only ever ended at one conclusion. Miranda was smarter than I'd given her credit for. She was figuring things out. The present told me as much.

Finally, accepting that I had slipped and allowed the vibrant woman to glimpse my past, I relinquished my mental search and opened the pack that sat against my thigh. The scent of wood reached my nose, pulling on memories of a long past memory. A boy and a girl tucked away in an attic on a rainy weekend. The boy drew for the girl and the girl watched intently, mesmerized by every stroke and shade.

I swallowed the memory with the emotions it incurred and flipped the latch set into the leather. I pulled a pencil at random from the pouch and sat back, pulling my knees up into a makeshift table. The end of the pencil tapped against my chin, unsure of what to draw. I thought for some time, but when I closed my eyes there was only a face that lingered there. And so I drew it.

I slid the pencil across the paper, letting the familiar lines of the face flow from my memory and out the tip. It took very little time at all for the unused skill to return. Like riding a bike, the cogs of my mind pedaled and the charcoal smudged and shaded until I was left with the likeness I sought. I smiled at the face that haunted my dreams of late, tracing the curve of its beauty with my fingers, blurring the edges until the picture had no sharpness left to it, only softness and beauty.

I flipped the page, unable to look any longer, and started again. I drew a different face, a new friend, and when I'd finished with the image of Miranda winding a long candy worm around one finger I flipped the page and drew another, another picture, another face, another memory. I drew and drew until my hand cramped and tears dripped to the paper, ruining lines I'd have to retrace later.

I drew until I could draw no longer, and then I fell asleep. One hand pillowed my head, the other cradled the portfolio like a child. Pencils and smudge sticks were strewn across the mattress, staining the white sheets with bits of black and grey. That night I dreamed in greyscale

The sky was black with clouds and thunder. Flashes of white blinked just at the edge of the horizon, warning of a storm to

come. Or had it already left? I wasn't sure. The white light of repetitive poles shone on the wet pavement as my sneakers padded along. I was alone on the street, hands in pockets, head down, walking nowhere.

My mind was busy, but I don't know with what. Something important I was sure, but at the moment I couldn't remember anything but a face. A face that was sweet and kind, with lips as soft as down feathers, softer maybe. I'd kissed those lips this night. I knew that much. I could still recall the pressure of them against my own.

I ran a pale grey hand across my lips, remembering the kiss that occupied my thoughts. They say love is blind, that it clouds the judgment. But I felt on fire, alive and vibrant, the world sharpened to pinpricks. I smiled at the beauty I saw everywhere. True beauty, not the manufactured stuff of obsession in our troubled times, but the beauty of a storm edged night, the scent of rain in the air, the mist of fog coiling in and around the buildings, tickling my skin where we met.

Everything was heightened. The world was a symphony and I was entranced. I was so wholly engulfed that I didn't hear the most important part, the rhythmic pounding of percussive feet. They were drowned out by the sing of light, like violins, by the tremolo of my racing heart. The conductor that was my mind urged the melody onward, but I forgot about the drums.

With a crash and a beat and thump their hands fell upon me, dragging me backward. I cried out, but a heavy hand came down across my mouth, stifling the sound. Fingers dug into my skin, raking scratches down my arm as I fought to pull away. The blood rushed in my ears like a roll of cymbals, and then, with a final crash, the world went dark.

I awoke to a dark room illuminated by a single white orb. The edges of it all seemed fuzzy and wrong, tilted in a way that didn't make sense. The hands grabbed me again, pulling me upward and righting the world with my body. Someone moved in the darkness, twitchy and nervous.

My head spun and the world seemed to come in and out of slow motion. Time seemed to flip back and forth, forward and backward. Nothing made sense. I both knew and didn't know what would happen. I didn't know where I was or who I was, a third party or a participant. I didn't know anything anymore. My world was numb and silent.

And all amidst that confusion the night passed, the acts committed put on repeat as I watched from every angle. I saw the faces, dark in the dim light. I saw the anger, the hate, the anticipation, the pain, the sorrow, the wish for death. I saw the face of a broken soul. I saw the world in black and white and then there was red.

The color that haunted my every nightmare poured from places that shouldn't bleed, from unnatural openings, from the hands of cruel men. I saw it drip to the ground; I saw it flung against the wall, spit on the shirt of another. I saw its horror everywhere. And then I saw nothing.

2 Days, 20 Hours, 3 Min...

A loud clang awoke me from the swirling black that choked me and made my head spin. I jerked upward immediately, momentarily disoriented by my surroundings. I looked down and froze my heart momentarily when I saw the face that haunted me staring back, eyes cold and evil, just like I remembered. I slammed the portfolio closed, banishing the face to another realm, and pulled a hand across my face. Someone cleared their throat at the cell door and I looked toward the noise.

"Good morning." Warden Green told me. He balanced a plate of yellow mush and grey tubes in one hand. My breakfast I supposed.

"Good morning." I returned the greeting, climbing from the bed and crossing to the bars that separated us. He slid the tray through the slot. I took it and set it on the edge of my bed.

"Not what you're used to of late, I suppose." He observed. Something about his gaze as it met mine wasn't right. There was hardness to his face I'd not seen before. Not even when Miranda goaded him. "It seems Miranda has gotten you quite spoiled." He smiled coolly.

"I suppose she has." I admitted, attempting to decipher the change in demeanor of the man in front of me. "But you're not here to discuss breakfast, are you?" I asked him, putting pieces together.

"I don't like the effect you're having on her." He told me. So he'd come to discuss Miranda.

"I wasn't aware I had an effect on her." I replied, the cold, calculating portion of my brain taking control of the conversation. "I was under the impression that she was an adult and that I was a project for work, nothing more." I smiled.

"You are far too intelligent to not deduce that Miranda has grown attached to you, like some sick obsession she won't let go of." He grumbled through clenched teeth. "It's vile how she protects you, how she acts as if you're…"

"Friends." I cut him off. His gaze hardened. "I suppose you could say we are. She's an intelligent and interesting human being, why would I not enjoy her company?" I asked, cocking my head to the side, playing the part.

"That's where we have the problem." He hissed. "I don't care that she finds you fascinating, that she's chosen to make you her pet project. I don't even mind so much that she's interfering with my work in the process." He paused, for effect I surmised. "What I do care is that you seem to be as fascinated by her as she is by you."

"Miranda is an intriguing young woman." I smiled, interlocking my fingers in front of me.

"Do you know what she asked me yesterday?" He asked. Clearly it wasn't something he liked. I shook my head no, smiling only the slightest to throw him off. I'd had enough of people trying to intimidate me lately. I couldn't do anything about the ones locked within my mind. I *could* do something about him. "I doubt that very much." He glared.

"Then do, pray tell, enlighten me as to what evil seed you think I've planted in the impressionable mind of young Miss Stevens." I smirked.

"You think you're so smart, don't you?" He asked. I laughed.

"I don't think. I *know* that I'm intelligent, more so than you. More so than most anyone I've ever met. I'm a genius, Jim, a certified brilliant mind with an IQ higher than you can comprehend. I don't see, however, what that has to do with a question she asked you." I spat, slicing at him with my greatest weapon. The only weapon I'd ever possessed really.

"She asked me if there was any way I could save you." He stated. His voice was cool, but just below the surface was the rage that fueled our confrontation. I truly believed had he had the power he'd have executed me on the spot. "She begged me to find a way to grant you a stay of execution." He continued. "Tell me you had nothing to do with that."

"It doesn't matter what I tell you." I shrugged. "You've worked it out in your mind that I'm corrupting the mind of your future step-daughter and nothing I say will change any of that. You can't change the mind of an absolute man."

“I don’t like you spending time with Miranda.” He admitted.

“So stop me.” I suggested. He scowled. “You can’t, can you?” I smiled. “You know as much as I do that Miranda will never stand for it. I surmise she has her mother’s ear as well, something that could either harm or help you.” I laughed, he glared. “How does it feel, warden, to be under the control of a woman half your age? How does it feel to hold no control over your actions?”

“Enough.” He growled. I laughed harder, stopping suddenly and closing the gap between myself and the bars that kept us apart. I wasn’t sure any longer which of us they were protecting from the other.

“You’re an absolute man.” I told the warden, just above a whisper. “You don’t seek absolution from me. You seek it *for* you. You need the surety that you are right in your thinking. I cannot give you absolution, James Greene. One can only find absolution of their own accord.” I turned and went back to my bunk, ignoring the man who remained at the front of my cage, the man with a fractured facade.

“The lawyer you requested will be here within the hour.” He told me. “I’ll have the guards fetch you when he arrives.” He turned on his heel, stamping down the empty hall with less determination than he approached with.

My hands shook as I picked up the sketchbook from where I’d tucked it under my pillow. I opened it, running my fingers across the face that softened my heart, a face that would have been ashamed of my recent behavior.

"Damn you for making me weak." I told the face. And then with a sigh I went to the cell door. "Warden Greene." I called out. His footsteps stopped and then returned. He stopped when he could see my face again, my hands draped through the bars as my shoulders gave up the arrogance they'd just held.

"I didn't ask Miranda to save me." I told him. He nodded as if he already knew. "I don't want to be saved." I admitted.."

"I know." He sighed, fiddling with his keys. With another heavy sigh he started to leave, turning back just enough to give me my absolution. "Don't worry, Dr. Andrews, you'll get your wish. There isn't anyone that can save you now."

2 Days, 14 Hours, 31 Min...

I drew some more after the warden left. I left the faces behind and drew places instead. My apartment in Essex, the lab where I'd discovered my most valuable work. I was putting the final touches on a house that held more memories than I could count when the guard came for me.

"Your lawyer is here." He told me. It was the one I liked, the gentle one who always seemed to forget to tighten the cuffs that last click. I tucked the drawing away and slid the pencil I'd been using back into its case. I walked over and slid my hands through the slot without him asking. He never had to ask.

As he slid the cold metal around my wrists I took the chance to read the name above the number on his badge. It never seemed to matter before, but for some reason I suddenly needed to know the name of the man that showed me kindness regardless of the fact that he hated me.

"Delgado." I read aloud. He flicked his eyes up to mine. "That's your last name, right?" He nodded, pocketing his keys and opening the gate. He gestured and I walked out ahead of him. When we got to the door that separated my hallway from the rest, I looked at him again.

"What's your first name?" I asked him. He studied me a moment, clearly trying to suss out my motives. I could see him determining if his name could be dangerous in my hands, but finally he sighed and with a shake of his head he answered.

"Carlos." He told me, opening the door and ushering me into the hallway that led to the interrogation room. "Why do you want to know?" He asked from behind my shoulder.

"Curiosity is a powerful force." I replied. "You've always been nice to me. I figured I should know your name." I explained. He hummed, stopping me as he opened the door to the small grey room with the grey table and chairs. A man sat in the place that was usually mine.

Carlos escorted me to the one usually occupied by a feisty brunette and asked the lawyer if he wanted me cuffed. He said it was fine, and after Carlos undid the restraints, he left us to our business. I placed my hands carefully into my lap and surveyed the man in front of me.

He was maybe mid thirties, not much older than I. He, of course, was beautiful. Most everyone was. He had a strong, square jaw that balanced well with the square set of his shoulders. His nose and cheek bones where sharp and angular and he had dark chocolate eyes. His equally dark hair was perfectly trimmed, each strand in its rightful place. His crisp charcoal suit was expensively tailored and he wore a shining gold band around his wrist. The watch must have cost several thousand alone.

He had a leather bound portfolio pad in front of him and a sleek silver pen poised in his left hand. He smiled up at me when he'd finished writing the date and time on the top of the paper next to my name. His teeth were just as perfect as the rest of him and I instantly hated him on principal.

"Good morning." He greeted with a well bleached smile. "I've been told you requested legal counsel. I'm Daniel Ardan." He extended a hand. I accepted it hesitantly. I needed him after all.

"Dr. Andrews." I introduced myself.

"Well, what is it that I can help you with today, doctor?" He inquired, clicking his pen. Part of me wanted to ram the thing into his throat. What did it matter if I took another life at this point? I was dead in a couple days anyway. Of course I'd never taken a life with my bare hands before. I wasn't entirely sure I was capable. It would also likely ensure I wouldn't see Miranda again until the execution, so I decided against it.

"I would like to create a last will and testament." I instructed the annoying man. He smiled and nodded.

"I can certainly help you with that." He answered. He pulled a briefcase onto the table and removed a handful of papers. "This is a list of the items seized at the time of your arrest." He handed them over. "I could possibly see about regaining some of the personal affects, but the papers and the laboratory equipment would be beyond my capabilities." He instructed. I nodded as I perused the list.

"The only possession on here I would want back would be my books, but seeing as how I won't be reading for much longer I'm not concerned." I told him, pushing the list aside. "My main concern is with the properties and bank accounts I possess." I continued.

"Yes." He nodded again, pulling more pieces of paper from his briefcase and looking them over. "A 1500 square foot penthouse in Brentwood, Essex. A time share, beachfront condo in Buenos Aires. A two bedroom home in Ridgefield, New Jersey. A savings and checking account with Brentwood Bank, over a dozen separate stock holdings in various companies throughout England and the United States, and an IRA, totaling $8,786,513.26." He listed. I shook my head at each.

"That sounds about right." I replied. "I also believe there was a car in the garage of the penthouse garage and the deed to the Thomas Facility." I added. He checked his papers, agreeing with me.

"Yes, a black 1968 Corvette Stingray." He read from the paper. "It was impounded, but it shouldn't be difficult to retrieve." He assured me. "As for the research facility, the labs were mostly cleared out, but it seems you still own the building." He stated, abandoning his papers and folding his hands across them.

"Excellent, shall we proceed with the official paperwork?" I asked, mirroring his posture.

"Yes, we shall." He clicked his pen again, poised to write. "How would you like your assets divided." He asked.

"It's quite simple, actually." I told him. "The time share can be released to the other owners to be dealt with as they see fit. The home in New Jersey should have been sold years ago. I simply never got around to it. Sell it and give the proceeds to the local children's hospital."

"All of the proceeds?" He asked. I confirmed with a nod of my head. "And the Thomas Facility?" He continued, head still bent as he wrote.

"The deed to the facility along with any remaining funds associated with it is to be left to Dr. Nigel Whitwill, along with three million of my personal fortune." I instructed. "The apartment in Essex and all it's contents, the car, and the remainder of my fortune, minus your fees, of course, will go to Miss Miranda Stevens." I told him.

"The reporter?" He asked, showing a flash of judgment for the first time since I'd entered the room, the first crack in this charming, arrogant armor.

"Yes." I told him. "She will be my primary benefactor." I told him.

"Very well." I agreed, scribbling down the last of my wishes. I knew he didn't understand. I didn't fully understand it either. There was just something about the girl that moved me. She'd been the first person in over a decade to surprise me, to make me rethink my judgment. She'd earned more than just the words I'd shared with her and the ones I'd yet to share. She deserved more than that.

"Is there anything I need to sign or release?" I asked the arrogant Mr. Arden.

"I'll have to have the papers drawn up and a quit claim deed pulled for the time share. Once I've obtained those I'll come back and have you sign them." He informed me. "I should be able to get them by tomorrow afternoon, the following morning at the very latest. Everything should be in order before…" He trailed off, feigning decency.

"Before I'm executed you mean?" I finished for him.

"Yes." He swallowed, pulling at his tie uncomfortably. "While we're on the subject, actually," he stated, tapping his pen against the pad in front of him, "we should probably discuss your plans for after the fact."

"Well, Mr. Arden," I sighed, "after the lethal injection I plan to be deceased." I teased him. He flushed and then relaxed when I smiled at him. "I'm assuming you meant what I wish to have done with my remains." I continued, easing the poor guy's anxiety.

"Yes, I know it's a delicate subject to discuss, but it's something you should plan for. Without expressed wishes your body will simply be buried in the federal cemetery in a plain marked grave." He told me. In all honesty I'd not thought about the after. I suppose he had a point. I hated the idea of them burying me like the others. The prison had claimed the last of my life. I didn't want them to have my body as well.

"I've made my peace with what is coming." I told the now nervous lawyer. "I suppose I'd like to cremated, ashes to ashes and all that." I told him.

"And what is to be done with the remains after cremation?" He asked, bent to take notes again.

"I suppose I will ask Miss Stevens to care for that as well." I sighed. "She's the only friend I have left." I said, more to myself than him.

"I'll see to it that she is named your next of kin and that they are aware of your wishes." He told me, the first kind expression he'd given me. "Is there anything else you need?" He asked. I shook my head no and he took his things and left.

Carlos came in for me a minute later, clicking the cuffs around my wrists yet again. With a gentle hand he led me back to my cell. Just as gently as he'd affixed them, he released my restraints and locked the door behind him. I rubbed my wrists out of habit and thought about the conversations I'd had that day until I heard someone clear their throat behind me. I turned and Carlos was still beyond the bars of my cell door.

"I went to see a chiropractor yesterday." He told me. I waited for him to continue and he did. "My back and hips haven't felt this good in over a year. I just," he sighed, looking at his hands and then back at me, "I just wanted to thank you." He told me. I smiled at him.

"I'm glad you're feeling better." I told him. He shook his head and left me. I looked out the window a while and then pulled my sketchpad from under my pillow. I pulled the pencils out and realized I'd worn them to stumps. Unfortunately the guard had taken the sharpener for fear I'd pull it apart and slice my wrists. I sighed and then had an idea.

I leaned my head out the bars as far as I could and called for Carlos. He came sauntering down the hall and asked what I needed. I asked for a favor, for him to sharpen my pencils for me, and he was nice enough to oblige. Five minutes later he returned with them and I thanked him profusely. He smiled and left me again. His was the first face I drew that night.

2 Days, 9 Hours, 0 Min...

At three o'clock sharp Carlos returned to my cell, accompanied by the ever insufferable Dr. Gunderson. She looked overdressed in her perfectly pressed linen suit and black pumps. The spike heel was much too high for the workday. Perhaps she was going someone after. Perhaps she was trying to reach my level. She'd never reach it mentally; I suppose I couldn't deny her the attempt to reach it physically.

"I thought I was rid of you." I grumbled just loud enough for her to hear. I could see the reaction in her eyes, but she managed to keep the rest of her under control.

"I heard you've had a difficult time of late." She oozed with fake concern, like a festering boil ready to pop and splatter feigned empathy all over me. It made me sick and it made me irritated.

"I'm fine." I told her, ignoring the fact that Carlos was standing awkwardly by the bars, cuffs in hand. He rarely had to request for me to come to the bars. I only held out for Chuckles. "I'm actually a bit busy at the moment, if you don't mind. Perhaps you could come back another time." I smirked at my drawing pad. "Tuesday works for me, if you're available."

"You'll be dead Tuesday." She stated, not at all the usually touchy feely I usually got from her. She was being unprecedentedly blunt. I liked it. It meant I was getting to her.

"Glad you see you're not pussy footing around any longer." I sighed, rolling until I was seated on the edge of the cot. I took as much time as I was able to slide each individual pencil back into its slot. I then folded the pad closed and laid them perfectly square against the corner of the bed.

"You could bring that with. Art is an excellent insight into the soul." She suggested. I stood and walked to the bars, leaving the portfolio behind.

"Good afternoon Carlos." I greeted the guard. "Did you have a pleasant lunch?" I asked him. He seemed taken aback, but shrugged noncommittally.

"Can we get on with it?" The annoying shrink asked. I sighed and slid my wrist through the bars, leaning so I could whisper at Carlos just loud enough for the blonde to hear.

"Some people just don't have any manners." I smiled. "It's a crime." The shrink huffed and Carlos stifled a smile. I knew I liked him for a reason. I followed the blonde down the hallway, Carlos bringing up the rear, and we quickly took our places in the interrogation room. I was only mildly happy to have my usual seat back. The view was still undesirable.

"So which doctor tattled on me?" I asked as the door shut behind Carlos.

"Both." Gunderson replied. "Honestly, I'm not even sure where to begin with you." She smoothed her jacket sleeve. "The last time we spoke you were blatantly combative and uncooperative. And yet I've heard that you are now chummy with that reporter girl. Some employees here even say you two seem like friends."

"I *like* Miranda." I told her, making it quite obvious that the same didn't apply to her.

"Oh, don't get me wrong, I'm elated that you're opening up to someone." She encouraged, completely missing the point. I sighed at her stupidity. "I just wish you'd be willing to discuss things so in depth during our sessions." She continued.

"I'm pretty sure there's a difference between a conversation with a friend and a bearing of your soul with judgmental psychiatrist whose been forced upon you." I replied, crossing my arms in my typically defensive stance. She never failed to bring out the worst in my temper. This time she sighed at me.

"I simply don't understand what I did to make you distrust me so." She shook her head as she straightened her notes. "Or is it that you simply distrust all psychologists?" She hinted.

"I've been to many shrinks throughout the years." I informed her. She looked hopeful for a moment that her theory might be right. It just made crushing it that much more satisfactory. "I never seemed to have a problem with any of them. I'm fairly certain it's just you." I smirked. She sighed again, flipping through a stack of pages scrawled with incomprehensible chicken scratch. Doctor's handwriting.

"Why don't we discuss the incidents of late?" She suggested. I didn't respond and she took it as a sign to continue. "Let's talk about the assault on Dr. Cichowski." She shifted in her seat, crossing her long, smooth legs.

"What's to say? He pissed me off, I took action, and I woke up with a killer headache for my troubles." I replied, pulling my arms tighter against my chest at the memory.

"I'd say there's more to it than that." She insisted. "Why did you attack him? What did he do to 'piss you off' as you say? Was it something he said?" She leaned back, studying, analyzing.

"Does it matter?" I asked, leaning toward her. If she wanted to play this game we'd play. But I wasn't someone who often lost. She sat up straight once more. Reacting exactly how I'd intended.

"I'd say it does." She replied. "We've spoken a dozen times over the course of your stay here. You've consistently been cool and calculated in every manner. You've gone so far as surly, but never aggressive. Even your crimes aren't of the violent nature. If someone managed to push you to the point of physical retaliation, I'd say it matters."

"I'd argue that considering I'll be taking my last breaths in just over 48 hours, any points or observations are null and void. Even if I were to take on a sudden violent streak it would only implore the conviction further." I shrugged. "What difference does it make if I'm temperamental so long as when my heart stops beating you can check that little box that says I was psychologically sound both when I committed the crime I was convicted of and when I was put to death for it."

"Don't worry, you can leave with a clear conscience." I assured her.

"Perhaps you can brush off the incident with Dr. Chicowski as a desperate act of a person looking at their last days on earth, but how do you explain the other episode? Dr. John Sanders reports that the guards found you in what was apparently a severe mental break, that you tried to harm yourself, and were so out of it you were unresponsive to any attempt to communicate." She read off the paper in front of her, paraphrasing I'm assuming.

"Well, for starters, Sanders is an idiot." I shrugged. "And furthermore, I did not suffer a psychic break. I had a night terror and wasn't unresponsive when the guards found me, I was still asleep."

"You claim you were experiencing a night terror that caused you to huddle in the corner and repeatedly bash your skull against a brick wall?" She asked, raising her eyebrows questioningly. She didn't believe me. I wasn't surprised.

"By definition night terrors are vivid hallucinatory dreams brought on by..." I started

"I know what night terrors are," she interrupted, "and their causes. I also know that they tend to not be singular events, so unless you're ready to tell me you've been having a string of violent, vivid nightmares..."

"I have." I interrupted, returning the favor. For the first time it seemed I shocked her. She closed her mouth quickly, breathing sharply. I didn't want to share, but I also didn't need her trying to psychoanalyze me. Nightmares could be explained simply by the stress of my impending death. Psychotic breaks were a little more complicated. I chose the lesser of two evils.

"You've been having nightmares?" She asked once she'd composed herself. "For how long?" She inquired.

"About a week." I lied. She didn't need to know I'd had nightmares my entire life. She didn't need to know anything about me.

"What are the nightmares about?" She asked, resting her chin on her perfectly manicured hands. I cursed mentally. Of course she'd want to delve into the deep, dark recesses of my apparently damaged mind. I suppose I shouldn't have hoped for anything less. After all she was a shrink, a shrink that seemed to have a personal mission in life to figure out why I'd gone postal and murdered several thousand people. It was also a personal mission of mine to not let the bitch into my mind. I needed a lie good enough for her to believe, but far enough from the truth to keep her off my back.

"I dream I'm falling." I told her. It wasn't entirely false. I'd dreamt of falling before.

"You dreamt of falling?" She judged. I could hear the suspicion in her voice. "People dream of falling all the time. It's a common nightmare. I'm not sure it qualifies as a night terror."

"I dream I'm falling into a grave." I added. "That hands are pulling me downward into hell." It was dark enough to qualify as a night terror, but a pretty blatant analysis.

Before she could read any more into what I'd said or not said, I stood and called for Carlos. He opened the door and I gestured that I was ready to go. He replaced the cuffs and directed me toward the door. Before I left, I decided to dig one last nail into the doctor. I peered over my shoulder at where she was scribbling in a black pad-folio.

"Gunderson." I called. She looked up and peered at me incredulously. "For the record, I am now and have always been of sound mind. Particularly when I released the virus. I was especially clear that day." I winked before I turned out the door and left the scowling Dr. Gunderson to her notes. I walked back to my cell with a smile on my face.

2 Days, 5 Hours, 41 Min...

After my less than pleasant chat with the ever irritating Dr. Gunderson, I was left aggravated and full of nervous energy. I tried to draw, but only ended up with three scratched out attempts. I resolved to let it go for the time being and deserted the sketch pad for the most recent book of crosswords Miranda had brought me. Twenty minutes later and I'd managed to fill in a total of four answers. I gave up on that as well. Clearly my mind was otherwise preoccupied.

I stood and went to the window, peering through the bars I grasped. The sun was setting on the westernmost edge of my field of vision. The pinks and oranges and plums that smeared the sky made me ache for a paintbrush and some oils. I'd always been more of a sketch artist, but on occasion I found the only way to truly capture the beauty of nature was with a brush and paint. Unfortunately I had neither the tools nor the canvas for such an attempt.

I abandoned the window as the last streaks of sienna bled from the horizon. I considered drawing for a moment but another glance at the discarded balls of paper in the corner discouraged me. I wasn't in the right mindset to accomplish anything of great creative or intellectual value.

I was tired and frustrated and just a little lonely. It'd only been one day since I'd seen Miranda, but already her absence was weighing on me. It was amazing how close I'd gotten to her in just a handful of days. I honestly considered her a friend, someone I could talk to, maybe even trust. I missed her without even realizing it. I was glad this day was almost over. I looked forward to breakfast with Miranda more than I cared to admit to myself.

I decided after a few nights of torrent slumber I could use a good nights rest and so I gave into the exhaustion that had settled into my bones. I slid my art supplies and crosswords under the bed and flopped down onto the flimsy mattress. Thankfully sleep took me quickly and I drifted off into my common companion of strange dreams.

I was sitting on a bar stool, glass in hand. The man that stood before me was tall with broad shoulders and a close cropped haircut. Each ear bore a gold hoop and a black and grey dragon wound around one arm, its head disappearing inside his t-shirt. He smirked lazily as he filled my glass again.

I felt the stool next to me shift and someone brushed slightly against my arm as they took their seat. I swallowed a sip of the golden liquid in my glass before I turned to my new companion. Miranda reached for her now room temperature martini as I faced her.

"Sorry I'm late." She smiled as she tipped the glass back, emptying the contents in one swift motion and chewing on the olive as she waived the bartender down for another.

"Someone's thirsty." I observed as her second martini slid across the polished wood of the bar. This time she chose to sip rather than gulp.

"I hate warm gin." She shrugged, swirling her new olive through the clear liquid in her glass. "How was your day?" She questioned. She was dressed nice this evening. Not her usual jean and sweater combination. She had on a knee length rose colored dress with brown suede boots whose heel was a little too high for daily wear. Her hair was moussed and her eyes were perfectly lined.

"Not bad." I smiled, sipping again from my glass. "So are you all dressed up just for me?" I asked.

"I had an interview." She answered.

"Must be someone important for you to break out the heels." I teased, swallowing the last of my chosen poison and gesturing for another round from the bartender.

"Not so much important as in need of swaying." She shrugged. A devilish smile played on the corner of her mouth. I had no doubt in my mind Miranda Stevens was one reporter who would go to almost any lengths to get a scoop.

"Miss Stevens, you're not insinuating you used your feminine wiles to coerce some poor sucker into giving you information, are you?" I feigned shock. I was certain she'd done it before.

"I would never do such a thing." She gasped, dramatically placing a hand over her heart. She managed to hold a blank face for a total of ten seconds before we both burst into a fit of laughter. I certainly liked how easily she made me laugh.

We sipped drinks as we talked, chatting about her day and mine. It seemed I'd been working on a new gene therapy technique that might lead to a cure for schizophrenia. I told

Miranda of the potential for human trials as early as a year from now. She seemed genuinely pleased for me.

We also discussed her current story. She was apparently within days of blowing the lid off of some conspiracy a local politician had been covering up. I warned her to be careful and she told me not to worry so much.

Everything about our conversation felt easy and relaxed, like we'd done the same thing a hundred times before. I could almost see it. The brilliant young scientist and the intrepid young reporter meeting for a drink at the end of their long week to catch up. Two friends who were completely at ease with one another in what was clearly a tradition.

When we'd sufficiently drunk ourselves into a comfortable buzz we departed and said our goodbyes outside the brick walls of the pub we'd been at. Miranda wished me luck in my experiments the following week and I warned her yet again to always be careful. With an eye roll and a slightly intoxicated wave she slid into the back of a yellow taxi cab and disappeared into the night.

I chose to walk home. The night air was cool but welcoming after the warmth of the bar. I could feel the effects of the alcohol swirling within me, making my head heavy and my thoughts erratic. I wasn't drunk, but I was definitely not at my highest clarity.

I rounded a corner, glad to leave the bright lights of the main road behind and sink into the shadows of the side street. The air was heavy with impending rain and the wind blew about me in warm gusts, bringing the scent of an early summer to my nose. I breathed deep.

The first drops of rain splatter the pavement at my feet. One by one they hit, faster and faster. The sky ripped open with a crack and the rain poured down on me. By the time I reached the house at the end of the block I was soaked through.

I stopped when I reached the edge of the porch light, breathing in the night and rain and damp earth. Everything smelled and felt alive. The heat and humidity had been eradicated by the storm and my breath came out in large puffs. I laughed at the amazement I felt, such a drastic change in atmosphere in such a short walk.

A few moments later a light flickered to life beyond the curtained window at the front of the house. A figure appeared in the doorway, peering into the darkness. I stepped further into the light so they wouldn't fear me. I took one more deep breath of the damp air and climbed the steps to where the love of my life waited on the threshold.

I wrapped my arms around them and laughed as they complained about the dampness of my hug. They laughed too, and that laughter was my home, my sanctuary. That laughter, that face, that being was my world, my everything. This dream was my happily ever.

1 Day, 15 Hours, 28 Min...

I heard the tapping of the guard's shoes just as I was putting the finishing touches on the sketch I was doing for Miranda. It was my fifth since I'd awoken from the dream of my perfect life. It may not have been much, but the simplicity of the dream left me feeling hopeful that I may find peace in another lifetime, that maybe one day I could get my happily ever after.

I'd been unable to sleep after for fear the sweetness of the dream would be wiped away by another nightmare. I'd finished four pages of crosswords in the expert section and finally pulled my sketchbook from under the bed.

I drew the dream first, piecing together what I could from my subconscious. An old brick pub scrawled from the tip of my pencil, worn from many years of patronage. A small home framed in lamplight, a man and a woman dancing in the rain. Last I drew a field full of bright flowers and flowing reeds, a silhouette in the distance, beckoning me onward.

When I'd finished I began the one for Miranda, a gift from me to her, a little piece of my past that could continue on into the future. A sort of legacy I suppose, though I guess I technically already had a legacy I was leaving behind, one of death and sickness and vengeance. Not that it mattered much. I had no one to leave my legacy for anyway.

Miranda and the guard, a newbie I'd only seen a couple of times in the last week, appeared outside my door just as I slid the last of my pencils into their rightful place. I tucked the pouch under my pillow and turned to my guests with a smile on my face.

"Nice to see you making use of my present." Miranda observed, smiling as well. She looked tired. The circles under her eyes were darker than before and her hair hung loosely around her shoulders. Even her sweater seemed to slump more than usual around her curvaceous frame.

"Nice to see you, Miranda." I greeted as I joined them by the bars. Without being asked I slid my wrists through the slot and the rookie guard slapped the cuffs on with more gentleness than I expected from someone his size. He was a big man, but it seemed he was a gentle giant.

He led us to the exit as I asked Miranda about the day we'd not spent together. She'd not said exactly what she'd been up to, but I got the sense it was something that had left her feeling both saddened and weary. Once we'd left the confines of the prison we took our usual seats at the picnic table.

"So what delectable treats have you dragged out today?" I asked once we'd settled into our usual seats.

"What makes you think I brought food?" She accused. A slight smile on the corners of her lips told me she was teasing me. It seemed she was as glad to see me as I was to see her. I leaned back and stretched my arms above my head, grateful to feel the sun on my back again.

"Well," I smiled, "considering I've yet to see you without food I just presumed you lugged something with you." I replied. She smiled fully at last and shook her head slightly.

"Well you know what they usually say about assuming." She joked as she pulled a bag from the bench next to her. I could still see the steam curling out from whatever it contained. My stomach grumbled in anticipation. "Someone's hungry." She observed as she doled out the meal.

"Let's just say I missed your food as much as your conversation." I answered. She slid a white cardboard container across to me along with a plastic fork. I lifted the lid to find pancakes, sausage links, and breakfast potatoes along with several packets of butter and syrup. I smiled at the sight. "Maybe more." I admitted to the delicious food in front of me.

"Well, glad to hear I'm missed I guess, even if it's just my ability to purchase good food." She smiled kindly as she slid a lidded Styrofoam cup across to me, my usual two sugars and one cream balancing on top. I thanked her with a nod and dumped the packets into the steaming coffee.

"There's something I should tell you." I said around a mouthful of syrup soaked pancakes. They dripped butter and tasted like heaven.

"Mmmhmm?" Miranda responded, her own mouth full of potatoes.

"I met with a lawyer yesterday." I continued. "We discussed my wishes for after…" Miranda's nod cut me off before I actually said the word execution. It seemed she didn't like the word any more than I did. "Anyway, I made up a will and I figured I should let you know about it." I shoved another forkful into my mouth.

"Why did you feel like you needed to tell me about it?" She asked, setting her fork down. "I mean don't get me wrong, I'm glad you're sharing." She smiled. I smiled back.

"I put you in my will." I told her. Her jaw went slack and her eyes got big. She was clearly not expecting me to divulge such information,

"You put me in your will?" She asked. I confirmed with a nod. "You didn't have to do that. I never expected anything more than conversation from you." She sounded guilty.

"I know, Miranda, but I don't have anyone left. You've been nicer to me than anyone has in a long time. I consider you a friend and when I'm gone I figured my possessions should go to someone who deserves them." I spoke to the pancakes, unable to look at her in the face. I was afraid she was offended by my suggestion. Perhaps I'd overestimated our relationship. "You don't have to accept anything if you don't want." I shrugged. I jumped a moment later when her hand fell on mine. I looked her in the eyes finally.

"I'm honored, Doc." She smiled. I smiled back. "Thank you." She added with a squeeze of my fingers. "So, shall we have a chat?" She asked, easing the uncomfortable tension that had settled around us. I nodded in agreement; glad to be headed toward another subject. "I was hoping you'd share the rest of Cal and Lily's story with me." She suggested. Again I nodded.

“No problem. I believe we left off right when Lily saved Cal.” I remembered.

“He drew her a picture and she told him it was the most beautiful thing she’d ever received.” She added. I smiled at her enthusiasm. She swallowed the last of her breakfast and then rested her elbows on the table top, coffee in both hands, poised to listen. I smiled again.

After Lily saved Cal from Anthony, Owen, and Will she tried to convince him to go to the hospital. He refused, but she insisted that he at least walk home with her and let her clean him up. He agreed, reluctantly, and after a ten minute walk they arrived at Lily’s home.

Her mother was working, like she did most of the time. Lily told Cal that her mom worked two jobs and sometimes picked up extra shifts at a local community center. Her mother was a dance instructor, ballet primarily. Cal smiled over the various photos of Lily in tutus as a little girl. Lily ushered him into the kitchen and pulled a first aid kit from the bottom of a cupboard.

“Let’s get you cleaned up.” Lily smiled at him. He was mesmerized by her smile. She pulled a small bottle of peroxide and some cotton balls from the white box and dabbed at the blood

on his face. He winced, but she comforted him. She told him she was sorry.

"It's not your fault." Cal told her. He still didn't want to look her in the face. He could feel the heat of embarrassment warm his cheeks. When she lifted on the hem of his shirt the heat intensified. He jumped and she smiled.

"I only want to look at your ribs." She promised. He hesitated, but another smile from her and he allowed her to raise his shirt up and peer at his sore rib cage. She gently probed at the sore spots with the tips of her fingers. His face felt like it was on fire and he felt an even more embarrassing sensation below the line of his belt. He hoped she didn't notice. "I don't think they're broken." She said, letting his shirt fall and wandering toward the freezer.

"They're not." He muttered, still looking at the floor. She returned, her pink tennis shoes slapping against he linoleum. She raised his shirt again and pressed a towel to his side, it was cold from the ice within it.

"Have you had broken ribs before?" She asked, letting him hold the towel and turning her attention to his face. Cal nodded in affirmation. "Did those jerks give them to you?" She inquired further, sounding angry and saddened at the same time.

Again Cal nodded. Lily rested her hand on his shoulder, looking at him until he met her gaze. "I'm so sorry they do such horrible things to you." She sniffed.

A single glistening tear rolled from the corner of her eye and down the side of her face, leaving a trail of mascara in its wake. Cal traced a finger down the path of the tear, wiping it away with his thumb. Lily rested her face against his palm and closed her eyes, sighing slowly. Cal swallowed hard. It had been a long time since he'd been so close to another human being. He'd never been so close with a girl; especially one so beautiful, both inside and out.

Lily asked Cal to stay, to have dinner with her. He obliged and after dinner they watched movies until the sun had long set. Lily's mother came home just after ten and greeted Cal warmly. She seemed grateful that her daughter had made a friend. Cal learned later that Lily had trouble making friends and didn't often open up to people.

Cal seemed to be that exception. The next day after school Cal went to his spot in the library and nearly dropped his books when he found Lily sitting on the table in his usual corner. She smiled when she saw him and he couldn't help but smile back. He was most certainly smitten.

That was the last day Cal went to the library to hide after school. Instead he met Lily around the backside of the school and they walked home together. Sometimes they went to Lily's house and watched TV. Sometimes they went to Cal's and listened to music in his room, doing homework and reading together. They frequently spent long periods of time without even talking to one another. They didn't feel the need. They immediately felt as close as people who'd known each other for years.

It wasn't surprising to either of them that one day they found themselves stretched across Cal's bed, snuggled into both one another and a good book, when suddenly the overwhelming need to be closer struck. Cal stopped reading as Lily slid her hand up his chest, directing his attention to her instead of the Bard. Minutes later the book was forgotten and the only reading that took place was the nonverbal cues from one another's bodies.

From that day on the two were utterly inseparable. Time spent watching TV or doing homework was frequently abandoned in favor of time spent kissing and cuddling, sharing one another's deepest secrets. Cal told Lily about his mother. Lily told Cal about her parent's divorce. They drew closer and closer each day.

By winter break they were inseparable. Even outside the confines of their homes they were constantly linked. People around town and in school began to notice, comment even, but they didn't care. When school let out Lily and Cal were elated for two whole weeks of time to themselves. Lily had to go away for the first few days in order to celebrate the holidays with her father, but she promised to come see Cal as soon as she returned.

Cal counted the days until she returned, and on the day she was due back he decided to surprise her. He pulled on his winter wear and trudged the six blocks to the local store. He purchased her favorite chocolates and a bouquet of the flowers she was named for.

He smiled as he headed back home, filled with anticipation. That excitement was quickly diminished as he turned the last corner of his journey and found three familiar faces glaring at him. Dread settled into Cal's stomach and he knew the blissful bubble he and Lily had been sharing was about to burst.

1 Day, 12 Hours, 12 Min...

My story was interrupted by Miranda's cell phone. She apologized and swiped the screen, walking a few paces away and listening to the caller on the other end. I sipped at my now cold coffee and finished the last of my potatoes, also cold. Deciding our meal was sufficiently completed I took to cleaning up our mess while Miranda chatted with whoever had called.

I peered around the vicinity I had access to, but didn't see any form of trash receptacle. I suppose there weren't usually things to throw away in this area. I decided to ask the guard for a garbage bag and to my surprise he actually went to the door and returned with a small rectangular trash can.

I disposed of my food containers and stale coffee and returned to the picnic table just as Miranda punched the end call button and sighed heavily at her phone. She returned and tucked the phone into her bag, apologizing again.

"You're popular today." I smiled, brushing crumbs off the table into my hand and depositing them into the trash. She shrugged. "Avoiding someone?" I asked as I rested my elbows back on the table.

"It's nothing important. Some TV person wants to interview me for the coverage of the execution." She sighed, looking guilty. I suppose she didn't want me thinking she was trying to exploit our connection.

"I take it you don't want to be interviewed?" I asked. She nodded.

"I prefer to do the interviewing." She smiled. "Besides, I don't want them scooping my story. It's bad enough they've worked out that I'm talking with you, I don't want them stealing my info." I nodded in understanding.

"Been keeping me a secret, huh?" I teased. She laughed.

"Just being cautious with who I divulge my information to." She replied. "A lot of people wouldn't understand." Yet again I nodded. I completely understood how people might react to a young woman occupying her days with a known terrorist. I wonder what they'd say if they knew that she enjoyed it. It was a good thing she didn't tell many. It made me like her more, trust her more.

"I have something for you." I remembered, pulling the paper from my back pocket.

"A present? For me?" She smirked, leaning forward over the table. She was genuinely excited to see what it might be. I slid the paper across to her and watched as she unfolded it. Her eyes grew and her face lit up. "It's beautiful." She gasped, barely above a whisper. "Doc, thank you so much." She smiled.

Her hand slid across the table and grasped my fingers, squeezing tightly. For a moment I thought she might cry, but she didn't. She just smiled and looked between the drawing and my face. Finally she released my hand and smoothed the drawing in front of her, looking at it with more intention.

She traced the lines of the willow that consumed much of the paper. Its branches arced to the ground that was covered in flowing grass and wildflowers. The edge of a fountain could be seen in the distance of the lower right hand corner. She looked at me when she'd finished her investigation.

"What is this place?" She asked.

"Somewhere that's special to me. A little piece of my past." I answered. Her smile grew in intensity.

"Thank you for trusting me with this." She said as she carefully tucked the sketch into her notebook and slid it all protectively into her bag.

"It just so happens I have something for you as well." She added as she pulled a book from her bag. "I found it while I was out and about yesterday and I thought of you." She slid the novel across the table to me.

The cover was worn and the edges of the pages darkened from numerous readings, but the binding was good. I'd read the novel countless times in my life. It had long been a favorite of mine. It touched me that Miranda had remember my reference to it.

"Anna Karenina." I smiled. "Thank you."

"I know it's old, but I thought it had character." She returned my smile.

"It's perfect." I promised, flipping the pages of the novel that was deeply imbedded in my past. I didn't even feel the tears fall. I only realized I was crying when I saw the drips splash against the page in front of my face. I wiped them away with one hand as I shut the book with the other.

"Doc, I'm sorry, I didn't mean to upset you." Miranda worried, fidgeting. I shook my head.

"No, it's ok." I pulled the book to my lap and looked at her forcing a smile through the tears. "Thank you, this means a lot to me." She smiled hesitantly and nodded.

"Are you getting hungry?" She asked. I nodded and she pulled her cell phone back out. "How about I order us some chow and you finish telling me about Cal and Lily while we wait for it."

"Deal." I nodded, resting my new possession next to me on the seat. My hand never left it again. My fingers traced the pattern of the printed cover as Miranda ordered our lunch. They found the torn corner and fiddled with the fabric there as I picked up the story where we'd left off.

When Cal rounded the corner to find those three boys waiting for him his heart pounded so hard he could hear it thumping in his ears. He was terrified. He knew they were waiting for him. He was the only one from school that lived on that block. He nearly dropped his shopping bag as he contemplated whether he could beat them to his door or not. He doubted he could.

Even as they slowly inched toward him Cal tried to work out if he could escape them, but in the end he knew he couldn't run. He knew they'd just catch him and it would be worse. For that reason he held his ground, swallowing the fear that was lodged in his throat and trying to calm his breathing. Neither helped much.

"Hello Freak." Anthony greeted, smiling like the cat who ate the canary. Cal felt a new kind of chill run up his back, a chill that went deeper than the winter air that nipped at his face. Cal didn't respond to the boy who'd spent years tormenting him. Instead he looked down at the ground and waited for it be over.

"Did you hear me, Freak?" Anthony asked, grabbing Cal by the elbow and spinning him into the waiting hands of his two companions. He yanked the bag from Cal's grasp and chuckled diabolically. "What do we have here?" He leered, digging through the bag.

Cal watched helplessly as Anthony pulled out the flowers and chocolates and tossed the empty bag to his feet. The flowers went to Owen, who stood on Cal's right, while Anthony ripped open the candy and took a sniff.

"Awfully nice of you to bring us a treat." He snickered, pulling a truffle from its place and holding it up between his fingers.

"They're not for you." Cal mumbled angrily. Why did they always have to pick on him? What had he ever done to them? Nothing. He'd never done anythin, except exist.

"Not for us, huh?" Anthony asked before popping the chocolate into his mouth and chewing slowly. He stared Cal down with every bite and then spit the lot at his feet. "Tastes like ass, anyway." He hissed.

Anthony slid the lid of the box under its base and tossed the lot into the slush covered street. Cal felt his face flush with rage. The boys just laughed. This was all a game to them. Anthony stepped closer to Cal and yanked the flowers from Owen's hand, sniffing them once.

"Oh, Fugly, you shouldn't have." He laughed and then his face twisted into rage that far surpassed Cal's own. "You really shouldn't have." He hissed in Cal's face. With a wave of his hand the other two boys pulled Cal around and forced him face down against a snow bank.

Owen and Will held him down while Anthony yanked at Cal's jacket. The snow bit into Cal's skin as they pulled his shirt *up to his armpits, pressing him harder into the icy bank. Cal heard Anthony snicker once more before he felt a sharp sting across his back. The scent of lilies permeated the air. Anthony continued until he'd beat the flowers to shreds against Cal's skin.*

When he'd finally finished he dragged Cal around, making him face him. Cal's throbbing back pressed into the bank, stinging where his skin connected with the snow. He couldn't tell if the dampness that trickled down his back was water or blood. He suspected both.

"Stay the hell away from her Freak." Anthony hissed.

"She's my friend." Cal whimpered back, knowing exactly who they were discussing.

"Not anymore." Anthony said with a shove. "Stay the fuck away from Lily or I'll kill you, and I'll make her wish she'd never met you." He spit in Cal's face, giving him one last shove into the snow before leaving him to cry in the street.

The flowers lay in pieces around him and the chocolates were buried under a layer of salt and sand filled slush. He wiped the salty water from his face and stood carefully. He tugged his shirt back down, pulling his torn coat around him and walked slowly home, contemplating the night's events.

He had no doubt in his mind that Anthony would make good on his promise. Cal had always feared that he would die by that boy's hands one day. He wasn't afraid, at least not more so than usual, not for himself. He worried for Lily. What would they do to her? Would they hurt her? Make her so miserable she moved away?

Cal couldn't live with the thought of either. He made his decision as he approached the place he called home. He wouldn't let them hurt Lily. He would tell her they couldn't see each other again. It would destroy him, break his heart into a million pieces, but he had to keep her safe. You protect the ones you love.

1 Day, 11 Hours, 14 Min...

Our lunch arrived in the hands of a boy who couldn't have been over the age of 18. He was small and skinny and seemed utterly terrified of me. He wouldn't even look at me directly as he skirted around the table and handed Miranda the paper sack full of food and the two drinks she asked for.

"Do you need anything else ma'am?" He asked her. I raised my eyebrows at the word ma'am and Miranda rolled her eyes.

"Sayid how many times must I ask you to stop calling me that?" She complained. The boy flinched and mumbled an apology.

"Sorry ma...I mean Miranda, can I get you anything else before I leave?" He asked again.

"No thanks kid." She responded. He nodded and started to leave. "Did you ask if Dr. Andrews needed anything?" She called to him. He froze, flinched again, and slowly turned toward me. I could sense the reluctance in his movements.

"Is there anything you need Dr. Andrews?" He mumbled, still unwilling to look at me.

"No, I'm fine, thank you." I smiled at him. He nodded and seemed all too glad to be able to leave. He practically jogged to the door that stood open for him.

"Cute kid." I observed once he'd left. Miranda shrugged as she pulled our dinner from the paper sack the boy had handed her. The spicy scent of Mexican food reached my nose, making me very hungry.

"He's learning." She sighed. "I told the paper I didn't need a new assistant, but they insisted. He seems nice at least, and he does what I tell him to, for the most part." She slid two paper rapped burritos to me, a packet of salsa verde on the top of each.

"Must be doing well if they gave you an assistant." I observed. She nodded.

"My coverage of a certain inmate has gotten me a lot of attention as of late. It seems a lot of people are fascinated by you Dr. Andrews." She smirked and I laughed.

"People are always fascinated with that which they find taboo or disturbing." I told her as she slid a churro on a napkin next to the burritos. I took a quick bite of it, glad for a sweet treat.

"Our society certainly is messed up." She agreed. She finally handed me one of the sodas she'd set next to the now empty paper sack.

"Society has always been messed up in some way. Humans have always been fascinated by violence." I told her. She looked as if she doubted me. I sat my drink down and continued. "In ancient Rome the crowds watched and cheered as slaves were forced to fight to the death or defend themselves against lions and other animals that'd been starved to madness. In the 14th century the English frequently used large workhorses to draw and quarter the prisoners they'd hanged. The crowds would watch as the bodies were pulled in four separate directions until they literally ripped apart. Beheading is still practiced in a few countries as a form of criminal punishment to this day. People have always and will always be fascinated with gore and violence. Unlike the rest of the natural world, human beings have violence ingrained in their DNA. We always have been and always will be a sadistic species."

Miranda sat quietly for a while when I finished speaking. She picked at the churro in front of her, chewing thoughtfully. I let her process; let her think about whatever it was that was playing on her mind. I bit into the spicy chicken burrito. Finally she sat dessert down and sighed.

"Question Doc." She said, eyeing me suspiciously. I surmised whatever her question was she didn't think I'd like it very much.

"Shoot." I said, shoving in another bite of my lunch.

"What you did, do you consider that to be an act of human nature, a sadistic act of violence?" She inquired. I'd been right to guess she was nervous about asking the question. She'd basically called me a sadist after all. I thought carefully as I finished chewing my mouthful of chicken and cheese. Finally I swallowed and answered.

"I suppose to most it would be. Strictly speaking, viruses exist in the natural world and are constantly evolving and adapting to become more effective, more deadly." I answered. "But considering I manipulated said virus I would have to say that, yes, I consider my actions to be violent and sadistic."

"Can I ask you something else, Doc?" She wondered. I nodded in compliance. "Do you regret what you did? Do you wish you could take it back at all?"

"I regret that people died." I admitted. I knew it would happen, it was inevitable, but that didn't mean I didn't feel bad about it. I wasn't a monster, though most thought I was. I had a conscience and I hated myself most of the time for the deaths I caused, but I took solace that it couldn't have been avoided.

"If there had been a way to achieve my goal without any death I would have done it." I continued. "Unfortunately that wasn't a possibility. There were too many factors to control for me to achieve such a feat. People died, I'm sorry they did, but as for the virus itself, no I feel no regret. I released the virus for a reason and I stand behind my conviction, selfish though it may be. I wouldn't take it back. I wouldn't change the past, even if I could." I answered. Miranda only nodded.

"You wouldn't even change it so you wouldn't be caught?" She asked, picking at her food again. I shook my head.

"I always knew I'd be caught, even before I released the virus. I knew from the moment I created it that I'd never get away with it." I told her. She paused a burrito halfway to her lips.

"Then why would you do it, knowing you'd be imprisoned? You're smart enough to know what you did would get you the death penalty." She asked.

"I did it because I knew I'd end up dead anyway, either by their hand or my own." I sighed. Miranda's face paled. "I wanted to die." I admitted aloud finally.

1 Day, 10 Hours, 3 Min...

Miranda sat in utter silence for a surprisingly long time. Her jaw hung open for several moments before she shut it. Even when she did she still remained silent, staring me down with eyes full of awe and wonder and deep sadness. She was shocked silent, even motionless, and so I let her sit. I let her process.

I'd not even meant to say the words. I'd never said them aloud before. Of course the thoughts were always in the back of my mind, the desire to be free of this world, to find peace after so many years of agony.

I'd never been a religious person. I didn't believe in heaven or hell. I knew enough that if such places existed I had no doubt I'd be headed for a quick drop downward. Lucky for me I didn't believe in the metaphysical. I didn't know what came after this life, only that whatever it was couldn't be worse. Even nothingness would be an improvement.

I contemplated this thought, this struggle with my doubt as I waited for Miranda to finish processing. For a moment I grappled with the fear that maybe I'd said too much, maybe Miranda wouldn't understand. My rational mind froze momentarily over the idea that maybe death wasn't better, maybe I *was* scared of what was coming.

Reasonably, I should be scared. I was going to die. In less than 48 hours I'd cease to exist and I had to face the unknown. That unknown was what truly scared me. I'd always known the answers, always had control over the situation. Even my death was carefully calculated. What couldn't be calculated, what couldn't be controlled or studied or comprehended, that scared me more than anything else. Thankfully Miranda's voice broke me from my thoughts before I got any further.

"What?" I questioned, not hearing what she'd said initially. She sighed and looked me straight in the eye.

"What happened to you?" She asked, eyes glistening slightly. I had a feeling she might cry soon. I didn't want her to cry for me. I didn't deserve her tears.

"It doesn't matter now. It's in the past." I answered, not breaking her gaze.

"I've spent hours upon hours with you. I've talked with you, I've listened, I've watched you. I feel like I know you almost better than myself." She told me. I listened intently. "You're a good person Doc, you have a big heart and you're not evil. I just don't understand why you would do something so terrible. It doesn't seem like you." She finally looked at her hands.

"Maybe you don't know me as well as you think you do." I suggested. She shook her head.

"My job has been to study you. To get inside you're head." She sighed. "Did you know I studied psychology before I decided to major in journalism?" She asked. I shook my head no. She nodded slowly. "I studied it for three years. Mostly because of my brother, but I learned a lot. I learned enough to understand people really well. I've always been a great judge of character, and I'm telling you Doc, you're not a murderer, not naturally at least." She sighed.

"But I am Miranda, I killed thousands of people, maimed even more." I replied. "I'm a terrorist, a convicted enemy of the state. Maybe I wasn't a bad person once upon a time, but I am now. I haven't been a good person for a long while." I looked away, unable to look at her any longer. Her eyes were too full of pity. I didn't want her pity. I had enough of it within in my own mind.

“It must have been horrible.” She muttered. I looked back at her, questing where she was going. “Whatever it was that happened to you,” she continued, “it must have been absolutely terrible to make you hurt people like that.” I nodded, confirming her suspicions but unable to will myself to tell her more.

“You’re lunch is getting cold.” I observed. She shrugged.

“I’m not really hungry any more.” She sighed, peering at the half eaten taco in front of her with disinterest.

“I’m sorry.” I apologized. “I didn’t mean to ruin your lunch.” She nodded, pushing it aside. She thought a while longer, picking absently at the corner of one flap.

“Are you scared, Doc?” She asked me.

“Scared of what?” I wondered.

“Dying.” She clarified. “Are you even a little afraid of what’s going to happen in a day and a half?”

“I’ve made my peace.” I answered.

“You can make peace with something and still fear it.” She insisted. I nodded.

“Truthfully, it’s not the death I fear.” I admitted. I shifted the empty soda in my hand, fiddling uncomfortably. I didn’t like sharing my feelings. I didn't do it often. "I know about the process. It won't be painful. I guess if I'm afraid of anything it's what happens after the injection, after I stop breathing." I set the cup down and placed my hands back in my lap.

"You're not religious." Miranda stated. She'd studied me enough to know as much. "What do you believe exists after death?" She inquired. I shrugged.

"Honestly, I don't know." I answered. "I suppose I'll find out soon enough."

"Well, when you do, can I ask a favor?" She requested, her face finally giving way to a bit of a smile. I accepted her question. "Let me know what it's like?" She smiled. I returned the gesture and the tension melted between us.

"I'll see what I can do." I joked. "Now, how about we talk about something a little less depressing?" I asked. She agreed.

She pulled out her cell and typed in a message. I assumed it was to her assistant. A few minutes later my guess was confirmed when he strolled across the lawn and handed her a fresh bag of tacos, two more sodas, and a small white box.

Miranda thanked her assistant, handed me one of the cans, and opened the box. Inside was a reasonably sized squared of chocolate cake. It was three layers tall with a ribbon of fudge in between each layer. The top was sprinkled with white and dark chocolate curls. It looked delicious.

"I thought we deserved a bit of a treat." She smiled, positioning the unfolded box between us and handing me a fork. I scooped a bite into my mouth and moaned in approval. Miranda giggled. It was a nice sound.

"Deserved or not, this is delicious." I offered, digging in for another taste. She did the same and in less than two minutes we'd consume the entire thing. Miranda went back to her lunch and I opened the can of Pepsi and took a swig.

"Better?" She asked.

"Much." I sighed. "So what shall we discuss next?" I asked. Miranda hummed into her soda. She contemplated the possibilities.

"I'd still like to hear more of Cal and Lily's story, but maybe we could talk about you for a while, fill in some of the gaps in my research." She suggested. I agreed and we began, the uncomfortable topic of death and the hereafter left for another day. The next day to be exact.

1 Day, 1 Hour, 7 Min...

Miranda and I filled in the minute gaps of her research for the remainder of the day. We chatted all afternoon and through our dinner of fried chicken, mashed potatoes and gravy, and corn on the cob. She even had Sayid bring us each a slice of still warm apple pie. We chewed and talked.

She asked questions and I answered. From time to time she'd ask me to share anecdotes from my life or explain something beyond what she already understood. I obliged as much as I was able to. Even geniuses don't generally remember every detail of their entire life. In fact, considering much of my life was spent within the recesses of my mind, I was less likely to remember the day to day events than most.

By the time I was escorted back to my cell that evening Miranda and I had sufficiently discussed the entirety of my life since the day I stepped into the hallowed halls of Yale University to the day I first laid eyes on the stubborn reporter.

I told her about college, about the people and the places and the experiences I had there. I told her about the first time I was drunk, a poor decision to follow a roommate to a frat party. I told her about my favorite classes, about the joy I felt when I first stepped into the laboratories in the Wright Building on Science Hill. I told her about the night classes I took in Green Hall to sharpen my drawing abilities.

I told her about my decision to transfer to Oxford, of the friends I made there. I told her about my difficult assimilation into British culture. I demonstrated my fairly impressive accent that I'd taught myself and explained how it often helped me smooth cultural misconceptions. I learned quickly that people were more likely to back someone of from their own culture.

I told her about my brief obsession with languages and told her a few choice phrases in Latin, Greek, and Mandarin. She laughed profusely when I translated the less than appropriate expressions. She insisted I teach them to her, as well as a few others she requested, and in less than an hour she was armed with a dozen phrases that would make a priest blush.

She was proud of herself and I enjoyed playing the role of teacher yet again. Thoughts of Nigel and the many others I'd employed flashed through my mind for the duration, bringing a myriad of feelings. I told Miranda about them as well. The ones I could remember at least.

When we'd exhausted one another and Miranda had as much information as she possible could hold on her little recorder, we went our separate ways. She bid me adieu and waved goodbye as she strolled down the hallways that would lead to the parking lot.

When I returned to my room my first instinct was to draw. I settled down into the corner of my cot, the drawing pad balanced on my knees and my spine rested against the corner post. I drew until my fingers ached and my pencils were dulled nubs. I tucked them away, and rested my head back with a sigh, gazing down at my completed work.

My hands were black up both sides from the loose charcoal and my fingers were smudged. I stared at the page in front of me, the soft curves and lines of the face I'd sketched. The angled features and soft, full lips almost felt real, like I could wipe my hand across the page and feel skin. I traced the feathered wings I'd drawn around the shoulders I once held tightly. I could almost feel the downy softness of them under my finger tips.

I touched them again, leaving grey smears behind. I closed the cover and tucked the book under my pillow. I pulled my knees to my chest and rested my head against them. I felt the tears swelling behind my eyes, but I held them back. I couldn't lose it now; I couldn't give into the fear, not this late in the game.

I swallowed the pain and breathed deeply until the stinging subsided. I kept my legs pulled up but rested my head back against the concrete. I needed to get myself together. I focused my brain, running through a series of random equations that were just challenging enough to keep me preoccupied. They seemed to help.

When I tired of math I turned to my book of crosswords. I'd finished most of the book, but there were a couple puzzles left untouched and a few unfinished. I pattered through them quickly, killing only about an hour. Finally, with nothing else to do, I wandered to the window, peering through the bars at the moon high overhead.

The stars were bright, only blocked by a scattered cloud or two. The moon was nearly full, waning in the late spring sky. I watched for a long time, carefully taking in every detail I could. It would be the last time I saw the moon, the last time I saw the night sky at all. After this night there would be no more stars, no more moonlight to make the earth shine in its silvery light. The next time the moon shone the sky there would be no more me.

I abandoned the moon and the stars, settling again on my cot. I lay on my back, my hands tucked up behind my head and my feet crossed at the ankle. I stared at the ceiling, trying to wrap my mind around the idea that in roughly twenty four hours I would be dead. It was an intense and strange concept to contemplate.

I thought about it from every angle possible. I ran over the procedure first, noting exactly what would happen within my body, what I might feel, what would occur in what order. I knew it was a fairly simple and painless way to die, a pinch of an IV, perhaps a little heat from the injection of chemicals. My breathing would slow, my pulse would diminish, and eventually it would stop all together. My heart and lungs would fail and my life would end.

I was comfortable with the way in which I would die. It was better than many alternatives. It wouldn't be painful like a gunshot, or as agonizing as wasting away from a disease. I'd die with my mind fully functioning, with my body under my own control, and with my business on this earth completed. I would be finished, completely.

I think it was that fact that seemed to unsettle me the most. I would be finished. I *was* finished. I'd done what I'd always wanted to do. I'd gotten my revenge. I was ready to die, ready to leave this place and move on to whatever existed beyond this world.

I'd speculated what might be waiting on the other side. I knew what I wanted it to be. The memory of a face came to mind, accompanied by a voice that made my whole body tingle with anticipation. I missed that face, the soul that resided there, warm and comforting and kind. I hoped with all I had that when I closed my eyes for the last time and shook off this mortal coil it would be that face that welcomed me to the hereafter.

I knew I probably didn't deserve that. I didn't deserve to ever see that face again, but I still hoped and wished and prayed to see the face that had been taken from me all those years ago. I felt the tears break free from the hold I'd had on them and slide down my cheeks as I prayed to whatever higher power there might be, begging to let me see that face just one more time. I cried and I prayed until I fell asleep.

23 Hours, 11 Min...

I dreamed of the place I'd drawn for Miranda. I walked along the path that led to the willow. The trees were just beginning to bud and the flowers had yet to peek their heads out from their winter hiding. The chill of spring was in the air and I drew my coat tighter around me.

I followed the path along the edge of the park, taking my time and watching the world around me. Though the air was crisp, the sun was warm on my cheeks, healing the earth from a long nap under the snow. I paused for a bit to watch a car drive by. The clean lines of the old convertible pulled at me, pulled on memories I'd prefer to ignore.

I left both the car and the memories behind and continued up the path. I stopped twice more along my way. A dog crossed my path, chased by a child with rosy cheeks and wild hair. Both disappeared around the bend, but left a smile on my face. I'd never given much thought to the idea of children, but for that moment I wondered what it would have been like to be a parent, to be completely responsible for another being. To be unconditionally loved.

I stopped again when I nearly stepped on a paper airplane. I picked up the folded paper and looked it over carefully. It was well designed. The aerodynamics were almost perfect. I carried it until I reached a small bridge that overshadowed a bike path. I stopped at its apex and released the airplane over the side, watching it glide through the air.

It landed at the feet of an elderly gentleman, who picked it up gingerly and smiled up at me. I smiled back and returned to the path. I followed it around the final curve and found the fountain I sought. Sitting on its edge was the person I hoped to find and my smile widened as I approached.

"Hello, my love." They called as I approached, holding their arms wide for me. I slid into the embrace as if it hadn't been decades since I'd felt their arms around me. I breathed them in, reveling in the fact that they always managed to smell the same to me, like mint tea and fresh ground ginger. It was an odd combination, one I'd never discovered the source of, but it was comforting.

"I've missed you so much." I whispered into the hair that tickled my nose. I felt them sigh against me, their chest rising and falling in tandem with mine.

"I've been waiting." They replied. Their fingers found my face, tracing the planes as if they intended to memorize every line and curve. I melted beneath their touch. My heavy heart lightened with every caress. Finally, seemingly satisfied with their examination, their lips fell on mine. The kiss was swift and sweet, but one I'd longed for achingly.

"I'm sorry I've kept you so long." I apologized, returning the kiss. They laughed against my lips, cheerful and bright, perfection to my ears. I'd missed that laugh most of all. It was both intoxicating and infections.

"You've got plenty of time to make it up to me." They smiled, lacing their fingers through mine. They pulled lightly on my hand and I followed them down the path that led to our favorite place. The branches of the willow swayed lazily in the breeze. Our arms swayed as well, hanging loosely in between us, as comfortable as if we'd never been separated a day in our lives.

As we approached the willow I stole a moment to study the being that walked beside me. Though their life had ended long ago, they seemed to have aged right along side me, though somewhat more gracefully. Stress and hardship hadn't worn on their face like it had mine. Their eyes were as bright as I remembered, eternally youthful, but I could see the distinct changes of age around their corners and along the lines of their cheeks and jaw.

They were taller than they had been when they were alive, only slightly, but enough that they stood at a different level than they once had to me. The hand that held mine was as soft as I remembered it and I ran my fingers across their knuckles, finding grooves and callouses that weren't there before, marks that were mirrored on my own hands. It was as if the part of them I'd held within me had experienced life through me.

I smiled at the idea of them walking beside me through life, my unseen but ever present companion. I only wished they'd been there for real, not only in spirit. They wiped a shed tear from my cheek as we approached our willow, smiling sadly. Their lips brushed the place their finger had wiped and they leaned closer to whisper into my ear.

"Wait here." They commanded. I didn't want to, but I obeyed, watching them slip into the branches. I waited eagerly to see what surprise must await me within our secret spot. I considered the possibilities, but ultimately didn't care. Whatever the surprise I knew we'd be together. We'd be happy at last. We'd be at peace. Their voice called to me finally and I stepped toward the willow, smiling wide.

I slid through the branches, brushing them this way and that as I went. They seemed to increase in number and thickness, growing deeper than I remembered. The voice called to me again and I quickened my pace. I was nearly jogging by the time they called a third time and yet I couldn't seem to find the end of the branches.

I pulled and pushed and ran toward what should be the center of the tree, but as I moved faster the voice seemed to grow more distant. Finally I broke free of the branches and came to a skidding halt on the edge of a precipice. I looked down into the endless black abyss and felt my heart sink. The voice called to me again, but this time it came from below, echoing along the stone walls of the hole in front of me.

I fell to my knees, fingers grasping the edge of the chasm, and I called back to them. Panic took hold of my chest, pressing tightly. I cried and cried, sobbing into the darkness. Finally I heard a voice behind me. A voice just as familiar as the one I called to, but instead of warmth and comfort this voice chilled me to the bone and stopped my heart mid beat.

I turned toward the second voice, fear coursing through me, my breath coming out in choked pants. I found nothing. Only the branches occupied my vision, swaying to and fro in the breeze that somehow permeated them. Had I imagined it? I could have sworn…

It called to me again, a ghost whispering along the breeze. Ice struck my face and I felt a pressure on my shoulders, like frozen hands grabbing for me. Before I could scream I was falling backward into darkness, flailing and reaching for safety that wasn't there.

I landed with a thud, surprisingly unscathed by the fall, and stared into the darkness around me. I could hear movement, the sound of footsteps all around me. I had the sense they were drawing nearer. I tried to stand, but couldn't. I scurried backward and came up against something hard. Again icy fingers encircled my arms and this time I was hauled upward onto my feet.

I tried to cry out, but something blocked my voice. I felt fabric against my tongue. I was gagged. I was also bound, my wrists tied tightly behind me. Something hard and cold bit into the skin there. My legs were free, but I had the sense that no matter how far I ran I couldn't escape what held me. You can't run away from reality.

The icy hands guided me through the darkness until something solid pressed against me. I felt the chill leave my arms, sliding upward and then the darkness lifted and a blinding light stung my eyes. I blinked, but the world seemed blurred at the edges. I could make out shapes and movement, but nothing definitive. The hands slid across me again, pulling at the knots that bound me, securing them one last time.

The next thing I knew it was as if I'd been pulled from my body, my consciousness rising until I hovered above the scene that was unfolding below. My vision cleared and suddenly the world was painfully vivid, sharp at the edges. I watched the remainder of the dream from above, wishing I was able to look away, but unable to.

I watched as three men drug a body through a door, a boy bound and gagged. The tallest of the boys pushed him none too gently against a wall. The boy slid to the ground when he was released, a groan releasing from his throat. It was clear they'd beat him. Blood dripped from a cut above his eye and speckled the collar of his shirt.

Another door opened and another body was pulled through, a girl this time, stumbling and shaking from fear. She was wearing jeans and a sweater, but her feet were bare and red from walking through the snow. Her hair was half pulled from the binder that wound around it and one sleeve of her shirt was torn. A bruise was blooming along her jaw.

The boy that was bound cried out when he saw the girl, tears falling from his eyes, but his cry was muffled by the tape over his mouth. The girl cried too but she didn't cry out. She didn't make a sound at all. The other boys laughed as they pushed the girl forward, slamming her against a table in the center of the room.

She winced when the table connected with her pelvis, but she didn't give them the satisfaction of a scream. Two of the boys held her there, pressing her face down into the rough wood, while the third, the leader, strolled over to the boy. He waved a gun and made a promise. He cracked the butt of the gun across the boys face and laughed when he bled, and all I could do was watch.

I watched as the boy with the gun joined the others with the girl. I watched as they pulled at her, taunted her, hit her. I watched as they tore at her clothes, slashing the fabric with a knife until she was left exposed. I watched as they threatened and promised and leered. I watched as they destroyed the girl one thrust at a time, laughing all the while.

The boy with the gun ripped the tape from the girls mouth and begged her to scream, ravaging her relentlessly until blood ran down her legs. When he'd finished he watched as the other two followed his lead, getting off on the torture they inflicted. I watched the light leave the girls eyes little by little, a tiny piece of her soul taken with each jolt.

Finally, when they'd had their fill, I watched as they hauled the boy to his feat, forcing him to watch as they turned the knife to her flesh. They cut the beauty from her piece by piece, slice by slice. I watched and cried and sobbed as they brutalized her in every way they could, making her love watch helplessly from the side.

I watched two souls die below me as three monsters emerged from their hiding place. The monsters reveled in what they'd done, pleased with their work. When the table had been painted red and no more damage could be done the monsters left. The boy fell to his knees and girl closed her eyes. Both wished they could die. So did I.

18 Hours, 6 Min...

I awoke with a gasp, a sob caught in my throat. My hand flung to the place where I could still feel the icy fingers gripping tight. I massaged the muscles until they relaxed and I managed to finally drag a solid breath into my lungs. I panted heavily, trying to wipe the images from my eyes. I slid a hand through my hair and down my face, closing my eyes momentarily. The instant I did a face appeared in the darkness, twisting the already growing knot within my gut.

I rolled and heaved over the side of the bunk, choking and retching until I was empty and then dry heaved twice more before I finally stilled. I rolled back onto the mattress and pulled the back of my hand across my mouth. My throat was raw and I the taste in my mouth was foul. The entire room was spinning.

I breathed, deep and rhythmic, until the spinning stopped and the world stilled again. Finally, certain I wasn't going to repeat my exorcism impersonation, I sat up, sliding my feet over the edge. I pulled my arms around myself, hugging tightly. I couldn't shake the terror that settled into my bones. I couldn't make the images go away.

I may not believe in heaven or hell, but I honestly believed with every fiber of my being that I had just witnessed my own personal version of each. I couldn't remember the last time I'd dreamt of that night, of the horrors I'd purposefully locked in my past. I'd left them there for a reason.

I physically shook as I rose from the mattress, unrolled the toilet paper from the spool next to the toilet, and laid it over the mess I'd made. I walked to the window when I'd finished, rubbing my arms in an attempt remove the chill that had settled into my core. I almost expected to see my breath hanging in the air when I exhaled.

I could see the first tinges of dawn along the eastern horizon. Day was coming. *The* day, my last. I breathed in the scent of impending dawn, hoping the sun would return warmth to my frozen body and burn away the nightmares.

I leaned my body against the wall and watched the day approach. Inch by inch it crawled across the earth. Slow, steady fingers easing their way toward me, waiting to choke the life from me and plunge me into whatever ecstasy or agony awaited at its end. At *my* end.

Dawn arrived and the sun climbed higher in the sky, streaking it with pastel hues. I sighed as the gold orb overcame the treetops and continued its ascension. I scoffed at the irony. The day grew to life as I demised, the consistent balance of nature. Light and dark, life and death, beginning and end. The image of yin and yang sprung to mind and I had the sudden urge to draw the symbol.

I quickly cleaned up the mess on the floor and slid my sketchbook from under my pillow. Only a few pages remained empty. I'd certainly been busy in the last couple days. I slowly flipped through the sketches in search of a blank page. One by one glimpses of my life passed. People and moments immortalized in charcoal and graphite. Each one pounded a new emotion into my chest, leaving me tired and sore, my stomach still rolling from the earlier dream.

Finally I reached the last pages of the book and found an empty space. I pulled a single pencil from the pouch, a soft leaded charcoal, and moved it across the page until the white paper turned inky black.

I blended the last few strokes as footsteps approached. The jingle of keys told me the guard was Carlos; he always fiddled with his keys, and the eager patter of tennis shoes told me he was accompanied by my favorite reporter. I blew the last bits of loose debris from the page as Miranda's face appeared beyond the bars.

"Good morning Doc!" She greeted with a wide smile. She was overdoing it for my sake. We both knew what this day meant. I'm not sure who was more uneasy about its culmination. "What's that smell?" She asked, scrunching her nose. Carlos also made a face.

"Good morning Miranda." I greeted, though less enthusiastically. "The smell is vomit. I threw up earlier." I answered, stealing a glance at the trash can I'd stuffed the soaked tissue into.

"You were sick?" She worried. Her hands wound around the bars as if she intended to reach through and comfort me. I smiled at the idea. "Was it something you ate?" She asked, though we both knew we'd eaten the same thing the day before. I shook my head.

"It wasn't physical sickness." I told her. "More psychological." I sighed and plodded over to the bars, sliding my wrists through.

"Another night terror?" She asked. I nodded and she did the same. "You ok?" She added.

"Good as can be expected, I guess." I shrugged as Carlos unlocked the bars. Miranda sighed and looked at the ground.

"Right. As can be expected." She mumbled to her shoes. She forced a smile and looked up at me again. "I got us breakfast, omelets with extra cheese and maple cured bacon. And fresh brewed coffee of course." My stomach growled at the thought. I was starving, but I wasn't sure my body would tolerate a meal. "Do you feel up to eating?" She asked.

"One way to find out." I shrugged and followed Miranda down the corridor to the yard exit. The door opened and I greeted the sun on my last day of life with the scent of bacon wafting to my nose. I vomited before we made it halfway across the yard.

15 Hours, 46 Min...

Miranda rubbed my back as I spilled the nonexistent contents of my stomach into the grass at our feet. I braced my hands on my knees and inhaled slowly through my nose, willing my stomach to stop rolling. I was pleased when it seemed to comply.

"Are you sure you're OK, Doc?" Miranda asked as we took our seats. I eyed the food and shook my head slowly. She quickly removed the container and the unholy smell with it. I took a whiff of the coffee, but decided it was best left as well. Miranda pulled her cell from her pocket and punched in a number. "Sayid I need a cup of mint tea and some soda crackers please. And a ginger ale for later." She nodded and hung up, smiling at me again.

"That's really not necessary," I told her, "but thank you." I slid a hand slowly across my abdomen.

"If you don't feel up to chatting we can..." She started.

"Pick it up tomorrow?" I interrupted, pulling one corner of my mouth skyward. She started to laugh, but then looked down. "Sorry." I sighed. Apparently it was too soon to joke about my death. I guess I didn't blame her. She'd still be alive in the morning.

"You said the issue was psychological." She recalled. "What did you dream that made you vomit?"

"Remember how you said I must have been through something terrible in order to make me do what I did?" I asked. She nodded. "Let's just say you weren't wrong and let's just say memories can be just as powerful twenty years after the fact." I sighed, pushing away the memory of the dream, and the nausea with it.

"I'm sorry that whatever it was happened to you." She said, grabbing my free hand across the table. "No one deserves to live through something so traumatic it makes them sick to their stomach decades later." I smiled and was immensely thankful when Miranda's assistant appeared and dispersed any further discussion of the thought. He also brought a large cup of peppermint tea, for which I was eternally grateful.

"Thank you, Sayid." Miranda chirped.

"Anything else I can get for you?" He asked. I noted he'd managed to drop the ma'am. I imagined a threat from Miranda was the reason. I didn't blame him for dropping it.

"No, thank you." She smiled. "I'll be here the rest of the day. Make sure any calls for me are sent straight to voicemail unless they're dire emergencies." He nodded his understanding and walked back through the door.

"I feel special." I joked, sipping the tea that was quickly relieving my nausea.

"You are special, Doc." She smiled. "You've changed my life." She shrugged, her eyes glazing over. "I'm going to miss you." She whimpered, chocking back a sob.

"Miss Stevens, I do believe you're about to cry." I attempted to smile. It wasn't fully executed.

"Oh I'm sure there will be tears before the day is up." She admitted. I nodded.

"No tears, Miranda." I begged. "Not now. Not for me." She sniffled and nodded, forcing a smile.

"Will you finish your story?" She requested. "I'm dying to know what happened to Cal and Lily." She insisted. I assumed she'd change her mind shortly. Nobody wanted to hear the truth of their story. It wasn't pretty. It wasn't nice. It was brutal and raw and painful. I agreed regardless. I'd promised after all.

"How about I talk while you eat? You shouldn't starve on my account." I offered. She accepted my proposal, pulled one of the Styrofoam containers to her, and flipped open the lid. I took another sip of my tea as she stuffed a forkful of egg and cheese into her mouth and then I began.

When Cal returned from his encounter with Anthony, Owen, and Will he found Lily on the front porch of his house. She was bundled up in a black pea coat and tall boots lined with fur. Her gloved fingers were wound around two steaming coffee cups and snowflakes dotted her hair. Cal couldn't remember a time when she was more beautiful and his heart sank further with every step.

By the time he reached the edge of the semicircle of light he was sobbing over what he was about to do. He knew he had to let her go, to save her, but it killed him to do it. She was his happiness, the only good thing he had left in his life. He was certain he would die without her love, but better him than her.

Lily saw his tears as he approached and stood quickly from her perch, setting the cups down on the stairs before racing over to him. She reached for his face, but he pulled away, sniffing against the cold and the pain. Her eyes were filled with worry and it made it worse.

She pleaded with him to tell her what was wrong, but he shook his head. He couldn't tell her, it would only make her more determined to stay together. She'd never been someone who backed down. She was stubborn to a fault. She'd insist that they stand stronger. She'd insist that the bullies would give up eventually. Cal knew they wouldn't.

As calmly and sternly as he could Cal told her she should go and that she shouldn't come back. Tears welled in her eyes and she asked him what was wrong. He lied; he said what he could to make her go, to make her angry. When her voice caught in her throat and the tears spilled over onto her cheeks he knew he'd succeeded.

He pushed past and started toward the house. He didn't get far. Lily was stubborn and proud, but she was also smart. She was extremely perceptive and Cal didn't even make it up the steps before she came bounding after him, seeing through his lie.

She refused to leave until he explained and after several failed attempts to convince her he was serious he caved and opened the door. She grabbed their now cold drinks and followed him in. Cal warmed up the cocoa she'd brought in the microwave while she peeled off her winter layers. When she'd finished and he'd retrieved their beverages she fixed him with a stern stare.

She demanded he tell her what happened and with a sigh and a sip of the delicious cocoa he told her what happened. Her face shifted from shock to terror to fury. She grabbed hold of his arm when he told her what they'd said and buried her head in his chest when he told her what they'd done and what they'd promised.

When he'd finished and tried once more, in vain, to convince her that separation was the best idea, she kissed him quickly. She ordered him to turn around and she carefully pulled his t-shirt up and over his head. Her fingers gently slid across his back and Cal winced when they reached the welts the boys had left behind.

When he turned back to face her, her eyes were filled with tears and her fingers were smudged with red. She said nothing as she retrieved the first aid kit from his bathroom and carefully cleaned and bandaged the cuts on his back. When she'd finished she kissed each of them gingerly and helped him back into his shirt.

Finally she spoke, pulling him close and apologizing through the tears. He comforted her, smoothing her hair and whispering that everything would be ok. He doubted it, but with her in his arms things always felt a little more optimistic.

Again he tried to press the issue of heeding the warning, but Lily would hear none of it. She told him that she wouldn't let such morons meddle in their love. They belonged together. They were soul mates. Looking into her eyes he couldn't disagree. He loved that girl with everything he had. He'd follow her through hell and back. He had a feeling he was about to.

Lily insisted on staying the night with him since his aunt was out of town. Cal could hardly protest. He was a teenage boy after all and his girlfriend was insisting on spending the night alone with him, something they'd never done before. He found that the idea frightened him nearly as much as the three boys had.

When they'd polished off three mugs of cocoa each and half a box of cookies, Lily switched off the TV and yawned that she was tired. Cal grew even more nervous. He nearly collapsed when she trotted off in the direction of his room. He had to hold on to the doorframe when he found her in his room, tying a pair of his pajama pants around her narrow waist.

She heard him swallow from across the room and giggled as she tugged her sweater over her head, exchanging it for a t-shirt she'd plucked from his hamper. When she'd finished dressing she crossed the room and dragged him to bed by his wrist. He tripped twice on the way. She laughed playfully both times.

They finally made it beneath the covers and Cal carefully wriggled out of his jeans. They snuggled in and promised never to leave one another. By morning they'd made a plan to escape together the first chance they had, taken their relationship to a new level, and spent the night in each other's arms.

Cal awoke with a smile on his face and the girl of his dreams in his arms, donning only the t-shirt she'd retrieved after they made love for the first time. He was perfectly content with her being both the first and last girl he would ever be with. When she awoke and kissed him he learned she felt the same. That morning their promise of escape progressed into a plan to elope as soon as they were both eighteen.

Cal and Lily spent the remainder of winter break exploring the exciting new aspects of their relationship and returned to school the following January closer than ever. Things went smoothly at first. Anthony and his goons were generally avoided and Lily and Cal delved deeper into their bliss and future plans.

As spring neared and Lily's eighteenth birthday inched closer they both grew more and more anxious. Rings were purchased, maps were procured, and Lily set the stage for her father to buy her a car for her birthday. She was apparently not beyond using his guilt to her advantage. Cal and Lily's happiness grew with their plan.

Unfortunately, like many things that reach skyward, their plans soon crashed and burned. As Cal feared, Anthony's threat was not idle. One night, when winter was driving its hold home, Cal and Lily were taken to a warehouse and Anthony made good on his promise to make them pay for their star-crossed love.

After that day everything changed. Lily and Cal were never the same, and by the time spring finally arrived and Lily reached her eighteenth birthday both their relationship and their plan was destroyed. Before the school year ended one was lost forever and the other was left permanently broken. The bullies had won.

12 Hours, 9 Min...

When I finished my story Miranda stared at me like I'd just kicked her puppy. Her jaw was slack and her eyes were wide. I think I even saw her lip quiver a bit. I let her have her moment. I'd never told anyone this story before, but like so many tragedies, I expected the shock of the ending. People were used to love stories ending in happily ever after that they often forgot that happy endings aren't all that common.

I finished my tea and tested my stomach with a bite of Miranda's bacon while she processed. After she regained control over her jaw she made as if to speak several times, but managed to say nothing. I restrained the urge to chuckle. It wasn't really appropriate, but she was being a bit dramatic. Finally she spoke.

"Seriously!" She exclaimed, her hands slapping down on the tabletop. "That's how it ends? That's it?!" This time I couldn't stop myself from laughing. "It's not funny!" She yelled. "It's terrible. That's a *horrible* story." I saw the tears trembling in the corner of her eyes, but she managed to hold them at bay.

"It's a true story. The truth isn't always pretty." I shrugged, stealing another strip of bacon. My nausea had finally dissipated and I was suddenly ravenous.

"I know, but seriously!" She gasped. "That's really how it ended? They were attacked and they broke up! Did their attackers even get caught?" She asked.

"No." I sighed. "Cal and Lily never reported what happened that night. It was too painful for them." I answered. She shook her head, sighing heavily.

"You said one was lost forever. Do you mean one of them died?" She inquired. I nodded that she was right. "Are you going to tell me which one?" She asked.

"Does it matter?" I replied. I was avoiding the topic, but I wasn't wrong. They were both in the past. Their story was long over. Who lived and who died wasn't really relevant. It didn't change anything now. Miranda groaned at my answer.

"Will you at least tell me how they died? Was it Anthony?" She begged.

"No, it was a suicide." I answered. Another memory threatened to surface, one that would surely upend the bacon I'd managed to consume. I swallowed slowly to force both back down.

"They killed themself?" She gasped, stunned even more. I nodded and she sniffled.

"That's a terrible story." She complained, crossing her arms over her chest.

"Life is terrible sometimes." I offered. She nodded and bit at her lip. I suspected the tears were wining. Luckily for her their decent was interrupted by the sudden appearance of Warden Greene. He called my name and as I turned to face him I saw Miranda wipe at her eyes. She was a softie after all.

"How can I help you Warden?" I asked with a smile. He stopped when he reached the edge of the table and sighed.

"It's nearly noon, Andrews. We have to escort you to the deathwatch cell now. You'll remain there until you're moved to the antechamber." He sighed. If I wasn't wrong he almost sounded apprehensive. Miranda remained silent, though I noticed she wiped at her eyes twice more while he spoke. I nodded in acceptance and stood. "Also, I should inform you that you have a visitor. He'll meet us in the cell. You can talk there if you wish." He added.

I nodded and allowed him to guide me toward the door. I wondered speculatively over who might be waiting for me. No one immediately came to mind. Throughout my entire incarceration I'd only had one voluntary visitor and she sat at the table behind me. I turned to look at Miranda as we left. She'd packed her stuff and was following us out.

"How about I go grab us some lunch while you chat with your friend." She offered. "You must be hungry." I agreed and thanked her. She even asked the warden if he wanted anything. He declined.

"Oh, one more thing Andrews." He added as they slid the cuffs onto my wrists again. "I need you to fill out your request for your last meal."

"Give it to her." I gestured toward Miranda with my chin. "She knows me better than anyone. I trust her choice will be satisfactory." I smiled. She returned my smile and her soon-to-be stepfather looked to her for confirmation. She accepted my suggestion and we parted ways.

I followed the warden down an unfamiliar set of hallways, holding onto my curiosity and the promise of lunch on the way. It was a good distraction from the fact that I was on my way to the last 'home' I'd ever know. Twelve hours. I had twelve hours left on this earth. It didn't seem enough and yet it seemed like an eternity. I felt conflicted.

Finally we reached our destination and the warden quietly excused himself, promising to see me soon and leaving me in the hands of the guards. They patted me down, ensuring I didn't have anything I could use to take my own life. They wouldn't want me offing myself before they had the chance. I smiled at the irony of it all.

When they'd sufficiently ascertained that I was unarmed they pushed a few buttons and led me through another series of doors and down a corridor of cells almost identical to the ones I'd left earlier that morning. They turned a corner and directed me to a cell toward the end of the L-shaped wing. I turned toward the entrance and found a man sitting on my bed I'd never expected to see again.

11 Hours, 58 Min...

Nigel stood as I approached. The guards un-cuffed me and asked if he wanted them to stay. He declined. I stared.

He'd changed since I'd last seen him. He was still the same awkward ginger I'd employed once upon a time, but he'd grown up. He smiled his crooked smile at me and asked if I'd sit with him. I took a seat on the opposite edge of the cot, giving him a last once over. Something about the way he carried himself was different, more mature. Hopkins had done him well.

"You look good Nigel." I said at last, returning his smile.

"Thanks." He said, shifting slightly. I was glad to see he still squirmed in my presence. I didn't miss the stuttering though. "I'd say the same to you, but you know..." He gestured toward me with one freckled hand.

"Are you saying orange isn't my color?" I joked. He looked shocked and then laughed.

"Well you may not look good, but you *sound* good." He observed. "I don't remember you ever joking around."

"I'm sure I didn't. I took my work seriously." I replied. "Perhaps too seriously at times." I admitted. "Nigel, I'm sorry if I was ever cruel to you. You were the best intern I ever had and I'm afraid I never truly appreciated that."

"Thanks." He accepted my poor excuse of an apology. To say I underappreciated him would be a vast understatement. "I kind of already suspected that you liked me, though." He smiled. "And if I hadn't, the call I got yesterday would have tipped me off."

"What call?" I asked.

"I received a call from a lawyer yesterday that seemed to think an old boss of mine intended to leave me a research facility and large fortune upon their impending demise." He answered. "Know anything about that?"

"Yes, I do." I nodded. "That would be my poor excuse for a lawyer that called you."

"By poor excuse, do you mean he was misinformed?" He asked. I shook my head quickly.

"No, I'm leaving you the facility and a portion of my funds. The lawyer is just an ass." I reassured.

"You're leaving me several million dollars?" He exclaimed. I could sense the shock in his voice.

"I am." I smiled.

"You can understand my surprise over this." He stated. I agreed. "I mean, I haven't even heard from you in almost four years. I read in a newspaper that you'd turned mad scientist and bio-hacked the world one day and that you'd been sentenced to death the next. And then the day before someone I once spent upwards of twelve hours a day with is to be legally murdered, I find out they're leaving me their most prized possession and a small fortune." He sighed. "Forgive a guy for being both shocked and a little skeptical."

"I missed you Nigel." I smiled at him. He flustered, his cheeks turning crimson. I laughed at the sight.

"You've changed." He observed. I though about it a moment and then shrugged.

"I suppose it's accurate to say I'm not the same person I was four years ago." I laughed. "Hell, I'm not the same person today that I was a week ago. Facing down death like a ticking time bomb will do that to a person."

Nigel nodded, looking away from me for the first time since I entered the cell. I could see the pity all over his goofy welsh features. My heart grew heavier. I didn't know how I felt about him pitying me. I didn't think I liked it.

"Don't feel sorry for me Nigel." I sighed. "I made my bed and I'm more than prepared to lie in it." I promised.

"It's a bit more complicated when that bed you made is a grave." He grumbled at the floor. I didn't know how to respond. We sat in silence for a while and then I took a deep breath and made him promise to leave the depressing thoughts behind. He'd made a pretty decent trip to visit me; I didn't want it to be a waste.

Instead of dwelling on the inevitable I asked him to tell me about his life. He was more than happy to oblige. I was more than happy to listen. It seemed he'd made quite a life for himself since I'd last seen him.

He told me about his research fellowship at Hopkins and the progress he'd made there. After that he'd taken a job at a genetics lab in Colorado. He claimed to like it there, although he was adjusting to the mountain weather slower than he wished. He had me in stitches over his tales of his first experience on skis.

Partway through his tale of how he nearly caused an avalanche I noticed a gold band on his finger that hadn't been there before. His face lit up as he told me about the feisty research assistant he'd fallen in love with during his time at Hopkins. It seemed his move to Colorado wasn't entire career driven.

His new bride was a native of the Rocky Mountain State. He told me that he still wasn't sure how he'd managed to convince such a woman to marry him, but he had and they were closing in on their second anniversary. They were also expecting their first child, a boy, and I couldn't help but smile at the joy that filled his eyes when he spoke of his unborn child. For a moment I was envious of him.

It seemed Nigel had obtained everything my life lacked. He'd found love, made a career for himself that was both financially substantial and satisfying, and he was soon to be a parent. I told him how proud I was, and how happy I was for him. He thanked me, both for my compliment and for everything I'd taught him.

"I wouldn't be where I am today if it wasn't for you." He sighed as he stood to leave. He had a meeting to attend, but he'd promised, despite my insistence that it was unnecessary, that he'd be there tonight.

"I'm glad you've found your own way, Nigel." I told him. "You should be proud of the man you've become. That kid's going to be lucky to have you, and I highly doubt that has anything to do with me." I smiled. He shrugged and hugged me before he left, surprising us both. We laughed as we parted. "Thank you for coming." I told him. "It means a lot." He nodded.

"I'm glad I knew you, Dr. Andrews." He smiled and stepped out the door. Before he disappeared down the hall he turned to me. "I'm going to tell my son about you, about the brilliant doctor who taught me everything I know." He smiled and waved goodbye. Before he exited the cell door he turned once more and asked me with a grin "Did I mention we're naming him Andrew?" He left before anything else could be said. I sat on the cot and wept.

10 Hours, 22 Min...

Miranda showed up about twenty minutes after Nigel left. I was still crying when she came and she sat quietly on the edge of the cot, rubbing my arm gently until the tears subsided. When I wiped the last of them away she smiled and slid an arm around my shoulders, squeezing gently. I was glad to have a friend like her.

"I brought you lunch. Do you feel like eating?" She inquired.

"Food sounds perfect." I replied. She flashed me a grin full of teeth and pulled a schmorgesborg from her bag. Nachos, chili fries, potato chips, chocolate truffles, chicken strips with several dipping sauces, soft pretzels, and a variety of bottled soda. I shook my head at her haul.

"You've been busy." I noted, grabbing a pretzel and a small container of what I assumed was some sort of cheese sauce. It was spicier than I expected and I grabbed a can of Coke to wash it down.

"Well, I figure if there was ever an excuse to pig out on junk food, dying was a pretty good one." She smiled, faintly, and then looked at me.

"You're a good friend." I told her, dragging a tray of nachos closer.

"So are you." She smiled. "I'm going to miss you." She sniffed and I shook my head.

"Nope, no tears." I insisted, forcing a smile. "Promise me?" She sighed, but nodded.

"Alright, I promise." She smiled, stealing a bit of my nachos. I happened to notice it was the one topped with the most cheese. She was lucky I considered her a friend. "So, Doc, t-minus 10 hours to go. What do you want to do with your last hours?" She inquired.

"Hmm, that's a very good question." I considered the possibilities.

"I'm up for anything." She smirked, winking ridiculously. "Well, within reason considering we're in a cell. So basically I'm up for whatever you want to talk about, whatever we can do with a deck of cards I swiped from the guard, and whatever we can eat." She emphasized her last point by plopping a fry in her mouth and chewing dramatically.

"Well, I'd say our spread seems adequate." I observed. She raised a finger and produced another container from her purse. It contained two large Ziploc bags, one of gummy bears and one of peanut M&M's. I grinned. "Alright, let's change that to satisfactory. I say we play a little poker and chat. Maybe you can tell me about your life for a change." I suggested. Miranda agreed and I dealt while she doled out the candy.

We bet with our sweets and nibbled on the chow Miranda had provided. She told me about her life, the town she grew up in, her friends, the college she attended (including a few less than legal exploits) and finally how she ended up at her current job. She also told me how she ended up working my story. I was thoroughly entertained on all accounts. She was an excellent storyteller.

Miranda was a card shark and as she nibbled on her poker winnings she told me about a new development at her work. She seemed reluctant to divulge at first, but eventually she told me that she'd been approached by a publisher about a possible book deal for her story about me.

I could tell she was worried about how I might react, but I insisted I wasn't offended and that it was her decision to make. Honestly I didn't care if she wrote a book about me. She'd sacrificed a lot of her time and money to get to know me; she should be rewarded for that sacrifice. She deserved recognition. She deserved a lot of things. I hoped she'd receive them all and then some.

At 5 p.m. the warden returned and informed me that there were some last rights related things I needed to complete. Miranda offered to go personally retrieve my last meal and return swiftly, with the promise of a rematch so I could win back some dignity. I made a silent vow to not hold back on her this time. I stood as she headed out and smiled sadly. I was definitely going to miss her.

"Hey, Stevens!" I called down the hall before she left. She turned back toward me. "You should do the book. If anyone's going to write my story it should be you." I told her. She smiled.

"You're sure you'd be ok with it?" She confirmed.

"I'd be honored." I promised and she smiled. I watched her walk away and waited with Warden Greene for a priest I really didn't need.

6 Hours, 33 Min...

The priest wandered down the hall shortly after Miranda left. I was still sitting on the edge of my cot, elbows on knees, head bent. I was exhausted. Between the sleepless nights earlier in the week, the nightmares, and a day of emotional discussions I was left feeling drained and anxious. I was so on edge I actually jumped when the warden's hand came down on my shoulder. He offered me a weary smile when I calmed myself and looked up at him.

"This is Father David." He introduced. "He's here to council you if you wish, and to administer any form of last right you may request. We weren't really sure of your religious affiliations so I hope this will suffice." He gestured toward the older gentleman dressed in the traditional black pants and shirt with while clerical collar.

"I don't have any." I sighed as I stood to greet the unnecessary visitor. I suppose in a way it was just the warden's way of being nice. It was also common protocol, last chance for absolution and all. I suppose it helped some people find peace. I just wasn't one of them.

"I beg your pardon?" The warden looked back to me from the priest. I sighed again.

"I don't have any religious affiliations." I reiterated. "I'm not religious."

"Oh, well, my apologies. I suppose I shouldn't assume such things in this day and age." He flushed and looked to the floor.

"It's quite alright. I suppose many inmates look for some sort of answer in the final hours. I understand that desire; I just don't believe the answer lies in some almighty deity." I replied, leaning against the wall and crossing my arms. Miranda could come back any time she liked. Surprisingly, however, it was the priest who spoke up.

"You may not believe in the 'almighty deity' like I do, but I was wondering," he smiled as he stepped quietly into the cell, "if you might wish to speak to me regardless. I'm an excellent listener for any who need to speak, regardless of their beliefs." He had a soft, warm voice and a pleasant demeanor. Somehow I found myself becoming more at ease in his presence. I decided a chat couldn't hurt anyone and so I shrugged in acceptance.

"Today must be an especially trying time for you." He offered, sitting gently on the edge of the cot and indicating that I should join him. I did as he requested. "Is there anything that worries you in particular?" He asked me.

"I guess the only thing I fear is the unknown." I told him, shifting to get more comfortable. He nodded in understanding.

"That is often what scares us most. As beings of higher intellect we tend to thrive on knowledge and understanding. It forms a sense of security in a way and when that security, that knowledge, is taken away we feel vulnerable and exposed." His words were nearly perfect, completely captivating what I felt. I was glad I decided to talk with him.

"I don't fear death." I said after a moment of thought. "Not the act of it, at least. I know I won't be in any pain. I know it will be swift, merciful. I suppose after what I've done I should be grateful for that much. I only fear what waits for me after, if anything waits at all."

"Do you feel remorse for the actions you took?" He asked me. I had to think about it for a while.

"Honestly I still believe my choices were justified, albeit for somewhat selfish reasoning, but as far as the lives I took, the blood upon my hands, yes I do feel remorse. I didn't want those people to die. If it could have been avoided I would have made sure it was." I responded, as honestly as I could. He only listened and nodded. He was right. He was easy to talk with.

"I assume you've considered the fact that all those lives, as well as your own, could have been saved had you chosen not to release the virus you created." He continued. "I make no assumptions about your life or your reasons for doing what you did. You're clearly a highly intelligent person and you seem reasonably sound of mind. I suppose I am simply curious as to what you think of yourself."

"What I think?" I repeated, unsure of the direction of his questioning. "Does it matter what I think?" He smiled, laughing softly.

"By three methods may we learn wisdom. First by reflection, which is the noblest." He offered.

"Confucius." I nodded, remembering the quote. He nodded in affirmation.

"He was a wise man indeed." He stated. I didn't disagree. Instead I thought for a moment, reflecting as he'd suggested.

"I knew the outcomes of my actions before I committed them. I could fairly accurately surmise the number of lives my virus would take. I chose to act regardless, to justify to myself that the positive outcomes of its release outweighed the loss. It's the reason they've labeled me a terrorist." I cringed inwardly at the word. "I'm not sure whether that knowledge made me more or less a monster." I finished.

The priest sat quietly for a while, considering my response. I took the opportunity to consider him in the return. He was a simple man. Not exceptionally tall and of slim build. He had short white hair that was just starting to thin and a well trimmed beard. His nose was too big for his face and hooked at the end. His skin was lined with many years of age, but his eyes were youthful still, their pale hazel bright with intelligence. Finally he met my gaze and spoke.

"I believe we alone know whether we are more monster or man." He stated. I nodded.

"I'd like to think I'm not as monstrous as the world seems to think." I admitted. "But I suppose only time will tell. If there is a God I'm sure I'll be judge accordingly in a few hours. I'll have my answer then."

"I suppose you're right." He smiled. "If there is a God." He winked and I smiled.

"May I ask *you* a question, father?" I requested. He accepted with a single nod of his head. "From your perspective, what can you tell me of heaven and hell?"

His smile grew and he clearly wanted to give me the answer I sought. I think we both realized that answer likely didn't exist, but he seemed eager to try regardless. He thought carefully for a bit and then returned his attention to me, preparing to speak.

"Do you know the bible at all?" He asked. I nodded. "Good, then you know how Christianity views these places." Again I nodded. "I suppose, in my humble opinion, I like to think of heaven as a place of ultimate peace. A place where all your earthly troubles are taken away and all your business finished at last. I'd like to think it's a place where you can be with those you love and exist in total happiness together." His thoughts drifted for a moment, seemingly occupied by something else, or perhaps someone else. I wondered who it might be that he hoped to see again in his place of peace.

"I suppose, then, that hell would be the opposite, a place of loneliness and despair." He concluded.

"Thank you, father." I smiled. He'd given me the best answer he could. In some ways he'd helped to ease my mind a bit. I was grateful.

"Please, call me David." He patted my knee. "I'll be here the rest of the day if you need me for anything further." He promised. I thanked him again and stayed seated as he rose to leave. A final question plagued my mind and I decided it hurt nothing to ask.

"Father," I called and then corrected myself as he turned, "David. Do *you* think I will go to hell?" I supposed I wanted his professional opinion.

"I believe that has a great deal to do with you, my child." He suggested. "Repent therefore, and be converted, that your sins may be blotted out, when the times of refreshing shall come from the presence of the Lord." He added.

"For God so loved the world, right?" I responded and he nodded his head slowly and stepped beyond the bars of the cell, turning one last time to wish me goodbye. "For what it's worth, I hope you're right." I told him and he left with a smile.

I wouldn't say I found religion, but it was nice to know that it was a possibility. The prospect of forgiveness eased the tension of my troubled mind. I could understand the appeal. I could see why so many flocked to such beliefs. Had I grown up in a different world I may have been more inclined to believe. As it stood, I remained a skeptic.

5 Hours, 57 Min...

"I think you're going to love what I've got for you." Miranda announced as she strode through the cell door. I was almost surprised that they'd yet to shut or lock it, but considering there were a total of six guards between myself and the nearest exit and no other inmates in the wing I assume they weren't concerned.

"I'm intrigued." I replied, standing to help her with the sizable load she balanced in her arms. A slender brown sack threatened to topple and I grabbed it before it could. When I found a wine bottle inside I was glad I'd saved it. It looked like a good vintage.

"Alright," Miranda huffed, catching her breath once she'd set everything down, "dinner is served." She bowed, enacting a poorly imitated Lumiere. I laughed at her and she stuck her tongue out at me.

"Well, Miss Stevens, what have you brought me for my final meal?" I inquired, helping her unpack. I quickly discovered a feast that made my mouth water. Still steaming filet mignon, cooked to perfection, filled my nostrils with delicious scents. The steak was accompanied by roasted baby red potatoes smothered in garlic, olive oil, and rosemary. They, too, smelled divine.

Another container revealed a large square of tiramisu for each of us, still cool to the touch. I closed the lid to keep it that way and slid it to the side. Miranda was working on the cork of the wine she'd brought. I was highly shocked the guards had allowed to her to bring a corkscrew into my cell. I had a suspicion, based on how frequently she looked around us, that she'd smuggled it in.

"Sorry I couldn't swing real glasses." She said, pouring a generous portion of the Cabernet into two paper cups. I chuckled as we clinked our cups and sipped the wine. I picked up the bottle while she retrieved silverware and read the label. It was a Mayacamas Cabernet Sauvignon, circa 1989.

"This is a $300 bottle of wine." I stammered. She only shrugged and handed me a fork and butter knife.

"Sorry, this'll have to make due. They wouldn't let me bring in a steak knife." She offered me a smile. I wiggled the bottle in my hand, reminding her she still hadn't answered. She took the bottle and smoothed her hand over the label. "It's a special occasion. I figured if you're going to go out, you go out with a bang."

"Miranda, this is too much." I insisted, but she shook her head.

"The wine was a gift." She informed me. "My grandfather gave it to me on my 21st birthday. He told me to save it for the day I knew my life had changed." She smiled and reached for my hand. I gave it to her. "You've changed my life so I figured it was a good time to crack it open." She sniffled, holding back tears again, and I squeezed her fingers tightly.

"Thank you Miranda. It means a lot. *You* mean a lot to me." I told her, finally releasing her fingers. She rolled her eyes and laughed, trying to lift the somber mood. She tucked the cork screw back in her bag as I attacked my steak with the butter knife she'd handed me. It was so tender I barely needed a knife at all. I plopped a generous piece in my mouth and sighed as I chewed.

"Good?" She asked, cutting her own into bite sized pieces. Apparently she wasn't as eager to dig in. Of course, she'd had breakfast. She'd also probably had steak in the last six months. I hummed in response to her question. She giggled.

"So how'd you manage to sneak that in?" I asked, gesturing toward the device she's returned to her bag as I skewered a chunk of potatoes. She smirked devilishly.

"I've got a few tricks up my sleeve." She replied, pushing said sleeves to her elbow and adding a wink. I shook my head at her while I chewed the perfectly seasoned potatoes. "It's not like I had a choice. How else was I going to open the bottle, my teeth?" She asked. I laughed, nearly choking on my dinner.

"Now that's a sight I'd pay to see." I snorted. She gave a noncommittal shrug of one shoulder and tucked into her dinner. We chewed and chatted and sipped our wine. By the time my steak was gone my glass was empty and Miranda wasn't hesitant in the least to refill it. I raised my cup to her and sipped away.

"Trying to get me drunk?" I teased.

"Hey, if anyone deserves to be drunk tonight, it's you." She suggested. I didn't disagree. I wondered a little if alcohol was technically allowed, but considering she'd not made much effort to hide the bottle I assumed the warden was both aware and condoning of the wine. It's not like a couple glasses of wine would make much difference in the end.

We managed to consume the entire bottle before the sun had set. We ate the entirety of our meal, Miranda gifting me a third of her steak that she couldn't finish, and had licked the tiramisu plates clean, savoring the last remnants of cocoa and cream.

We sat on the floor for the duration. I rested my back against the back wall; Miranda leaned against the cot. When we'd cleaned our plates and finished the last of the snacks that remained from earlier in the day, we sipped the last glasses of wine and talked about nothing in particular.

It was nice to just talk, to visit without the pressure of expectation or speculation. There were no questions, no digging for information. In fact, we didn't discuss anything to do with either of our lives. We discussed music and art and movies. We discovered a mutual fondness of the classics. We were both big Audrey Hepburn fans. Miranda told me that she'd named her first pet Cat, though it was technically a hamster.

Time passed both slowly and seamlessly. We talked and listened in turn, and laughed copiously. Things were easy. It was the perfect conversation after the perfect meal, the perfect last day.

As the time went, Miranda checked her watch more frequently. I knew she was aware of the time, fretting the impending midnight. I ignored the dials on her wrist. I didn't need to know how close we were. I didn't want to worry about how little time I had left. I didn't want to worry about anything. I just wanted to be.

About ten minutes after Miranda checked her watch for what must have been the twentieth time, I heard the first footsteps echo down the hallway. Miranda stopped midsentence, her mouth closing tightly, and a moment later the warden and Father David appeared in the doorway.

"It's time to move you to the antechamber." Jim told me. I nodded and stood swiftly, brushing off my pants. Miranda sat a moment longer, pulling at the sheet of the cot. Finally, with a gentle hand from the warden she stood. I noticed she didn't look in my direction.

"Are you ready, my child?" David asked me. I found the question both odd and comforting. How could anyone be truly ready for death? And yet I knew, somehow, that I was.

"I'm ready." I replied, stepping past Miranda and directing my wrists toward the guard that accompanied the two men. He started to cuff me, but the warden stopped him.

"I don't believe there's any need for those." He told Carlos. He smiled at me before he backed away and let me through the door.

1 Hour, 4 Min...

Warden Greene led the way and Father David followed close behind him. I kept my distance respectful and my pace calm and even. They'd given me the respect of not being cuffed and I didn't want anyone getting suspicious that I might take advantage of that.

Miranda came with us as well, walking by my side and looking at her feet as she went. I tried to think of a way to comfort her. I thought about reaching out to squeeze her shoulder, but figured a twitchy guard might misread the gesture. I decided to stay still.

Finally we reached the room they called the antechamber. Carlos unlocked the door and Warden Greene ushered us all inside. He gave Miranda a questioning glance, but allowed her to follow regardless. Inside only the five of us, plus a guard I didn't recognize, remained.

It was a small room, about the size of a large office, with a table, a couple chairs, and a rolling tray covered in various medical objects. The table held a clean pair of nurses scrubs the color of a midday sky and a pitcher of water with a stack of Styrofoam cups. I ran my hand across the clothing while Father David poured Miranda a glass of water and ushered her to a chair. Apparently he thought she looked unwell.

"You can change into them a little later." The warden told me, patting me on the shoulder. I nodded to let him know I followed. I was a little surprised that the color they'd chosen was one that would have once been a color that I'd frequently wear. Blue always made my eyes look brighter.

"If no one wishes my further guidance I think I'll go offer council to those who've gathered for witness." David suggested. We all agreed and he left. Carlos and the tall guard I didn't know returned to their military like stance on either side of the door. I did notice that my favorite guard looked less than enthused about his post. The other seemed indifferent.

"How many people will be out there?" I asked, unsettled by the silence in the room. Warden Greene inhaled sharply, running a hand through his salt and pepper hair.

"I don't know an exact amount. I'd guess a couple dozen. We can't seat more than thirty in the viewing room." He answered.

"Ok." I acknowledged.

"You saved me a seat right?" Miranda asked. It was the first she'd spoken and her voice came out shakily. She gripped the cup Father David had given her tightly in one hand and squeezed her opposite bicep with the other. I could see the indents where her fingernails dug in.

"There's a seat saved," the warden confirmed, "should you choose to occupy it."

"I'll be there." She insisted, sipping the last of her water and tossing the cup into a small trash can under the table. She resumed her stern stance with her hips leaned against the table. She still maintained her distance from me. I didn't blame her.

The warden sighed and rubbed the bridge of his nose. When he finished he looked at me. I could see the war in his eyes. He didn't like someone he cared about suffering, especially because of me. I saw the pleading in his eyes and I gave a subtle sign that I understood.

"Miranda." I called, resting my hand gently on her shoulder. Finally she looked at me. I could see the pain in her eyes. It hurt me more than I expected it to. "You don't have to take that seat. You don't have to do this."

"I want to." She insisted. "You deserve to have someone out there who's there for you, who's going to mourn you." Her voice caught on the word mourn. The warden walked away, unable to stand the pain in her voice any longer. I leaned against the table next to her.

"I appreciate that." I told her. "It means more to me than you can know, but I'm honestly telling you that if you don't want to be there, I will in no way be hurt or offended. I'll completely understand." She nodded.

"I need to be there." She whispered and I knew there was no changing her mind. I conceded and waited for her to speak again. The warden still paced along the far corner of the room. "Are you scared?" She whispered after a while.

"No." I lied, she glared at me, and I sighed. "A little." I admitted. She leaned closer to me and stretched her neck. I was amazed that of the two of us she seemed the most uneasy while I seemed the calmest. I suppose I'd accepted the resoluteness of it all.

We sat in silence for the majority of my last hour. Miranda scooted slowly closer until finally she leaned her body against my side, cupping her fingers around my mine. I took solace in her proximity, finding comfort in the fact that at the end, even after all I'd done, I had a friend by my side. The weight of her shoulder leaned against mine was an unexpected comfort.

The warden remained distant, pacing and anxious, constantly checking his watch. When he'd notice me watching he made a better attempt to not watch the clock. I was grateful for that small show of respect. I didn't expect anything from any of them at all. No one offers respect to villain of the story.

Finally the warden checked his watch a final time and started back to our side of the room. Nearly simultaneously I heard the approach of others outside the door. Miranda quivered at the same time I held my breath. The door opened and Warden Greene welcomed a man and a woman into the room with us, both in crisp white scrubs. The warden sighed, though I wasn't sure if it was out of sadness or relief.

"Dr. Martin, Miss Kim, welcome." He greeted our new guests. He showed them where the tools they required lay and turn back to Miranda and I. "I'm sorry Miranda; I have to ask you to leave now." He apologized. I felt her body tense where we still touched.

"Jim." She begged, he opened his hands to her. We all knew it wasn't his call. It was protocol. In fact I'm sure her presence in the antechamber in general wasn't covered under usual protocol. That was a favor from him to her. "Can I have a moment to say goodbye?" She requested. He allowed it. I turned to her and forced a smile.

"Thank you for everything." I told her, squeezing the hand she still held.

"I'm sorry Doc." She mumbled, looking at our interlaced fingers rather than my face. I could hear the crack in her façade mirrored in her voice.

"Don't apologize Miranda, there's nothing you could do. There's nothing anyone could do. I made this mess; I have to face the consequences." I told her. She shook her head. I started to continue, but she interrupted me.

"I'm not apologizing for not being able to save you. I'm not stupid. I know there's nothing I could do." She said. I waited, confused, and let her explain. "I'm apologizing," she continued, "because I'm breaking a promise to you." She laughed halfheartedly and finally looked me in the face. Tears streamed from her eyes and down her cheeks.

My heart ached for her. I would be dead soon, very soon, but she would live on. I knew she'd grieve for me and it hurt me more than any other action I'd taken. For this I felt true remorse. For this I *was* the monster they claimed me to be.

Unable to do or say anything else I wrapped my arms around her and hugged my friend. She placed a kiss on my cheek and hugged me back, squeezing tightly. We embraced one another for a long moment of silence, weeping together and saying goodbye the only way we could. Finally I stepped back, forcing her to release me, and I smiled softly at her.

"I'm better for having known you." I told her, fully releasing her at last.

"Ditto." She sniffed. Before anything further could be said, or more tears could fall, she turned on her heel and stalked out the door. Surprisingly I felt a slight weight lift when the door shut behind her. I suspected it would return shortly.

"Andrews." The warden called. I turned to him. He handed me the blue scrubs and pointed to a small bathroom through a narrow doorway. I looked down at the clothes and back to his face. "It's time." He sighed. I nodded and went to change.

This was it, the last moments of my short life. I'd never considered it short before. I was young, true, only 36 years old, but I'd lived a lot in those years. I'd traveled the world and experienced many cultures. I'd never felt incomplete or unfinished. My task was done. It was time to face the end.

I was ready to go, as ready as I could ever be. I slid the blue fabric over my body and took a final glance in the mirror. I traced the place where a scar once lined my now perfected features. I was ashamed to this day that I'd erased it, that I'd given into the pressure. It was one act I'd never forgive myself for.

A knock came at the door and I breathed deep. This was it. This was how it ended. My story was finished, the final keystrokes of the final chapter. I was complete, now it was time for my soul to be free. With that resolution I took a final deep breath and opened the door.

12 Min...

The door opened and I stepped into the last room I'd ever see. A large silver table stood in the middle of the cold, tiled room. Monitors and trays of tools and syringes lined the wall to the right. The doctor who'd recently joined us in the antechamber, along with his assistant, began the preparations. I heard the hum of machines as the assistant flipped the switches of the monitors.

Jim led the way to the left side of the table. The wall ended approximately three and a half feet up and a large sheet of glass separated us from the viewers who sat beyond. It was empty for now, but I could hear the buzz of people nearby.

My hands were cuffed in front of me again, more for show to the onlookers than actually necessity. I wasn't going to run. Even if I did, where would I go? I had no doubt the tall guard wouldn't hesitate to put a bullet in me if I even thought of making a break for it. I had no intention of trying to escape. I was ready for this.

As Jim checked the final details I tried my best to resist the urge to scratch. After I'd emerged from the bathroom of the antechamber the doctor, whose name I'd already forgotten, had his assistant affix me with a myriad of electrical probes to monitor my heart rate and brain activity. I had three sticky circles of wired plastic affixed to my temple and chest. They were more uncomfortable than the cuffs.

I wiggled and shifted behind the warden as he spoke quietly with Carlos and a man in a suit I'd never seen before. I assumed he was in charge of overseeing the execution. Had to make sure they killed me correctly. Your typical bureaucratic bullshit. Finally they finished and the warden approached me.

"We're about to open the doors. I'll address the viewers, read the sentence, and then you'll have the opportunity to say something if you wish. Then the doctor will insert the IV's and..." He trailed off.

"And they'll inject the cocktail that will kill me." I finished for him. "I know how it works."

"Alright then." He sighed and I was alone again, standing centered in front of the silver table. It was cold where it pressed against my back. I stared at the floor in front of me as the warden gave the order and the door was opened, the shuffle of people reaching my ears.

A tap on the glass pulled my attention upward and I found Miranda's eyes as the guard ushered her away. I could still see the imprint her hand had made on the glass, the fogged outline of five petite digits. I hitched a corner of my mouth to smile at her.

The warden cleared his throat and drew the attention of the crowd. Only Miranda and I looked elsewhere. She looked at me, her last glimpses of her friend. And I looked at her, the one person in the room who cared that I was about to die. That cared more than being glad at my riddance, at least.

"Greetings." He called. "Ladies and gentlemen, we are ready to commence." He cleared his throat again and reached for a paper at his side. "We commence today in correspondence with the death warrant handed down by the admirable Judge Winters to be enacted here, at the time of twelve a.m. on the twenty fifth day of April." The crowd silenced at his words and he continued.

"Dr. C. L. Andrews. You have been tried in a court of law by a judge of the State of California and by a jury of your peers. You've have been convicted of the crimes of intentional homicide, release of a biological weapon into unprotected society, and treasonous acts against the United Nations of this world. You have been sentenced to die by lethal injection." He paused, placing the warrant back where it had been.

"Do you have any final words you wish to share?" He asked. His attention turned to me, and with it, the entirety of the crowd beyond the window. Two dozen sets of eyes stared at me. Most were resolute and anxiously awaiting my demise. I avoided looking at Miranda for the time being. I spotted Father David by the doorway and he gave me a soft smile, placing his hand on his heart. He was a good man.

In the far side of the second row of viewers I spotted a crop of rust colored hair. Nigel blinked at me, wiping the tears from his eyes as discreetly as he could manage. I hoped he'd find happiness and soon forget all about me.

I left the woman I knew would never forget for last. Her eyes were shiny with tears and she clutched her bag so tightly against her that her knuckles were turning white. I watched a tear slide down her face and I felt one teeter on the corner of my eye. She mouthed something to me and smiled as the tear released. I'll miss you too, Miranda.

"Dr. Andrews." The warden encouraged. I swallowed and nodded that I was ok.

"I know you all see me as a monster." I said calmly. "I don't blame you. You're not wrong. I've done horrible things. I make no claim to innocence and for those who were harmed by my actions I honestly say I'm sorry for your pain. I do not regret my actions or dismiss my reasons for them. I only request that you remember that no being on this planet is truly and completely evil. We are complex beings, melded by experience and emotion, unpredictable and often unreasonable. I only hope that one day the world can see past the darkness of my actions and see the light of truth and meaning that awaits beyond."

The room stayed silent and, after a painfully long pause, Warden Greene gestured for Carlos to approach and I was guided to the table. The tall blonde guard held my arm while Carlos un-cuffed my wrists and helped me onto the table. I lay back against the icy steel and watched the lights on the ceiling while they reaffixed the cuffs, securing each of my arms to the table sides.

Everything seemed to come to a crawl. The world moved in slow motion, but my mind raced faster than it ever had before. Everything became instantly sharp and clear. The lights hummed above me. The people in the viewing room shuffled in their seats, their clothing rustling softly. The machines droned on around me and someone muffled a cough.

I heard the scrap of metal and someone approached from my right. I looked up into the face of the doctor. He made no attempt at feigned compassion. He was as cold as the table I lay on. I didn't care. It didn't bother me now. Nothing did. Nothing could.

I watched as he carefully swabbed the inside of my right elbow and swiftly injected the 18 gauge hypodermic needle, securing it with a strip of medical tape. I winced slightly from the pinch, but it was hardly painful. He returned to his tray, retrieving another, and slowly walked to the other side of the table and repeated the procedure there.

Both IV's inserted and set, he returned to his tray, carefully measured three syringes from three small vials and laid them out neatly. Sodium thiopental to sedate me, pancuronium bromide to slow my breathing, and the kicker, potassium chloride, to stop my heart. It was a fairly straightforward procedure.

I turned my attention from the doctor and peered at the warden. He was looking between his watch and the clock on the wall. It read 11:59. Lastly I stole a final glance at Miranda. I half expected to find the chair empty, but there she sat, eyes red and face tear-soaked. I breathed heavily under the weight of the guilt. I turned away and focused on the clock just as the hand ticked to twelve. This was it.

I saw Jim Greene nod out of the corner of my eye and heard the doctor shuffle beside me, but in that instant I became selfish. I couldn't look away any longer. I turned my head and found Miranda's eyes. She was sobbing, her shoulders shaking. Father David had a hand on her back. I was glad she had someone to comforter her. I wished I had the same.

I focused on the one comfort I had left, Miranda. In just minutes my heart would stop and I would be gone forever, extinguished from this world. It may have been selfish and cruel, but in that moment I needed Miranda's face to be the last one I saw on this earth.

Finally, after several beats of my heart pounding in my ears, I felt the burn of the injection as they administered the first dose. I turned my face skyward, my muscles relaxing and becoming too tired to turn my head any particular direction. I was tired. I was ready.

The world blurred at the edges and I stared into the light. It was bright and warm and unyielding. With the sting of the second injection the light intensified, spreading out across the ceiling until it filled my vision. Inside the light was a face I'd longed to see for longer than I'd hoped. It smiled at me and stood, shrouded in pale, warm light. A hand reached out for me, calling me upward.

"I'm coming, Cal." I whispered as I closed my eyes. I didn't need to watch any more. I was done with this world. My work was finished. My suffering was over. The last sound I heard was the drone of the heart monitor.

My life was over, but my legacy would live on. One day they'd find a cure for my virus, a way to stop the havoc I'd wreaked, maybe even reverse it. It didn't matter, the damage had been done. My lesson had been taught. The world would never see beauty the same way again, for how can beauty be discerned when the majority of the world was unable to view it. My virus had left the world blind, and I was free at last.

Epilogue: 1 Year Later...

I pulled the map from the passenger seat, double checking I was taking the right exit. I turned on my blinker and pulled onto the 95 Expressway toward Ridgefield Park. Once I entered the town the directions weren't hard to follow. In fact, they'd been much more difficult to come by than actually act out.

I pulled into a small parking lot and crawled from my rental car, shielding my eyes from the bright summer sun. Across the street the park was bustling with children playing, couples picnicking, and dogs chasing sticks. On the far corner stood a large willow, the branches waving in the breeze. I was in the right place.

I walked around the car and crossed the street. As I approached the willow I worried momentarily about the prospect of possibly interrupting a pair of unsuspecting teens, but when I pushed my way through the branches I was glad to find their interior uninhabited. I walked to the base of the tree, resting my hand on the trunk.

"I miss you Doc." I whispered before I pulled a small pocketknife from my purse. I rammed the tip into the bark and worked the blade until I was damp with sweat. Finally, finished with my task, I stepped back to admire my work. It was childish, but the sight of the initials C. D. and L. A. encircled within a heart made me smile. Cal and Lily's love was now eternalized in their favorite place.

I slid the knife into my pocket and gave the willow one final glance. I followed its lines upward, peering up into its vastness. It truly was a peaceful place. No sounds of the outside world reached my ears. I knew why it was sacred, and was even more honored to have its likeness framed above my mantle.

I returned to my car and turned the ignition. The clock read just after noon. I should have just enough time to complete my real reason for my detour to the small town.

The cemetery was easy to find and I climbed again from the rented sedan and started down the hill dotted with headstones. It only took a few minutes to locate the one I sought.

Calvin Lester Danielson

Beloved son

January 22, 2016 – May 12, 2034

Lost, but never forgotten…

I kneeled gently beside Cal's grave, setting the box I'd carted from the car next to me. I pulled out the flowers I'd purchased at the local grocery store and laid them in front of his stone. Then I opened the box and retrieved the reason I was there.

"Hello Cal." I smiled. "I know we never met, but I feel like I know you. Someone who loved you very deeply told me about you and about your love. I know you and Lily were separated far too soon, and I know that life was hard, for both of you, but she loved you so much. I could tell every time she spoke of you." I patted the urn in my lap.

"I know you're together now, wherever we go after all of this. I hope you're happy. And I hope Doc knows I miss her. I miss her so very much." I sniffed. I wiped the tears and ran my fingers over the urn that held all that remained of my friend. The inscription twinkled in the midday sun.

"Nothing is more creative,

nor destructive,

than a brilliant mind with a purpose."

Catherine Lily Andrews

March 3, 2016 – April 25, 2052

A kind and brilliant woman who will be truly missed.

A single tear splattered against the bronze and I wiped it away before I twisted off the top and scattered the contents over the grave before me. When the urn was empty I returned the lid and the empty canister into the box it had come in.

"Sorry it took me so long, Cal. You weren't an easy guy to find, but after all this time I just thought you and Lily deserved to be spend eternity together." I looked to the sky, hopeful that they were both looking down on me. "You deserve to have some peace after everything you've endured." I sighed and stood, brushing off my knees and looking down at the grave, dusted now with Doc's remains. My phone rang, breaking my reverie. I answered.

"Miranda they're asking where you are." Sayid whispered. I could hear him fretting through the phone and I rolled my eyes. He needed to grow a backbone if he was going to make it in this industry. "Please tell me you're on your way." He begged. I sighed, but smiled at his expense.

"I'm on my way." I promised. "I just had to take a detour to drop off a friend." He sighed and I'm pretty sure I heard his blood pressure drop. "I'll be there soon." I hung up, pocketing the phone.

"We'll meet again one day." I promised Doc.

I climbed into my car, found my way back to the freeway, and drove until New Jersey faded behind me and the New York skyline loomed into view. Thirty-three minutes later I pulled up in front of the Manhattan Hilton. Sayid greeted me at the door and practically shoved me into the elevator. He squirmed all the way down the hall to the meeting room and practically hyperventilated when I paused outside the doors.

"You're not chickening out are you?" He gasped.

"Depends." I shrugged. "How many are there in there?" I asked. He paled and I laughed. "Relax kid, I've got this." I smiled and grabbed the door handle. As I pushed it I turned and winked at my assistant. "Seriously, Sayid, decaf." He didn't look amused.

A fellow reporter and friend met me inside the door and led me down the aisle lined with flashing cameras and recording devices. I took the stage and waited for the announcer to introduce me. My palms were sweating and I was starting to shake. My very first press conference. It was intense.

"Ladies and gentlemen of the press, it is my pleasure to introduce renowned journalist and author of the best selling biography *Truth Beyond the Terror: The C.L. Andrews Story* Miss Miranda Stevens." The bulbs flashed and the crowd clapped thunderously as I approached the podium. I thanked the announcer and looked into the crowd. A hundred faces awaited my speech. I swallowed hard.

"Good afternoon." I greeted. "Thank you for being here today." I felt the panic rise in my chest and had a momentary flashback to a particularly painful moment of horror in high school speech class. My hands slid along the edge of the oak podium and my voice caught in my throat. Thankfully I heard a voice in the back of my mind, reminding me just how intrepid I could be, and I closed my eyes for a moment, thanking Doc for having my back even now. I breathed deep and began.

"Most of you know me as the reporter that interviewed Dr. Catherine Andrews. You know the story. A few of you have probably read my book. Everyone knows about the brilliant young scientist that went mad and unleashed a virus on our world, changing our society forever. The story is true. It's powerful. But I'm not here to talk about that story. I'm here to tell you another story, one of love and loss, of pain and sorrow and darkness. I'm here to tell you the true story of Dr. Catherine 'Lily' Andrews, because there is much, much more to this woman than you know..."

To the intrepid Miss Stevens,

By the time you discover this letter at the back of my sketchbook I will be gone. Firstly please don't grieve for me. Death is not something I fear. It is freedom, long awaited. Over the past weeks I've grown fonder of you than I ever expected. I honestly consider you a friend, and a good one at that. On one of our early visits I began a story, one of love and loss, of pain and sorrow and darkness, though you didn't know that then. In all honesty I'd never intended the story as anything more than a ploy to keep your questions at bay. Somewhere along the way, however, my perspective changed. You changed it. Relentlessly you pushed me and demanded that I share my life with you. And I have, more than you know.

The story is true, every single word of it. It's my story. It's the past you tried so hard to discover and that I'd fought so hard to bury. I applaud your determination. Because of that attribute and the unknown reason behind the bond that we formed I decided one day that you were someone worthy of my story, someone I could trust. I gave you my secret and I'm entrusting you with the final details now. I know you'll do the right thing.

I loved Cal with every fiber of my existence. He was the most brilliant and most beautiful soul I've ever met. His mind made me feel inferior and his talent for art was far beyond my own, though he did teach me a thing or two (which I'm sure you've glimpsed by now). The tale of our love I shared with you happened just as I said it did. I moved to Ridgefield Park the summer before my senior year. I felt alone and angry and frustrated until the day I met Cal. He made me smile and he filled my life with joy and love.

Anthony and the other two are real. On the night of February 7, 2033 they abducted Cal and I and took us to an abandoned office owned by one of their parents. They raped me and beat me and used a knife to cut my face and my chest, leaving me scarred and broken. They made Cal watch. They destroyed everything good in our world. They killed the man I loved that day, even if they didn't know it. The following May Cal stole the gun his aunt kept in her room and took his own life. He called me to say goodbye and I reached him only moments too late. I've never been able to erase the image of my love lying in a pool of his own blood, the scent of gunpowder still in the air. My life was never the same again. I was never the same.

You wanted to know why I did what I did, this is it. The fear of anything that isn't perfect and beautiful stole the man I love. It drove three men to vicious acts that destroyed my life and my sanity and left me hateful and lessened. I'm not saying it justifies anything. I'm not making excuses. You wanted to know the truth, and now you know. You were right. I did suffer something terrible. I'm not sure what I did was the right thing, or whether it even did any good. For all I know fifty years from now people won't even remember my name. Either way, you know the reason now.

I know watching me go won't have been easy for you. In all reality the only one it will be easy for is me. I've waited for this, for the day I might finally be reunited with my sweet Cal, after nearly two decades. I miss him. I have nothing left for me in this life. Please don't mourn me, please don't be sad. I'm free now. I'm not alone anymore, I'm not afraid, or broken, or in pain. If the afterlife brings me to Cal, then I am at peace. If it doesn't, then it doesn't really matter. Please know that your friendship made my last days worthwhile. You brought me happiness and laughter I thought I'd never find again. You are a truly magnificent person. Thank you, Miranda.

Yours,

Doc